D1628127

BARKING up the RIGHT TREE

LEIGH RUSSELL

A POPPY MYSTERY TALE

cmc

First published in 2023 by
The Crime & Mystery Club Ltd.,
Harpenden, UK

crimeandmysteryclub.co.uk
@CrimeMystClub

© Leigh Russell, 2023

Original artwork by Phillipa Leigh.

The right of Leigh Russell to be identified as the author of this
work has been asserted in accordance with the Copyright, Designs
and Patents Act 1988.

All rights reserved. No part of this book may be reproduced, stored
in or introduced into a retrieval system, or transmitted, in any form
or by any means (electronic, mechanical, photocopying, recording or
otherwise) without the written permission of the publishers.

Any person who does any unauthorised act in relation to this publication
may be liable to criminal prosecution and civil claims for damages.

A CIP catalogue record for this book is available from the British Library.

This is a work of fiction. Names, characters, places, and incidents either
are the product of the author's imagination or are used fictitiously,
and any resemblance to actual persons, living or dead, businesses,
companies, events or locales is entirely coincidental.

ISBN
978-0-85730-543-5 (Paperback)
978-0-85730-544-2 (eBook)

2 4 6 8 10 9 7 5 3 1

Typeset in 11.1 on 14.5pt Sabon
by Avocet Typeset, Bideford, Devon, EX39 2BP
Printed and bound in Great Britain by Clays Ltd, Elcograf S.p.A.

MIX
Paper from
responsible sources
FSC® C018072
www.fsc.org

Critical Acclaim for Leigh Russell

'A million readers can't be wrong! Clear some time in your day, sit back and enjoy a bloody good read' – **Howard Linskey**

'Taut and compelling' – **Peter James**

'Leigh Russell is one to watch' – **Lee Child**

'A brilliant talent in the thriller field' – **Jeffery Deaver**

'Brilliant and chilling, Leigh Russell delivers a cracker of a read!' – **Martina Cole**

'Leigh Russell has become one of the most impressively dependable purveyors of the English police procedural' – *Times*

'DI Geraldine Steel is one of the most authoritative female coppers in a crowded field' – *Financial Times*

'The latest police procedural from prolific novelist Leigh Russell is as good and gripping as anything she has published' – *Times & Sunday Times Crime Club*

'Another corker of a book from Leigh Russell... Russell's talent for writing top-quality crime fiction just keeps on growing...' – *Euro Crime*

'Good, old-fashioned, heart-hammering police thriller... a no-frills delivery of pure excitement' – *SAGA Magazine*

'A gritty and totally addictive novel' – *New York Journal of Books*

Also by Leigh Russell

Geraldine Steel Mysteries
Cut Short
Road Closed
Dead End
Death Bed
Stop Dead
Fatal Act
Killer Plan
Murder Ring
Deadly Alibi
Class Murder
Death Rope
Rogue Killer
Deathly Affair
Deadly Revenge
Evil Impulse
Deep Cover
Guilt Edged
Fake Alibi
Final Term

Ian Peterson Murder Investigations
Cold Sacrifice
Race to Death
Blood Axe

Lucy Hall Mysteries
Journey to Death
Girl in Danger
The Wrong Suspect

The Adulterer's Wife
Suspicion

This book is dedicated to the real Poppy.
You know who you are.
(Well, you probably don't, but I have told you.)

It is also dedicated to Michael, Jo, Phillipa,
Phil, Rian and Kezia.

Prologue

'IT'S ALL RIGHT FOR you. I've got my work to think of. Not everyone can swan around doing nothing. How am I supposed to concentrate with you hanging around all day?'

Ben glared at me, as if it was my fault my employers had gone out of business less than six months after giving me a job. He was probably afraid he would end up having to support me. He always was tight-fisted.

'I won't get in your way,' I assured him. 'Honestly, I won't make a sound. You won't even know I'm here. I don't mind staying in the bedroom while you're working.'

He grunted, and carried on packing his clothes. He didn't seem to notice he was using my case, but I didn't let that distract me from my attempt to persuade him to stay. I put my arms around him from behind, as he leaned forward over the bed, but he pushed me away.

'You can carry on using the table. We'll manage,' I insisted. 'It won't be for much longer, a few weeks at the most.'

'You don't know that,' he replied. 'It could be months before you find another job.'

'That only happens to people who are fussy. Seriously,

how long can it take, as long I'm prepared to accept anything I can get?'

'Who knows? No one knows what the hell's going on these days. In any case, we have to be realistic. What are the chances you'll find another job that pays as well? You might be prepared to accept just anything, but I don't want to see you reduced to doing some crappy menial work just to make ends meet. You deserve better than that.'

1

IN MANY WAYS I was lucky. Admittedly my boss had been forced to let me go, as he had put it, but losing my job was no big deal. If anything, I was relieved at being saved the stress of having to make a decision about whether to pack it in or soldier on. Ben had encouraged me to keep going and I had stuck at it, mainly to please him. Less easy to shrug off was my boyfriend's decision to walk out, once he realised I would be at home all day. I wasn't sure exactly what he did, but he worked online from the kitchen table.

If I'm honest, I think we both realised our relationship hit a rough patch once I lost my job. We had got along well enough before that, when we were going out every weekend, and enjoying a few drinks with friends on weekday evenings. Life had been a blast for us, and we were young enough not to think too far ahead. I had just assumed we would end up together, slowing down when we were ready, and maybe buying a home of our own, although it was hard to see how we could save enough for a deposit when we spent every penny we earned. Sometimes I daydreamed about moving out of London to a quiet little village where white ducks scudded around a pond and we went for long walks and spent our evenings snuggling in front of a cosy fire.

That was our life until I lost my job, and we found ourselves spending more time together, with a lot less money. Before that, our flat in Finsbury Park had been an ideal base for our busy lifestyle, even though we only had one bedroom. That was all we had needed, because we were hardly ever there together, except to fall in and out of bed. Ben worked from home but he only needed his laptop so that was no problem. Overnight everything changed. I would have adapted without too much fuss, but it turned out that wasn't good enough for my boyfriend. And so, after living with me for nearly six months, Ben packed his bags and walked out a week after I lost my job.

His abrupt departure left me devastated. I lay in bed weeping for days after he left, making only a desultory attempt to find another job online. My sole consolation was that my mother didn't know about the split. My sister, Susie, called me one evening, and I blurted out the devastating news. We had always been close, even though she was ten years older than me, and we rarely saw one another since she had married and moved to Colchester. She had always been unfairly critical of Ben, and she sounded guardedly pleased when she heard that he had left me. But my mother adored Ben. She was bound to make a terrible fuss if she knew we had broken up. She didn't really know Ben very well, but he was a man, and that was enough to make him eligible in her eyes.

'You get a ring on your finger before he changes his mind,' she told me on more than one occasion, her eyes bright with concern.

'For goodness' sake, mum, this is the twenty-first century, not a Jane Austen novel,' was the pithiest response I could come up with.

My father was no help, muttering irritably about young people and fecklessness. So when Ben walked out, I was keen to keep the break-up from my parents, and swore my sister to secrecy. I saw no point in sharing the news with anyone else in my family. Instead, I reassured my mother that all was well with me, when nothing could have been further from the truth.

'Ben's fine,' I lied. 'My job's great.'

It was hard enough coping with my heartbreak without having to fend off my mother's fussing. It wasn't as if she was likely to turn up unannounced and discover that Ben had moved out. I did try to find another job, but it wasn't easy, and with no income it was difficult to scrape together enough to pay my rent, let alone go out. The few girlfriends in whom I confided didn't offer much support. They listened to me before launching into monologues about their own preoccupations: they were frustrated with their jobs, disappointed in their relationships, excited about their holidays, each of them engrossed in her own concerns. I wondered if my friends had always been so self-absorbed, or if the recent pandemic had turned us all into narcissists.

While others were flying around the world on long-awaited holidays, my bank account was virtually empty. It was an effort to look smart for job interviews, but there was nothing else for it if I didn't want to be thrown out of my apartment. Changing my clothes and putting on make-up was easy enough. Keeping my shoulder-length hair looking tidy was more of a challenge. But the last thing I wanted to do was crawl back to my parents' house, an utter failure at twenty-four. So I tied my wild red hair back in a ponytail and tried to smile, even though I felt like crying.

One afternoon I returned home from a depressing interview at an employment agency to find a letter in my mail box telling me that my great aunt had passed away, leaving me as her sole heir. At first I assumed it was a scam. I had only met Great Aunt Lorna a few times, when I was very young. All I remembered about her was that she had seemed very sad, and she had given me a little bag of boiled sweets and asked me to write to her. My mother took the sweets away from me because, she said, they were bad for my teeth. I never discovered why our family had fallen out with my great aunt after my grandmother died, but I felt sorry for her and wrote to her for several years, without receiving a single reply. I put my own address on the envelopes and my letters were never returned, so I assumed they were delivered. Years passed and my letters grew less and less frequent, until eventually I stopped writing to my great aunt altogether.

Dropping the letter on my bed, I changed into comfortable pyjamas and made myself a cup of tea before calling the executor as instructed. To my surprise, I was given an appointment with a partner at the offices of a West End firm of solicitors. With nothing else to do, I looked up the address they had given me, and confirmed that the phone number I had called was genuine. Intrigued, and more than a little excited, the next morning I put my interview suit back on, pulled a brush through my hair, and went to meet my great aunt's executor. The offices of Williamson, Prendergast and Glynn were situated in a swish glass-fronted building in Central London. A receptionist took my details, and handed me a visitor's badge.

'Take the lift to the sixth floor,' she instructed me, opening an electronically operated gate.

On the sixth floor, another receptionist directed me to Mr Williamson's office. I knocked and entered to see a grey-haired man seated behind a large wooden desk, which looked quite out of place in its modern setting. Over his shoulder there was a view of London through a huge window.

'Emily Wilson?' he greeted me.

'Yes, that's me.'

Mr Williamson nodded and invited me to sit down before telling me that my great aunt, Lorna Lafferty, had altered her will some years ago, naming me sole heir to her estate. He was sorry to tell me that she had recently suffered a fatal injury as the result of a fall. After reiterating his condolences, he confirmed that my elderly relative had left me her house.

'A house?' I repeated, unable to take in what the clipped voice was saying. 'What do you mean?'

He gave the address of a property in a village called Ashton Mead, which allegedly now belonged to me. For a moment, I thought he might be trying to sell me a house. That was a joke, seeing as I couldn't even afford to pay my rent and it was only a matter of time before my landlord started kicking up a fuss.

'I haven't got any money,' I stammered.

It was almost impossible to believe what he was actually telling me.

'There's no mortgage on the property,' he went on impassively. 'We can put the house on the market for you if you like.'

'No,' I blurted out without thinking about what I was saying. 'That is, at least let me look at it first. I mean, that's all right, isn't it?'

'The property is yours to dispose of as you wish.'

'So you're saying it's really mine? My house?'

'Yes, according to the terms of the will. It's extremely straightforward,' he added, his tone almost accusing, as though he thought the house would be wasted on a simpleton like me. 'You are the sole beneficiary.'

I had never really known whether my great aunt had received my letters or not. Now I had my answer and it came in the form, not of a letter, but a house bequeathed to me in her will. At the age of twenty-four, single and unemployed, all at once I owned a house in a village I had never heard of, somewhere in Wiltshire. To say I was shocked would be an understatement.

'The property is yours to dispose of as you wish,' he told me calmly, as though acquiring a house completely out of the blue was an everyday occurrence. 'There is one condition,' he added in his unemotional drawl. 'Your great aunt has stipulated that you take care of any pet she might own at the time of her death.'

I couldn't remember her owning a pet, and hesitated. 'What happens if I don't want to look after her pet?'

'Then the house is left to another relative, providing he or she is willing to care for your great aunt's pet.'

'What kind of a pet is it?'

'The will does not specify. All I can tell you is the terms of the will.'

To be given a house was an almost unbelievable stroke of good fortune, but my aunt's pet could be a problem, and I needed to find out more before committing myself. It was important to be clear about my position before sharing the news with anyone, especially my mother who was bound to be strident in her views about what I should do. Feeling awkward, I explained that I would like time to think it over, and Mr Williamson nodded.

'Take as long as you need,' he said.

I left, promising to return in an hour. Resolved to say nothing about my inheritance, I phoned my mother as soon as I could. It would have been difficult to hold a conversation with traffic roaring past, but I found a quiet alleyway and made the call from there. To my relief, she answered straight away.

'What are you talking about?' my mother demanded when I put my question to her. 'Why on earth would you want to know? I've no idea if my Aunt Lorna had a pet, and I can't for the life of me imagine why you would be interested in anything to do with her, especially after all this time. I haven't heard from her for at least twenty years. What's going on, Emily?'

With some difficulty, I did my best to jog her memory, telling her that I recalled my great aunt had owned a dangerous pet, like a rat or a snake, or even a tarantula. That was a lie. I had no such recollection.

'A snake?' my mother repeated, sounding even more bemused. 'A tarantula? I think I would have remembered if she owned a tarantula.' She laughed. 'Really, Emily, I do wonder what you're talking about sometimes. You and Ben haven't been experimenting with drugs, have you?'

Feeling optimistic that my great aunt's pet might be harmless, after all, I decided there was only one way to find out, and phoned Mr Williamson. The woman who took my call explained that Mr Williamson was with another client.

'Can you tell him I'd like to go and see the house before I make up my mind?'

'Mr Williamson has left the key at reception for you,' she said, and she rang off.

Having collected the key to the house and booked a train ticket to Swindon, I prepared for an excursion that was hopefully going to change my life. Afraid of having to cope with yet another disappointment, I tried to keep my expectations in check as I set off, with a sleeping bag and a suitcase. It was time to view my property.

2

As the train approached Swindon, I struggled to control my excitement at the prospect of seeing my great aunt's house, because it wasn't my great aunt's house any more, it was *my* house! I had held back from researching the village, because I wanted to see it for the first time as it was in the real world, not in an image someone else had posted online. Leaving the train at Swindon, I enquired where to catch a bus to my destination and, half an hour later, set off on the final stretch of my journey to the village of Ashton Mead. The bus meandered along twisting country lanes through gently undulating fields and picturesque hamlets. Having lived for so long in London, it was strange and wonderful to see fields and trees and gently rolling hills passing by the cloudy window of the bus. I did my best to take it all in, but was too preoccupied to pay much attention to the view.

The closer the bus drew to my destination, the more apprehensive I became, although there was no reason for me to worry. The lawyer had made it clear that having inherited a house of my own, I was under no obligation to accept the bequest. I knew it would be crazy to turn down the offer of a house, but there was still the mystery of

Great Aunt Lorna's pet. With any luck it would turn out to be a cat, old and lazy, and content to doze all day. That would suit me very well. A cat might be a poor substitute for Ben, but at least it wouldn't break my heart, and it might be agreeable company. By the time I arrived at my destination, my doubts had been swept away by a surge of optimism and I couldn't wait to see my new home.

It was a bright morning in early April, the sky blue with a scattering of white clouds, when I stepped down from the bus in Ashton Mead. My first view of the district where my great aunt had lived was encouraging. The village was a collection of quaint cottages, clustered around a brick-built bridge across a narrow river. As yet, I had no idea which of the houses belonged to me, but I was in no hurry to find out. According to my phone app, the entire village consisted of no more than half a dozen streets that fanned out from the river. It would probably take less than an hour to explore the whole place on foot.

The contrast with the streets of London was stark. At midday on a Monday, the village appeared to be deserted. Removing my raincoat, I walked away from the bus stop down a street lined with shops. A sign in a grocery store window promised 'Best Fresh Produce in Ashton Mead', probably not a difficult boast to fulfil. Next to it was a tea shop decorated in bright yellow paint, with a yellow and white awning. Beyond that were a butcher's red frontage, and then a fancy-looking hair salon. A pub stood on the corner, at a bend in the road. Large and square, its window boxes were packed with flowers that made a colourful display. The whole street looked cheerful and well maintained, like an illustration of a village in a children's book, almost too picturesque to be real.

I made my way along to the pub and back down to the grocer's, which was the only place that looked open. In the stuffy interior, shelves were packed with a miscellany of groceries: magazines, biscuits, bread and chocolate near the counter, with vegetables and all kinds of packets and cartons and tins further back. An assortment of toiletries and cleaning materials were stacked in the corner furthest from the entrance beside which a grey-haired woman in a grey cardigan was seated, the first person I had seen since my arrival in the village. A magazine lay open on the counter in front of her. She rustled the pages as I entered, and didn't look up.

'Hello,' I greeted her.

The woman raised her head and scrutinised me through narrowed eyes, as though she suspected me of pilfering. I half expected her to challenge me to empty my pockets.

'Yes?' she said. 'Can I help you? Are you looking for anything in particular?'

She peered at me over the top of her rimless glasses as she waited for a reply.

'Actually, I'm not looking for anything,' I said. 'That is, I am, but not in here. I'm looking for a house, Rosecroft.'

'Rosecroft?' she repeated, with a slight shake of her tight grey curls. 'That's Lorna Lafferty's cottage, but it's empty now. The owner passed away. You're not after buying Miss Lafferty's place, are you?'

She looked at me with a calculating expression, weighing up my faded sweatshirt and worn jeans, my dishevelled hair, and the hint of panic in my eyes. There was no point in equivocating. If I decided to stay in the village, the local shopkeeper would learn the truth about me soon enough. If I took one look around my new house and decided to return to London straight away, then it hardly mattered what she thought of me and my unexpected windfall. As soon as she heard about my inheritance, the shopkeeper became very friendly, introducing herself as Maud and insisting on calling me by my first name. Shaking my hand across the counter, she told me how sorely my great aunt would be missed.

'There's the big supermarkets in Swindon, of course,' she went on, once she had finished extolling my great aunt, 'and we can't pretend to compete with them on stock, but if there's anything you need, anything at all, you only have to ask and we can get it in for you the next day. So you never need to leave the village unless you want to. Not for your shopping needs, anyway. We're your local, and you'll be surprised what you can find here. You won't find better quality anywhere. It's all fresh. And there's nothing you might be in need of that we don't supply.' She gave a toothy smile. 'We take good care of our local customers. Ask anyone in the village.'

'Thank you. It all looks lovely,' I replied. 'I don't need anything at the moment, but I'll certainly be coming here when I do. Can you give me directions to Rosecroft, please?'

It was thrilling, asking the way to my own house. That's what it was. *My* house. Following Maud's directions, it took me less than ten minutes to find Rosecroft. I loved it at first sight, at least from the outside. It felt as though I was coming home. Like most of the buildings in Ashton Mead, Rosecroft was constructed of pale yellow bricks, with a steep sloping roof, and it had old-fashioned latticed windows. There was even a white picket fence, albeit in need of repair, and trailing around the front door a climbing plant was covered in buds. The path to the front door was bordered by rose bushes interspersed with other plants that might also flower. Making a mental note to find out whether they were actually weeds, I walked up to the front door with a sick fluttering in my stomach. This was it, my very own house, and it was more beautiful than I could have hoped. I loved it, and felt a pang of regret at having stopped writing to the old lady who had bequeathed me such a wonderful gift.

There was only one other house in the narrow lane where my great aunt had lived. On the other side of the lane, a gently sloping grassy plot led down towards the river. As I was rummaging in my bag for the key the lawyer had sent me, I had a curious feeling that someone was watching me. Looking round, I was just in time to see my next door neighbour's front door close. It was natural that my sole neighbour would be curious to see who was moving in, and I was equally interested in them. So far I had caught no more than a fleeting glimpse of a figure. There would probably be an opportunity for us to meet, because I intended to stay in Ashton Mead, at least until the following day. My only concern was that I had yet to discover the truth about my great aunt's pet. If it turned out to be an aggressive and uncontrollable dog, it might lose me my inheritance. My excitement tinged with trepidation, I turned the key and opened the door to my house.

Inside Rosecroft, I quickly discovered that the place wasn't quite as welcoming as it had appeared from the street. A small hallway was lit only through a fanlight in the front door. When I flicked the light switch, nothing happened. Using the torch on my phone, I peered around, hoping the electricity hadn't been turned off. The first door I saw led me to a front room, packed with heavy dark wooden furniture. Grimy windows let in very little daylight. The house had only been empty for a few months, but dirt appeared to have accumulated there for years. Evidently my aunt had not done much cleaning. Given her advanced age, that was understandable. Reluctant to touch anything, I explored the rest of the ground floor, feeling like a trespasser. There was a second reception room, slightly larger than the front room, and a square kitchen big enough for a wooden table and four chairs. The kitchen was not as filthy as the other rooms, and I suspected my aunt had spent most of her time in there. On a worktop next to the sink was a small fish tank. Relieved, I watched a solitary goldfish glide lazily up and down, shifting direction with an occasional flick of its tail. This was going to be even less trouble to care for than a cat.

'Hello,' I said, grinning. 'What do you think about you and me living here together? We're going to get along just fine, aren't we?'

The fish flicked its tail and continued on its journey around the glass tank. I watched it for a moment, wondering if it realised how circumscribed its movements were, and whether my own life was really any different.

The back garden had gone to seed. Knee-high weeds flourished on what had once been a patio behind the house, and nettles and brambles had taken over at the far end. Between these two patches of wilderness was an overgrown area of long grass riddled with weeds. A faint breeze ruffled the tops of a row of tall poplars planted along the back fence, but where I was standing the air was still. It was very quiet, with a silence I had only heard in my home in

London during the lockdowns. Along the right hand side of my property a high metal fence separated my garden from next door, and I wondered whether my neighbour kept some kind of livestock, or perhaps a large dog. The other fence belonged to me. Wooden, with a few panels missing, it was more in keeping with the house than my neighbour's smart metallic fence. As I stood gazing around the garden, a cloud drifted in front of the sun and I shivered.

Going back indoors, I climbed a narrow staircase and found two rooms as neglected as most of the ground floor. Cobwebs thick with dust draped the windows and hung from the ceilings, and every surface was covered in a layer of dirt. Finding a pane that was less grimy than the rest, I peered next door but my view was partially obstructed by the high fence and it was impossible to see the whole of my neighbour's garden. All I could see clearly was the top of a tree that towered above the high fence. Turning my attention to my own property, I realised that only one of the bedrooms was habitable. This must have been where great aunt Lorna had slept. It was terribly sad to think that she had died alone among strangers. Even her own niece had not known about her fatal accident.

In the kitchen, I was relieved to find the electric kettle worked. The hall light was probably just in need of a new bulb. Shrugging off my melancholy mood, brought on by thinking about my great aunt, and the overwhelming task of sorting out the house, I returned to Maud's emporium. She was ensconced behind the counter, engrossed in a glossy magazine.

'You've decided to stay, have you?' she enquired, as she rung up the items in my basket. 'I thought you might.'

I nodded, paying for my purchases.

'I'd better give you these, then,' she said, rummaging in the till and picking out a set of keys. 'Unless you'd like me to keep your spare keys here?'

Unsure what to say, I stammered my thanks and watched as she returned the keys to her drawer. Seeing my surprised expression, she explained that she had been feeding the fish before I arrived.

'But I don't suppose you'll be needing me to do that any longer, not now you're here to take care of things.' She smiled ingratiatingly at me. 'If there's anything else you need, you only have to ask.'

What I really needed was someone to help me clean my house, but I doubted that was the kind of help Maud was offering. I went back to Rosecroft with a little tub of fish food, tea bags, milk, bread, cheese, a few light bulbs and several boxes of matches for the gas hob and oven, and set about making myself a simple supper. Having eaten, I turned my attention to giving my notice on my flat in London. There was no one significant moment when I reached my decision, but at some point I had decided to stay in Ashton Mead. If it turned out to be a terrible mistake, I would have to look for another home, but Finsbury Park was too expensive for me anyway, even if I managed to find another job straight away. In the meantime, I had one month in which to return to London, pack up my few belongings, and return my keys. The momentous decision reached, I hesitated for only a moment before hitting the send button to my landlord. Having spread my sleeping bag on the bed, I lay down and closed my eyes. The mattress was comfortable, but I was too excited to sleep. After a while I gave up trying, googled how to look after goldfish, and started making plans for the future.

In my mind I revisited each of the rooms in the house. I had to keep reminding myself that these were *my* rooms in *my* house. In the morning, after unpacking the few possessions I had brought with me, I would go to the shop and buy a stack of cleaning materials. I was determined to make Rosecroft habitable and stay there, at least until I had worked out a plan. Once everything I now owned had been thoroughly washed and polished, swept and scrubbed, and the garden brought under control, it would be a beautiful cottage. Even if I didn't decide to live there permanently, I could find a tenant, or sell it. But first I was going to stay there for a few months and make it presentable, inside and out. It was the least I could do to repay my great aunt for her generosity. Even though she would never know about my efforts, I owed it to her to look after her house, and the little fish that had meant so much to her she had refused to hand over her house to anyone who wasn't prepared to look after it. Having researched the life expectancy of goldfish, I googled pet shops in the area, determined to buy a proper fish tank. Eventually, I dozed off, still thinking about my fish and wondering if she ever fell asleep while swimming round and round her bowl.

3

THE FOLLOWING DAY, I set to work, starting in the kitchen. Hardly the most fastidious of people, even I baulked at what looked like mouse droppings tracing an erratic route across the red flagstones of the floor. In daylight which shone dimly through windows covered in a film of grime, cobwebs were visible, weighed down with dust. In a broom cupboard I came across an ancient feather duster which was more or less intact. Starting at the top, I did my best to remove the cobwebs hanging from the ceiling. After a while my arms were aching and my hair was full of dust, but the ceiling was clear. I was desperate to wash my hair but I pressed on, wiping greasy worktops, scouring filthy corners, laboriously working my way down to the floor. By the time I turned up at the shop for a third round of cleaning materials, Maud was treating me like an old friend, and she even gave me a discount on some of my purchases.

'You're doing a lot of cleaning,' she remarked as she handed me my bags. 'Must be hungry work.' Grinning, she popped a pork pie into my bag and refused to let me pay for it. Her kindness cheered me up more than she could have realised.

On my second evening, I ventured out and ate at The Plough, where I learned the corpulent landlord was called Cliff. He had a bald pate, smiling blue eyes, and ruddy cheeks. Tufts of ginger hair which stuck out above his large red ears combined with his bulbous nose to give him a slightly comical appearance. He chatted effortlessly as he served drinks without glancing at what he was pouring. Despite his apparent carelessness, I never saw him spill a drop. His assistant, Tess, was a stringy woman of indeterminate age, who seemed to be brimming over with nervous energy. As surly as Cliff was welcoming, she had a habitual scowl on her face. Initially worried I had inadvertently annoyed her, I soon realised she was crabby with everyone.

After a week, my arms were stiff from sweeping and scrubbing, and my nose felt as though it was stuffed with dust, but the house was beginning to look tolerably clean downstairs. By the end of two weeks I was able to relax my efforts, and start rifling through my great aunt's belongings. It felt voyeuristic yet it was compelling, like working on an archaeological dig, or sifting through items in a charity shop, hoping to find some long lost treasure. There were dusty boxes of photos, some so old they were black and white or sepia. I recognised my grandmother in a few and toyed with the idea of keeping them for my mother, but in the end I discarded them all, afraid of raking up forgotten animosities.

Having fallen out with her aunt after my grandmother died, my mother had been far from pleased on hearing that Lorna had left Rosecroft to me in her will.

'Why would she leave it to *you*?' was her initial reaction on hearing my news.

'Thanks for the congratulations,' I muttered, too softly for her to hear.

Along with batches of photos, many of them in their original yellow Kodak folders, I came across a tattered black notebook in a drawer beside the bed. The cover of the book was unassuming, apart from the one word 'Diary' printed in gold lettering in the top right hand corner. My curiosity was instantly aroused. Resisting the temptation to start reading at once, I waited until I had undressed and was in bed, comfortably propped up against a few pillows. With a cup of cocoa gently steaming on the bedside table, I settled down to study the contents of the diary. It was disconcerting, reading the words of a dead woman I barely remembered.

After my anticipation, the diary proved a disappointment. If Lorna had any sensational secrets in her life, she had not recorded them in her diary, which was filled with shopping lists and jottings about wildlife. Nevertheless, I scanned through the pages, learning about my great aunt's life in Ashton Mead. Some of her notes were repeated. She had written out a list of different garden birds which she ticked off, presumably when she saw them. A 'big fox' that lived in the vicinity was frequently recorded as crossing the lane or foraging in my great aunt's garden. For some reason, the fox seemed to worry her unduly. Towards the end of her records she mentioned several times that it disturbed 'P', which was presumably a reference to one of the birds that regularly visited her garden.

Towards the end of the book, I came across a few other cryptic remarks which caught my attention. 'No sign of S', my great aunt had noted in her spidery handwriting. A few pages later, half hidden among shopping lists and other notes, there was another comment, 'Still no sign of S', and a little further on, 'Worried about S.' There followed several pages of shopping lists, until the mysterious S cropped up again in the last few pages: 'Asked about S' and 'Can't find out anything about S'. I wondered why 'S' had vanished without any explanation, and why my great aunt had been so worried. Perhaps this mysterious S was the reason she had never married. Speculating about the identity of S, I fell asleep.

After a fortnight spent cleaning and sorting out, I had finally swept away every cobweb, sprayed the ants that had taken up residence along one wall of the kitchen, and thrown out dozens of bin liners filled with my great aunt's belongings: homemade grey and beige clothes that even a charity shop would struggle to sell, musty old books stained with mildew, and numerous china ornaments, many chipped or cracked and mostly hideous, relics of a solitary life. As far as I could tell none of them was worth anything, and I consigned all but a few to the bin. There was no place for useless clutter in my house. Mr Williamson had been in touch to confirm my acceptance of the terms of my great aunt's will, and Rosecroft finally belonged to me. After all my efforts, I felt as though I had earned my residence there. It was time to take stock of my life and decide what to do next. I liked Ashton Mead and decided to stay put, at least for the time being.

I fell into the habit of wandering along to the pub for a leisurely pint in the evening. The bar was spacious, furnished with comfortable well-worn chairs of dark wood with maroon leather seats. The polished tables were stained with many rings, in spite of a generous supply of coasters. No large screen television dominated the place, and a single fruit machine was discreetly placed in a corner so as not to intrude on those wanting to have a quiet drink. It was a relaxing place to sit for an hour or two after supper, and I had nothing to hurry home for. Besides, I was getting to know a few of the regular locals. I wasn't used to living on my own, and even an hour of sporadic and perfunctory chat was welcome company.

Apart from Cliff and Tess, there was an old man who never budged from his corner table in the pub. He was there every evening, although I never saw him arrive or depart. I guessed he was at least eighty. When I asked him, he replied that he was as old as his tongue and a little older than his teeth. He cackled as he threw his head back and opened his mouth to display his few remaining teeth. I never once saw him on his feet. Whatever time I arrived, he was there, sitting in a corner of the bar, wrapped in an old raincoat, hunched over a pint. From time to time, Tess or Cliff would take him a glass of beer, although I never saw him signal that he was ready for another pint, or part with any money.

With the initial phase of my cleaning finally completed, a cream tea at the Sunshine Tea Shoppe seemed like an appropriate way to celebrate. The café lived up to its name, as a splash of dazzling yellow in the High Street. Below the bright yellow awning, the exterior wall was painted pale primrose. Stepping across the threshold was like entering a giant daffodil. The floor was tiled in yellow and white, the walls were painted a pale lemon colour, and the tablecloths were yellow and white checked gingham. There was no one else around so when the waitress came bustling over, we fell into conversation. Hannah was tall and voluptuous, with curly blonde hair and a friendly open face above her bright yellow apron. She proved as easy to talk to as her welcoming smile promised. In all the excitement and activity of moving into my new home, I had scarcely thought about Ben, but now I found myself telling Hannah about my recent failed relationship.

'That's men for you,' she replied with a cynical shrug.

It turned out Hannah owned the tea shop, and she told me how she had come to open it with the money she had acquired from a divorce settlement.

'He was older than me, quite a lot older, and I never should've married him. It was a damn fool thing to do, but you don't think, do you? Well, I didn't. He seemed so kind and sensitive and warm and funny. They all do, I suppose, until the honeymoon period is over then – pouf! The magic's gone and you see each other as you really are. Not that my ex was a bad guy. He was generous to a fault. But he just couldn't keep his pants on. After his third fling, I'd had enough. That wasn't my idea of a marriage, and I told him so. He wasn't even surprised. He'd been through it all before, more than once. He tried to talk me into staying, but it was over. Anyway, if your experience was anything like mine, you're better off without him. I'm sticking to the single life from now on. Much less bother. Still, my ex was loaded and I came out of it with enough money to open this place and be independent of the lot of them.' She grinned. 'It's not exactly a goldmine, but it's a good little earner in the summer months and we make enough the rest of the year to keep ticking over.'

Chatting to Hannah made me realise how lonely I had been. Busy with sweeping and scrubbing, and hauling black bags out to the bin, I hadn't noticed the passage of time but since my arrival in Ashton Mead the only person

I had exchanged more than two sentences with face to face was Maud. My mother had recovered from her initial shock on hearing about my move, but she hadn't forgiven me for choosing to move out of London, and our telephone conversations had been brief. I didn't mind. She only nagged me when we did speak.

'I'm just saying it because I worry about you,' she would insist.

'Mum, I'm twenty-four. I can look after myself.'

'Clearly,' she would reply in a tone heavy with sarcasm.

Hannah and I hit it off, and when she suggested we meet for a pint later on, I agreed at once. 'That way I can chat without being at work,' she said, as if any explanation was necessary.

'Fair enough.'

When we were seated in the pub that evening, Hannah asked me about my work. I explained that I was between jobs, having recently become unemployed.

'It wasn't anything I'd done,' I told her. 'The company was in financial difficulties, and I'd been there less than six months, so when my job went down the pan, I got nothing.'

'What was the job?'

'I was working for a marketing company. I studied marketing for my degree and thought I was working my way up the career ladder, you know. My last job was quite a step up from my first, but in the end it didn't go anywhere.'

'Which went first, the job or the boyfriend?' Hannah asked.

'The job, and next thing I knew, he was packing his bag.'

'He sounds like a right bastard, dumping you when you'd just lost your job.'

'Something like that, I suppose,' I replied. I hadn't thought of Ben's departure in such harsh terms before, but Hannah had a point.

'So what wind blew you here to Ashton Mead?' she asked.

I explained that while I had been casting around for some direction in my life, I had unexpectedly inherited a house in the village.

'To be honest, I've no idea what I'm going to do now I've moved here,' I concluded.

'Well, I hope you stick around,' Hannah said.

I was living in a house of my own, and now I had a new friend as well. Life was certainly looking up. I wondered what Ben would say if he could see me settled in my own home, and realised I no longer cared about his opinion. I had moved on, and for the first time in my life I felt truly free. Like Hannah, I was living an independent life, and it suited me just fine.

It amused me to think that I had exchanged Ben for a goldfish.

'I'm much better off without him,' I told my little companion. 'And at least you're not going to walk out on me,' I added.

My new pet glided past me with a flick of its tail.

4

THE NEXT MORNING, THERE was a knock at my door. Opening it, I saw a frail old woman gazing up at me. She had curly white hair and sharp blue eyes that twinkled when she smiled. At her side a small brown and white dog was straining at its lead, eager to come in the house.

'Hello,' I said, returning her smile warily. 'Can I help you?'

I expected she was a friend of my great aunt, and wondered whether she had heard that Lorna was dead. The old woman handed me a shopping bag she was carrying and introduced herself as Catherine. My assumption was confirmed when she explained that she had been a close friend of my great aunt.

'I'm Lorna's great niece,' I replied, hesitating to add that Rosecroft now belonged to me.

'I'm so sorry,' she said. 'She was a wonderful woman. You must miss her terribly.'

Not wishing to admit that I had scarcely known my great aunt, I muttered vaguely that her death had been a sad loss for us all, and that it was lovely to meet one of her local friends.

'Do you live in the village?' I enquired politely.

'No, but we're not far away. It's just a few stops on the bus, so it's really quite convenient. My sister and I used to visit Lorna regularly, and Poppy, of course. We did, didn't we?' she asked, addressing the little dog. Catherine looked up at me. 'Isn't she adorable?' she asked, seeing me looking at the dog frisking at her feet. 'She's still only a puppy. Go on, give her some attention. I can see you want to, and there's nothing she likes more than being made a fuss of. Don't worry, she won't bite. She's a gentle little soul, poor thing. And you do need to get to know her.'

As she spoke, she stepped forward and the little dog nuzzled my ankles and looked up at me, mewing like a kitten. I bent down and patted her head, which she rubbed against my legs as though we were old friends before rolling over onto her back where she lay, blinking up at me. She had soft white fur, with brown patches on her back. Through the thin covering of fur on her underside her pale pink flesh was visible, dotted with dark grey markings.

'Lying on her back like that is a submissive position,' Catherine said. 'She wants you to pet her. She's very friendly. You can tickle her tummy. Go on, she loves it.'

Bending down, I scratched the dog gently under her chin.

'We've been taking care of her ever since poor Lorna was taken,' Catherine went on. 'Now that you're here, we're going to miss her, of course, but she's a lively little thing and we're getting on, and we don't have the energy for a puppy. And now, I really must be going.' She put down a second bag she was holding. 'There's some food in here for her, enough to tide you over. We don't need it now. And there's a few of her favourite toys in the bag. She loves things she can chew on. You have to watch her or she'll be chewing the legs of the furniture. And I wouldn't leave your shoes lying around.' She smiled affectionately at the little dog. 'You're a naughty little thing, aren't you? Oh yes, you are.' As I struggled to comprehend what Catherine was saying, she turned to me again. 'She's what they call a Jack Tzu, a cross between a Jack Russell Terrier and a Shih Tzu. You're going to be surprised when you find out how clever she is.' She grinned and lowered her voice. 'We're convinced she understands everything we say. Don't you?' she added, turning to look down at the dog with a smile.

'Wait a minute,' I cried out, finally finding my voice. 'What do you mean? I don't want – that is, I can't –' Just in time I stopped myself, as the truth struck me. 'Did you say you've been looking after this puppy since my great aunt died? Did she belong to my great aunt?'

But I had already guessed the answer.

'Yes, Poppy was poor Lorna's dog,' Catherine replied, with a sad smile. 'We would have returned her to you sooner, but Maud thought you might need a few weeks to settle in and sort the place out, and we agreed that was only fair. She told us how busy you've been, looking after the place and cleaning it up. And we didn't want to be preemptive. After all, we didn't know whether you were going to stay.'

I stared at her, aghast. Refusal to look after the puppy would mean losing Rosecroft, just when I had begun to feel at home there. Seeing my horrified expression, the old lady chuckled.

'Don't worry, you'll soon get used to her. She's house trained, and you'll find she's a very clean dog. She has to go for a walk twice a day, and if she needs to go out in between, she'll let you know, and there's a roll of bags for her business in there.' She indicated one of the bags she had been carrying. 'Don't forget, she has to go out twice a day, whatever the weather. She doesn't like going out in the rain, so you may need to coax her because, well, she has to go. And she needs to be walked every day. You know, she needs exercise or she can become overexcited.'

'How far can she walk?'

Catherine hesitated. 'Oh, for about half an hour,' she muttered, suddenly seeming less self-assured. She took a plastic bag and a little net out of her bag. 'I'll just collect my fish. I was a bit nervous about keeping Poppy in the house with him. Poppy can be a bit naughty, can't you, you little rascal?'

'What about your fish tank? How are you going to carry it?'

'Oh, Maud gave me that,' she replied. 'We've got a proper tank at home for him, but it was too heavy to move. He'll be glad to get back home.'

There was nothing else for it but to thank Catherine for taking care of the puppy, take Poppy's lead from her, and accept that the little dog was now my responsibility. Dumbly I followed Catherine into the kitchen, with Poppy trotting eagerly in front of me. Together we watched Catherine scoop the goldfish out of its glass bowl and drop it neatly into her plastic bag which she had filled with water.

'There,' she said. 'That's that. I'll be off now. I need to get him back in his tank as soon as possible. It's not good for them to be kept in plastic bags for too long, you know.' She glanced at her watch. 'There's a bus in ten minutes so I have to hurry.'

'Are you sure you wouldn't rather take Poppy with you?' I asked in sudden panic. 'I'd hate to take her away from you if you'd like to keep her.'

'Oh dear me, no. We're too old to cope with a puppy.' She sighed. 'But bring her to see us soon, won't you?' She reached down to pet the dog. 'We're going to miss you.'

It was on the tip of my tongue to cave in and beg her to take Poppy with her, but I had fallen in love with my new home. If I refused to take care of my great aunt's beloved pet, I might lose Rosecroft. Besides, Poppy seemed like a friendly little dog. She surely couldn't be too difficult to look after, once we had grown used to each other. It had taken Catherine less than a minute to transfer her goldfish into a bag. Clearly she was an efficient woman who had managed to cope with a puppy despite her age. I hoped she hadn't blundered in leaving my great aunt's puppy in my hands. I had never owned a dog before, and the prospect scared me. Still, I had come to Ashton Mead looking for a new challenge. It seemed that fate had granted my wish.

After Catherine left, Poppy sat in the doorway of the living room, watching me cross to the sofa and sit down. Her head tilted inquisitively to one side, and her bright black eyes remained fixed on me, as though she was considering whether to trust me. While I was dithering about what to do with her, she seemed to reach a decision. Bounding over to me, she sprang up on the sofa, settled down with her chin resting on my leg, and fell asleep.

Listening to her faint snoring and watching the gentle rise and fall of her back, I felt an overwhelming sense of relief that she seemed to like me, even though I didn't want her and had no idea what I was going to do with her. I studied her white legs and tail, and the light brown patches on her sturdy back. Unlike her body coat, the fur on her head was long and curly, with delicate strands that hung down over her face. She seemed happy enough, but I was unfamiliar with dogs and wondered how she would cope once she realised my great aunt wasn't coming back. I spent the next hour googling how to look after a dog. Every time I shifted on the sofa, Poppy's ears twitched, but she didn't stir from her position.

'How difficult can it be?' I muttered to myself, scrolling through a profusion of websites.

One thing soon became clear: Poppy was going to require a lot more attention than a goldfish. I was still researching 'How to look after dogs' when Poppy woke up, sprang to the floor, and raced over to the bag Catherine had left for her and began to chew it furiously. I snatched the plastic away and she whimpered.

'Okay, okay, I know you're hungry,' I told her.

My problem was that I didn't know how much food to give her. Catherine had told me that the food she had left would last for a while, but what did that mean? Several websites advised against overfeeding dogs but how much was too much? Googling advice on feeding dogs, it was soon obvious that online guides were no help. Recommendations were based not only on the breed of dog, but also on a combination of its age and weight. All I knew was that Poppy was a puppy.

In the end I found an old plastic bowl in the kitchen and dished up half a tin of her food. It appeared to be minced up meat of some kind, so I cleared a shelf in the fridge for the rest of her tins, thinking I would make myself a mug of tea while she was eating. By the time I had finished putting her food away, her bowl was empty. I emptied the remainder of the tin into her bowl and she walked away from it, without a backward glance. Clearly half a tin was enough for one meal.

My next task was to take Poppy out for a walk, and hope she would empty her bladder and bowels outside. To my relief, she did both. So far, so good. Great Aunt Lorna would have been pleased. Maybe this dog owning lark wasn't going to be too difficult for me after all, I thought, as I picked up her little brown poo in a bag, and looked around for a bin. Of course there wasn't one in the lane, so I took it home and deposited it in the bin in my front yard.

By now I was worn out with the excitement and stress of having a dog unexpectedly foisted on me, so after supper I deposited the dog on the sofa where she had slept so happily earlier on, and went upstairs to bed. Poppy scampered after me. I carried her back downstairs and shut her in the kitchen for the night but she barked and whimpered so pitifully that in the end I went downstairs to reassure her that there was nothing to be frightened about. I had to pick her up and hold her close to me for a few minutes before she stopped trembling.

'You poor little thing,' I murmured. 'You're missing Lorna, aren't you? I'll leave the door open and you can come and find me if you feel scared. I won't be far away. I'll just be upstairs.'

As soon as I left the room, Poppy darted after me, clambered up onto my bed and promptly fell asleep. I was loath to wake her so, pleased that she had calmed down, I gave in and went to bed with Poppy curled up at my feet. It was comforting to know she was there with me, and I fell asleep resolving to train her to sleep in the kitchen. But not yet. First she needed to settle in and become used to me as her new owner. And I had to admit the situation worked both ways, because I found her presence reassuring.

Woken by a wet tongue licking my cheek, I checked my phone and groaned. Six o'clock was far too early for me to be awake. Poppy had been with me for one night and already she was causing me problems. I was desperate to go back to sleep, but Poppy seemed equally desperate to be taken out. Not wanting to risk any accidents, I pulled on my clothes and we left the house for her morning excursion. On our way back from a walk all round the village, we bumped into the village postman, Pete. Tall and wiry, his grey eyes peered down at me through his rimless spectacles.

'I see you have a dog,' he said in his soft voice.

With a rueful smile, I told him Poppy had been my great aunt's dog.

'I thought I recognised her,' he said, smiling. 'Oh well, as long as she doesn't start biting my ankles when I deliver your post, we'll get along just fine.'

'She won't,' I promised, hoping that was true.

I really knew nothing at all about my dog, but I was learning fast.

5

IT DIDN'T BOTHER ME that after a few weeks in the village I still hadn't met my next door neighbour. People are entitled to lead reclusive lives, and an unsociable neighbour was preferable to having a busybody living on my doorstep. All the same, I was curious to find out who was living in the house next door. On my way home from taking Poppy for a walk one day, I spotted a woman walking through next door's gate carrying several shopping bags. She must have gone to the Village Emporium the minute Maud opened up in the morning, because it was still early. Appearing to be struggling with heavy bags, she clearly heard me call out 'Hello', because she halted abruptly at the sound of my voice. But then she continued on her way without turning round. Impelled by curiosity as much as cordiality, I repeated my greeting.

'Can I help you with your shopping?' I called out over the low hedge that bordered our paths.

The woman stood as though frozen, her head lowered, her face concealed beneath a mop of dark hair.

'I've just recently moved in here,' I added, waving my arms around, although she must have noticed me coming and going.

Still she kept her eyes fixed on the ground. The encounter was becoming awkward and, besides, Poppy had begun to whine and pull at the hem of my trousers as though she wanted to drag me home.

'Stop it, Poppy.'

As I looked down, tugging at the lead, my neighbour scuttled to her front door, flung it open and slammed it behind her, leaving me feeling curiously disconnected from my surroundings, as though this was all a dream. Poppy's barking recalled me to my surroundings. Thoughtfully I went inside.

Warmer weather had arrived at last, the change in the temperature happening almost overnight. Throughout April the dismal weather hadn't bothered me much, since I was mostly indoors cleaning, painting walls, and sorting through my great aunt's belongings, all of which was time consuming and exhausting. I was proud of my achievement, and wished Ben could see me now. My only concern was that my funds were running low. If I didn't manage to find a job soon, I would be reduced to cadging off my parents.

As though the atmosphere was sensitive to the date, the first of May dawned bright and warm, with a distinct hint of summer in the air. I spent a couple of hours in my overgrown back garden. There was no private garden attached to my lodgings in London, and I found pulling up weeds surprisingly satisfying, although it was going to take me a long time to make it anywhere near tidy. Poppy snuffled and scurried around in the garden while I worked. She seemed to like eating moss which I didn't think would do her any harm, although I googled it just to make sure. Occasionally a squirrel darted up a tree or across the grass and she tried to give chase, but I kept her on a long lead so she couldn't run off and disappear. As soon as I could afford it, I was planning to mend my broken fence so she could run around the garden untethered.

After a while she settled to scrabbling at the earth right at the edge of the garden. When I pulled her away, she whimpered and strained on her leash, seemingly determined to tunnel underneath my neighbour's high metal fence. I wondered what might be concealed on the other side of the fence that interested my dog so much. Speculating about the mysterious secret my neighbour could be hiding, it struck me that my great aunt had died as the result of a fall, not long after she had acquired a dog who was keen to tunnel under the metal fence. Catherine had told me the dog was intelligent. Was it possible Poppy was trying to gain access to my neighbour's garden in order to expose a nefarious secret hidden from the world? The more I speculated about it, the more likely an explanation it seemed both for the unusual metal fence, and for my great aunt's unexpected fall down the stairs.

After a while I took a break and went to the shop, partly to look for gardening tools, but also to question Maud about my elusive neighbour. I was relieved that my dog could accompany me into the shop as long as I was holding her. Poppy didn't protest when I gathered her up in my arms, but lay against my chest with her head resting on my shoulder.

'Wrong?' Maud echoed, shaking her grey curls and pushing her glasses back in place as she rang up my purchases. 'What makes you think there's anything wrong with her?' She squinted at me inquisitively, and I could almost imagine her pointy little nose twitching, eager to sniff out gossip.

'She just seems a bit antisocial. Not that there's anything wrong with that,' I added quickly, not knowing how friendly Maud was with my mysterious neighbour. 'Does she live there alone?' I asked, determined to find out more information.

'Yes, that is, she does now. She came here – oh, it must have been about fifteen years ago.'

I gave a little laugh. 'You know, I don't even know her name.'

'She's called Alice,' Maud told me promptly.

'Alice,' I repeated softly as I tapped my card on the reader.

Knowing my neighbour's name didn't really give me much to go on, but it felt like the beginning of a connection with her. The next time I caught sight of her, scurrying in or out of her house, I would be able to call out to her. 'Hey, Alice, can I help you with your shopping?'

I turned my attention back to Maud who was holding out my receipt.

'Did Alice come here alone?'

'Alone? No, she came here with her daughter who was a small child when they first arrived in the village.'

That surprised me, because I had only occasionally glimpsed one woman entering or leaving the house.

'Did her daughter die?'

'Die?' It was Maud's turn to look surprised. 'Oh no. We would have known.'

I suspected that was true, and had already made a mental note to reveal as little as possible about my own life to the shopkeeper. Anything I told her in confidence would no doubt be shared with the whole village in next to no time. Maud seemed puzzled by my questions. Perhaps she was unsettled by the suggestion that something might happen in the village without her knowledge.

'So where is Alice's daughter now?' I persisted as I packed my shopping into my bag with one hand while Poppy wriggled and whined to be put down. 'Only I've never seen her and I'm living right next door. Did she go away to university?'

'Sophie? She went away travelling about a year ago, and she's not come back since.'

Tess from the pub came in and I had the impression Maud was relieved at the excuse to end our conversation. Intrigued, I went home, wondering about my antisocial neighbour who hid herself behind an impenetrable metal fence.

That evening, in the pub, I met up with Hannah who made a great fuss of Poppy.

'She's gorgeous,' she crooned. 'She was Lorna's little dog, wasn't she? My mum and I have been wondering what happened to her. We were talking about her only this morning.'

After explaining how Catherine had been looking after Poppy, I repeated the questions I had put to Maud that morning. Hannah confirmed that my neighbour had arrived in Ashton Mead about fifteen years ago. 'Sophie was a few years below me at school, although of course we knew each other, both living in Ashton Mead. But we were never friends. I don't think we've exchanged two words since we left school. To be fair, we hardly spoke when we were at school either. Sophie was sweet, but she was quiet and pretty boring, to be honest.'

I could imagine Hannah, outgoing and gregarious, having little time for a shy younger pupil at school.

'As for Alice, she's always kept to herself, and since the lockdowns she's been more reclusive than ever.' Hannah's normally cheerful features creased in a faint frown. 'I think the lockdowns affected people in different ways. I couldn't wait to start seeing everyone again, but some people seem to have withdrawn from society altogether. It must be miserable, living such a solitary life, but it seems being in lockdown suited some people. It would have driven me nuts if I'd been on my own, but I've been living with my mother since my divorce, thank goodness. I would have found it really hard on my own.'

'What's Alice's daughter like?' I asked, determined to stick to the subject that was intriguing me.

'Sophie's all right, I suppose.' Hannah smiled. 'I mean, she's not weird like her mother. She was always a bit quiet, but nice enough. I never had any reason to dislike her. She was never what you might call popular, although I don't think anyone disliked her. She was a bit of a nonentity, really. Not much personality and absolutely no sense of humour. You couldn't have a laugh with her and she never wanted to go out anywhere. To be honest, I've no idea what she did for a social life.'

Before Hannah could say any more, a customer entered the pub. Noticing Hannah, he waved, and came over to join us. Without realising it, he had just given me another reason to stay in Ashton Mead, at least for the time being. Not the kind of man you would notice in a crowd, Toby was tall and slim and his hair was jet black. But it was his blue eyes that arrested my attention. He seemed to smile at me with a sense of intimacy, as though we had known each other all our lives. Afraid I would blush, I looked down, and felt my cheeks turn warm. Toby was the first even vaguely attractive man I had seen since coming to Ashton Mead, and I fumbled for words when he spoke to me.

'Is this your puppy?' he wanted to know.

'Yes.'

'She's adorable.'

He leaned down to scratch the top of Poppy's head. As she closed her eyes in ecstasy, I explained how my great aunt had died, leaving me her house and her dog.

'Ah yes, Lorna Lafferty,' he said. 'I thought I recognised her dog. I heard about what happened to her. I'm sorry for your loss.'

'To be honest, I hardly knew her, even though she left me her house.'

Born in Ashton Mead, Toby told me he had left the village to go to university. He had fully intended to move out of the area, possibly to London, on graduating.

'That was four years ago,' he concluded ruefully. 'I came back to visit for a week, and I'm still here. I never got further than Swindon.'

I nodded in appreciation of his words. 'I know,' I murmured.

'But you've done the exact opposite,' he pointed out, and I felt my face turn red. 'Not that it matters,' he added quickly, seeing my embarrassment. 'But if you've never crawled back to the place you came from, and been unable to move on with your life... well, you're lucky.'

I had to agree about that. 'It's almost too good to be true,' I concluded. 'Rosecroft is perfect. I mean, it was quite neglected when I moved in and I had to spend weeks cleaning it up, just to make it habitable. But I love it. I still can't believe my luck.'

'I'm sure it's no more than you deserve,' Toby replied politely. 'Will you be living there alone, or will a partner be joining you?'

'I don't have a partner,' I replied reluctantly.

It wasn't that I was still loyal to Ben, or was hoping he would follow me to Ashton Mead. On the contrary, I had been too preoccupied with housework to even think about him. The truth was, since moving to Ashton Mead, I had never been happier. But meeting Toby made me question whether I really wanted to live by myself for the rest of my life. The thought of having male company in the evenings, and through the night, gave me a yearning sensation. And Toby really was very attractive, in a quiet sort of way. Where Ben was brash and vain about his appearance, Toby had the unassuming air of a man who was unaware of his own good looks

I was tempted to invite him back to Rosecroft, to see my house, when Hannah returned from the bar with a tray of drinks and crisps, and the conversation moved on. My two new friends chatted companionably while I sat listening. But once or twice Toby turned to look at me and my spirits gave a little flutter as our eyes met in a smile. As for Poppy, she seemed blissfully happy with Toby and Hannah taking it in turns to pet her and play with her in a corner of the pub.

6

THE FOLLOWING AFTERNOON I called into the tea shop to see Hannah. As well as wanting to see my new friend, I was curious to find out whether Toby was single. For a few minutes there was no opportunity to mention him because Hannah launched into a diatribe about being rushed off her feet, taking orders, preparing them, and serving them.

'I have to do everything myself,' she concluded, with a grimace. 'It's too much.'

The café was empty, so I wasn't quite sure why she was complaining, but at least she was happy for me to take Poppy inside with me.

'Mostly customers don't object to well-behaved dogs,' she told me. 'But let's sit in the corner and have a cup of tea. That way no one will notice her until they're inside, unless she starts barking.'

'She won't,' I assured Hannah. 'She's very well-behaved.'

To my relief Poppy obediently curled up quietly in the corner and fell asleep.

'Toby seems nice,' I said, casually, when Hannah finally stopped grumbling.

'Yes, he's lovely, but he's got his hands full looking after his mother.'

'Looking after his mother?' I echoed.

Hannah nodded. 'You know his mother's in a wheelchair?'

I shook my head. That was the trouble with living in a village where everyone knew everyone else. Other people expected me to know all about the other local residents.

'That's why he goes to see her all the time. He's not happy about her living in that house, with only strangers looking after her, but she refuses to move. She insists she can cope with living independently, but if he wasn't around, I don't think she'd be able to stay there.'

Hannah's eyes narrowed and she looked at me shrewdly. 'He's a really great guy, but I don't think he's looking for a relationship right now.'

I nodded, wondering whether Hannah might have her own reasons for trying to warn me off Toby.

'I tell you what,' she went on with sudden eagerness, 'if you're feeling lonely –'

'I'm not feeling lonely –' I replied, but she ignored my interjection and carried on talking.

'The point is, I could really do with some help.'

Seeing my baffled expression, she proceeded to offer me a job. 'The pay's not great, but it'll be fun working together.'

There was only one problem with Hannah's plan: I didn't want a job in her café. In fact, I had no ambitions to work in any café whatsoever.

'If I'm ever looking for a job as a waitress, I promise to offer my services to you first,' I assured her.

Hannah cheerfully batted away my objections.

'At least you can try,' she said, grinning. 'You need a job and I need someone to come and help me out. This is

51

perfect! Both our problems sorted in one fell swoop. It's pure genius!'

I didn't even need to think about it. 'I appreciate the offer, really I do, but how can I leave Poppy? She hasn't got used to me yet, and she's been moved around from Lorna to Catherine and now to me. She must be feeling unsettled and it wouldn't be fair to leave her on her own all day.'

We both glanced at Poppy who was dozing contentedly in the corner.

Hannah didn't seem at all put out by my objections.

'You can tether her in the yard at the back,' she said. 'I sometimes leave my mum's dog out there. It's perfectly safe, and there's an awning she can shelter under if it rains, and you can pop out and see her whenever you want.' She smiled. 'You'll have to come up with a better excuse than that if you want to avoid working. Besides, where else are you going to get a job that lets you bring your dog with you, right here in Ashton Mead?'

She had a point, so I agreed to consider her offer, my reluctance mingled with relief that I would be earning again. Now that I no longer had to pay rent, my wages would more than cover my bills. Hannah flung her arms around me, and nearly stifled me with her warm embrace. As I struggled to extricate myself, I couldn't help laughing at her enthusiasm.

'I promise you'll thank me,' she said, finally releasing me. 'It's no good being shut up alone indoors all the time. You can't spend your life cleaning your house. And anyway, I'm telling you, you're going to love it here. It's a great place to work. You'll get free tea and cakes every day.' She patted her stomach with a moue of dismay. 'But seriously, the work's not hard. I'm telling you, this is going to work out brilliantly for both of us. It's going to be fun!'

Although naturally cautious, my experience with Rosecroft had taught me to be open to new adventures, so I repeated that I would consider the offer. Feeling unusually bold, I treated myself to a full cream tea and Hannah refused to charge me. She seemed to assume that I had agreed to work for her.

'I'll deduct it from your first month's pay,' she said, grinning. 'Now you're going to have to work for me for at least a week or I'll tell everyone what a scrounger you are.'

'That sounds like way below minimum wage, even with your expensive cream tea,' I laughed.

Contrary to my expectations, I enjoyed working in the tea shop. With the arrival of better weather, Ashton Mead became busy with people driving through on their way to the south coast, or Wales, or other holiday destinations. We were generally kept busy from lunch time onwards, and often in the mornings as well, with travellers coming in for a late breakfast. Hannah extended her opening hours, the till rang almost continuously, and I understood how the tea shop managed to turn over a profit even though some months were quiet. We worked hard, but we entertained ourselves, laughing discreetly at some of the odd customers who came in throughout the day. Hannah enjoyed likening them to fictional characters. One morning a stout man with a shiny bald pate came in for breakfast with a very thin companion.

'They look like Jack Sprat and his wife,' Hannah whispered to me behind her hand.

I corrected her, pointing out that in the rhyme, Jack Sprat ate no fat and his wife ate no lean. Laughing, she called me a pedant. Shortly afterwards, a man came in with a large flesh-coloured plaster on his temple.

'Now here's Jack but where's Jill?' Hannah muttered under her breath.

As she spoke, a woman came in and sat down beside him and Hannah smirked at me, as though her theory had been confirmed. It was a silly game, but it kept us amused.

Whenever I wasn't working at the café, I would be playing with my dog, and learning how to take care of her. Poppy had a tendency to go slightly crazy, running round in circles chasing her tail, and barking at her own reflection in the mirror. She was very affectionate and jumped up whenever she saw me, licking my legs and doing her best to hold on to my trousers with her teeth. However excited she was, she never bit me, and gradually we learned to trust each other.

I learned that Jack Tzus, with the body of a Jack Russell terrier and the shaggy head of a Shih Tzu, were a hybrid breed known for their lively and inquisitive nature. Poppy and I soon slipped into a comfortable routine where she did exactly what she wanted, while I made sure she was fed and exercised and couldn't get lost. One Monday, after the café closed, Hannah volunteered to give me a lesson in controlling my dog. Poppy was energetic and could be very wilful which, I gathered, was a common trait in Jack Tzus. Naturally friendly, she was still young, and needed to learn to obey my commands so we could co-exist comfortably. My little dog's welfare depended on me, and I was determined to do my best to give her a happy life, and avoid having to discipline her.

We stepped out into the yard behind the café. With Poppy on her lead, Hannah showed me how to teach her to come when I called her name, and to wait when she was told to stay where she was. Hannah told me the key to issuing clear instructions lay in hand movements, not words. Remembering Catherine's claim that Poppy understood everything that was said, I thought Hannah might be underestimating my dog.

'Poppy's very intelligent,' I said. 'She understands what you say.'

'She's a dog,' Hannah protested, laughing.

Just then, Poppy sprang to her feet and scampered away from us. Caught off guard, I let her lead slip from my grasp. Before I realised what was happening, Poppy dashed out of the yard. Hannah and I raced after her, but she had disappeared. Appalled that we had lost her, we ran off in opposite directions, calling her name. Poppy had only been mine for a short time, but I was already attached to her. I was devastated that she had wanted to run away from me, and terrified she might come to harm out on the road. We couldn't run around indefinitely, so when Hannah eventually phoned me to say she could see no sign of Poppy, we agreed to go home and make some 'Missing' notices to display in the village.

Struggling to control my tears, and desperately looking around for my little companion, I returned to Rosecroft alone. A fluffy brown and white bundle was sitting patiently by the front door, waiting to be let in. Usually Poppy would jump up in excitement when she saw me. This time, she sat perfectly still, gazing at me with an innocent look on her face, as if to ask how anyone could suspect she had done anything wrong. She needn't have worried. I was too happy at seeing her to scold her and, besides, it had been my fault for leaving the gate ajar and letting go of her lead. Scooping the little runaway up in my arms, I felt a rush of happiness as I hugged her.

That evening I took Poppy to the pub with me and we sat in the garden with Toby, who played with her, dangling a chew toy at her.

'She's much more interested in that little patch of earth than in this toy,' he laughed, as Poppy scrabbled furiously in the soil. 'She's like a kid in a sandpit. I can't remember when I last had such a good time.'

Excited that Toby wanted to spend time with me, I was scarcely aware of Poppy digging in the earth behind me.

'She's good fun,' I agreed, hoping he would reassure me that he was enjoying my company, rather than Poppy's.

When he replied, 'She certainly is,' I had to force myself to smile to conceal my disappointment.

We chatted for a while. He told me about his mother, who had been injured in a car accident and was paralysed from the waist down.

'She's remarkably cheerful, considering,' he added. 'She hardly ever lets it get her down.'

In return I explained how I had acquired a dog along with Rosecroft, and my initial mistake in thinking my great aunt's precious pet was a goldfish.

'It's lucky you like dogs,' he said, laughing at my story.

Poppy had abandoned her digging and now lay curled up at my feet, her eyes closed.

'I didn't, not really, until I inherited Poppy,' I confessed.

As though she was listening, Poppy's ears pricked up.

'Do you know my next door neighbour, Alice Thomas?' I asked Toby, when there was a pause in our conversation.

'I know who she is, yes.'

I glanced around before leaning across the table and confiding my suspicions to Toby.

He seemed amused. 'And what dark secret do you think she has concealed behind her metal fence?' he asked. 'Is she cultivating dangerous drugs? Or fencing stolen goods?' He laughed at his pun.

'It just seems a bit of a coincidence that my great aunt had a fatal accident a couple of months after she brought a dog home with her. I mean, she wasn't ill, or she wouldn't have bought a puppy. And the postmortem said she died after falling down the stairs at home. But what if Poppy was trying to get under the fence, and my great aunt followed her and discovered what was going on, and Alice needed to get rid of her?'

'What was going on?' Toby raised a quizzical eyebrow. 'What exactly do you suppose was going on in Alice Thomas's back garden? Do you think she was –' He broke off and glanced around surreptitiously. 'Do you think she was disposing of dead bodies behind her metal fence? And Lorna pole vaulted over the fence to find her dog?'

'Is it a coincidence that her daughter has disappeared? What if Alice buried Sophie in her back garden and Poppy dug up the body? You've got to admit it's possible –'

I broke off, as Toby burst out laughing. 'Has anyone ever told you that you have a very active imagination?'

'It could be true,' I retorted, stung by his scepticism.

'What do you think, Poppy?' Toby said, turning to my dog. 'Do you think she's barking up the wrong tree?'

Mortified by Toby's amusement, I conceded that such

terrible crimes didn't happen in places like Ashton Mead, at least not in the real world. In any case, sitting in the fading sunlight with my little dog at my feet and Toby smiling at me, I was too content to fret about what might have happened to Alice's daughter. When Ben had walked out on me, I thought I would never feel happy again. As it turned out, I couldn't have been more wrong. In the space of a few weeks, I had acquired a house, new friends, a job and a dog.

Life was good.

7

AFTER NEARLY TWO MONTHS, my life in Ashton Mead had settled into a comfortable routine. My only disquiet centred on my next door neighbour. All I had been able to learn about Alice was that her daughter was away travelling. Everyone in the village knew Sophie, but no one was able to tell me very much about her, and no one seemed to know exactly where she had gone. When I had first moved to Rosecroft, the fence between Alice's property and my own had intrigued me. I couldn't work out why anyone might want a fence like that in Ashton Mead. Now, every time I went out in the back garden, Poppy would run straight over to Alice's fence and whimper, for no apparent reason. My dog's obsession with the fence fuelled my own curiosity.

'It's not as if there's a crime wave around here,' I said to Hannah one day. 'She can't be worried about her security, can she? So why do you think it's there?'

Hannah shrugged. 'It's just a fence. It's her garden. To be honest, I didn't even know it was there until you started going on about it. Why shouldn't she put up a fence? What's the big deal?'

'It's not a normal fence,' I replied, irritated that she was so uninterested in something that intrigued me.

Preoccupied with Poppy, I soon forgot about my neighbour, but my curiosity was rekindled by seeing her coming home with several shopping bags over her arm. I was just setting off for work, but halted in surprise on seeing her walking towards me. Since I was standing between her and her front gate, she had no choice but to stop. Poppy growled; when I stepped forward, she let out a frenzied bark and seized the hem of my trousers in her teeth and tried to pull me away. Ignoring Poppy's antics, I tried again.

'Hello, Alice,' I greeted her in a loud voice.

It had occurred to me that perhaps the reason she hadn't responded to my earlier greeting was because she was hard of hearing. On the few occasions I had spotted her from a distance, her bowed shoulders and shuffling gait suggested a woman older than the forty or so years she appeared to be close up. She had dark eyes and a thin pointed nose, and looked somehow faded, as though she might once have been lively and attractive. All of this flashed through my mind as we faced one another in the street.

'I'm Emily,' I called out. 'I've moved in next door to you. I live at Rosecroft,' I added, jerking my head fatuously in the direction of my house.

Even the most socially diffident of people could hardly refuse to acknowledge so friendly a greeting. The woman tilted her head back slightly so she could look at me. With a wariness that was almost palpable, she glared at me while I repeated my greeting.

'Yes, yes,' Alice said testily, breaking her silence at last. 'I know who you are. I heard all about you from Maud.'

While my neighbour was speaking, Poppy rose up and pressed her front paws against my legs, as though she wanted to push me towards Rosecroft. Leaning down to tell Poppy to desist, I saw Alice spin on her heel and turn away from me. With the movement, one of her shopping bags swung on her arm and tilted. Several apples and oranges burst from the bag. Cascading to the ground, they rolled along the pavement in a colourful jumble. Poppy immediately gave chase, tugging at her lead and letting out a frustrated yelp each time she nudged a piece of fruit with her nose and sent it spinning out of reach.

'I'm sorry, I'm really sorry,' I stammered, pulling on Poppy's lead to stop her from reaching any more of my neighbour's fruit. 'She's not disobedient, really she's not. She thinks it's a game.'

I lunged at Poppy, but she was too quick and darted out of reach. She was having far too much fun to stop. Eventually I seized her and held her under one arm while Alice retrieved her fruit. I crouched down and gathered up those I could reach with my free hand, and dropped them into a fallen bag. Most of the oranges appeared to have survived intact, but a few apples had become bruised in their tumble, and one or two had bite marks from Poppy's exuberant assaults on them.

'She was just playing,' I repeated as I put Poppy down. 'She didn't mean any harm. I'll pay for the damage.'

Alice sniffed disapprovingly. 'You should keep your animal under control.'

Poppy backed away from my neighbour, crouched down and began to growl, baring her teeth. I had never seen her behave so aggressively before.

'She's only a puppy,' I retorted, stung by the implied criticism of my dog handling. 'And anyway, you were the one who dropped your shopping. It was hardly Poppy's fault if you dumped a load of apples right in front of her. It's only natural she'd want to play with them. She's a puppy and that's what puppies do. So you've got no cause to complain. In fact, you're the one who should be apologising. We live next door to each other and you've been avoiding me ever since I moved here.'

Alice seemed taken aback by the vehemence of my attack. 'That's not true,' she responded coldly.

'Well, maybe not deliberately avoiding me, but you haven't exactly welcomed me to the village as a neighbour should. You don't seem to want to even say hello when we see each other. Given that I've moved in next door to you, and we're bound to bump into each other from time to time, that's hardly neighbourly. We live next door to each other, so we might at least try to be civil to one another.'

Alice frowned. 'I had no intention of being uncivil,' she said.

That was a blatant lie, but I let it go. At least we were talking now.

'Do you have any pets?' I enquired.

Unless she had a dog, or perhaps chickens, I could see no reason for the metal fence which had piqued my curiosity, but I hadn't heard any animal noises coming from her garden.

'No,' she replied.

'I work at the tea shop,' I went on, hoping that by sharing something about myself it might encourage her to be more forthcoming. 'You should come in for tea one day.'

'I have a kettle,' she replied, deliberately missing the point. 'And now move aside so I can go home.' She might deny being uncivil, but that didn't alter the fact that she was being rude to me.

Realising that I had returned to my earlier position in front of her gate, blocking her entrance, I hesitated. I could hardly prevent her from entering her own home, but I didn't want to lose the opportunity to look around inside her house.

'Would you like me to help you take your shopping inside?' I asked, keeping hold of the bag of fruit I had gathered from the pavement.

She scowled at me. Poppy began growling again and Alice seemed to reach a decision.

'I don't want that feral dog coming in,' she said, glaring sourly at Poppy who was barking furiously again.

'I can tie Poppy up outside for a few minutes,' I replied, keen to see inside Alice's house. 'She won't be any trouble. You keep to the path and no digging in the earth,' I told my dog sternly.

As though she understood I was cross with her, Poppy hung her head, but she kept her eyes fixed on Alice. I hoped she wouldn't begin burrowing among the plants as soon as my back was turned, and followed Alice without much confidence that Poppy would sit still while she waited for me to return. There were plenty of plants within reach that she might be tempted to dig up, but I wanted to see inside Alice's house, and decided not to worry too much about her front garden. It was her back garden that interested me. If I could only get a glimpse of it from inside the house, I might solve the mystery that had been puzzling me since I moved in. Until I saw for myself, I could only speculate about what might be hidden on the other side of the fence bordering my garden.

Clutching a bag of bruised fruit, I followed my neighbour, ignoring the sounds of frantic barking that started up behind me as I crossed the threshold. It struck me that Poppy seemed to want to warn me not to go inside, but I dismissed the thought at once. If Alice *was* hiding anything, Poppy could have no more idea what it might be than I had. But I intended to discover the truth.

8

I EXPECTED ALICE'S HOUSE to resemble Rosecroft, but the two properties were designed very differently. Where Rosecroft had a small hall, my neighbour's front door led straight into a living room which was shrouded in semi-darkness, since the front window was concealed behind thick velvet curtains. A window at the side of the house was also hidden behind long drapes. Alice switched on a central light and I saw the room was furnished with pink and purple chintz-covered chairs. A dark wood coffee table stood in the centre of the room, within reach of both chairs and the matching two-seater sofa. Beneath it, covering most of the carpet, was a heavy patterned rug.

Alice led me to her kitchen at the back of the house, and instructed me to put my shopping bag on the table. This proved tricky, as the table was covered in a random collection of crockery and cutlery, carrier bags and packets of biscuits, trays, tins and a variety of vegetables. Once I had deposited the shopping, I tried to look outside without betraying my interest in her garden which, from what I could see, was even more overgrown than mine, with tall grasses and giant nettles and other plants that I assumed must be weeds since clearly no one had been taking care of the place for a while. Other than the proliferation of weeds, there was no sign of anything unusual out there, and no indication of why anyone would want to protect it with a metal fence.

Frustrated by my failure to discover what dark secret might be hidden in Alice's house, I tried to broach the subject that was puzzling me.

'You've got a very strong fence out there,' I ventured.

Alice paused in putting her shopping away and visibly tensed.

'My fence?' she repeated, turning away from me to continue with her task. 'Can you pass me the milk from that bag?'

'Yes,' I ploughed on. Aware that I must be sounding faintly ridiculous, I was glad Toby could not hear me. With a sudden flash of brilliance, I tried a different approach. 'It's just that it looks really strong and I need to replace my own fence on the other side. It's falling down. You must have noticed. So I wondered where you got your fence from, and how much it was. It's unusual to see a metal fence, isn't it?'

'Is it? Yes, I suppose you could be right. The old fence was falling apart and I wanted something that would last. Galvanised steel panels are not only strong, they're maintenance free. They don't need varnishing, they're sturdy and storm resistant, and they don't rot. They're cost-effective as well, because they go directly into the ground. It makes so much sense to me. To be honest, I'm surprised more people don't go for them.'

Alice's explanation sounded like an advertisement for metal fences. Murmuring about how fascinating that was, I turned away from the window, disappointed to discover the truth was so much less dramatic than the scenarios I had dreamed up. Even if I hadn't just lost interest in Alice's secrets, it would have been difficult to pursue the topic without exposing the reason for my interest so I let it drop, instead asking whether there was anything else I could help her with. Alice smiled wistfully.

'You remind me of my daughter,' she said with a curiously yearning expression on her face. 'She always likes to help people.'

'Where is she?' I asked. 'Is she at university?'

Maud had already told me that Sophie was away travelling, but Alice seemed keen to talk about her daughter. Listening to her was the least I could do. Of course, Alice had no inkling I had suspected her of harbouring an unspecified dark secret, but I couldn't help feeling guilty all the same, and made up my mind to be kind to her.

'You must miss her dreadfully,' I said.

'She's a wonderful girl,' she said, her expression softer and somehow less distant.

'You must be lonely without her,' I said, beginning to glimpse a possible reason for Alice's withdrawal from society.

'Yes, but she's having an amazing time, exploring so many different places,' she said brightly.

'When did she leave?'

Alice sniffed, and her expression grew guarded again. 'As soon as she finished school, she was planning her trip. Of course her travels had to be modified because of the pandemic, due to all the restrictions. At the moment she's in India and making her way to Thailand and Vietnam.'

'It must be tricky getting around,' I said.

Alice shrugged and turned away. 'Oh, there's always a way if you look for it.'

'I suppose so,' I agreed. 'So do you Skype with her, or have Zoom calls?'

'No, but she writes to me. I get letters from all over the world,' she added, her eyes bright with excitement just thinking about the letters she received.

'How wonderful. Not many people take the time to write letters these days.'

'It is really lovely. I don't know what I'd do if she stopped writing to me.' Her voice faltered slightly.

'What does she say in her letters?'

Genuine interest must have shown in my face, because Alice smiled shyly. 'I could read some of them to you, if you like.'

All the time we were talking, Poppy had been barking frantically, which was unlike her. Anxious to see what she was up to, I thanked Alice and agreed to return another day, without my dog. Taking my leave, I was mortified to see an array of leaves and bright red petals strewn beside the path. Scolding Poppy, I replaced the ruined geraniums as neatly as I could, and hurried away before Alice noticed the mayhem in her flowerbeds. I hoped it wasn't a foretaste of things to come when I had mended my fence and could leave Poppy to amuse herself in my garden. In the meantime, she seemed quite happy to spend time out in the yard at the tea shop. I was a little nervous about leaving her alone in the house, but my curiosity to find out more about Alice and her absent daughter overcame my qualms about abandoning my dog.

'What I want to know is, how is Sophie getting around

with all the travel restrictions?' I asked Hannah, when we had a free moment in the tea shop that afternoon.

'People manage,' she replied, lifting a tray of scones out of the oven, red-faced. 'It's hardly our business what Sophie wants to do, anyway.'

Hannah's scones made the heat of the kitchen worthwhile. I had tried to copy her recipe, but my scones lacked the light texture of my friend's, although mine were tasty enough. Hannah assured me it was just a question of practice, but in the meantime, she continued making batches of scones and cakes for the tea shop customers, while I was supposed to be practising baking at home.

'But don't you think it's odd?' I persisted.

'What's odd is that you are so interested in what Sophie's up to, when you haven't even met her,' she replied tartly. 'Now, is that tea ready yet? We have customers waiting and you're going to want to run out to play with your dog soon, so come on, let's get to work.'

'And what has Poppy got against her? She's such a friendly dog usually,' I said, unwilling to let the subject drop.

'She obviously senses your unease around Alice,' Hannah replied.

That made sense. Poppy was a very sensitive and intelligent dog.

'Now can you please get on with setting the tray before all the customers get fed up with waiting and walk out?'

9

DISMISSING MY SUSPICIONS ABOUT Alice, I turned my attention to work. It was a Bank Holiday weekend, and we were busy. The afternoon was exhausting, and I was on my feet, rushing backwards and forwards to the kitchen where Hannah was toiling at the oven and the sink, and running outside to check on Poppy in between orders. The day seemed to last interminably but finally Poppy and I were on our way home. I couldn't wait to have a long soak in the bath and put my feet up, while Poppy seemed determined to stop and to sniff at each tree and lamp post, and every clump of weeds and patch of grass. Before supper, we went out in the garden. My decision to forget about Alice was tested, because Poppy remained fascinated by the metal fence. At every opportunity she scampered over to it and scrabbled at the earth, as though trying to tunnel underneath it. She seemed particularly interested in the corner of the fence at the far end of the garden.

'What can you smell, Poppy?' I asked her quietly. 'What's on the other side of that fence?' I heaved a sigh. 'If only you could talk.'

Once again I began to suspect that something really

might be hidden in Alice's garden – something that could conceivably have been buried just when Sophie had disappeared. Hard though it was to believe that Alice could have done away with her daughter, I was feeling increasingly uneasy about living next door to her. It seemed likely the 'S' about whom my great aunt had been concerned was Sophie, and living next door to her, Lorna would surely have noticed what was going on. She had been mystified. But then I remembered the letters Alice had mentioned and realised that my idea couldn't possibly be true. Unless someone else was sending Alice regular letters from overseas, and Alice was lying about the identity of her correspondent, Sophie was clearly alive and well and away travelling overseas.

The following Sunday I went to The Plough for lunch and was pleased to spot Toby seated by himself in a corner of the garden. My mood lifted further when he waved and smilingly called out to me to sit at his table. As soon as I caught sight of him, I had intended to join him, but it was nice to be invited. I tried not to allow myself to believe he had gone there hoping to see me.

'I thought Hannah might be here,' he said, dashing my secret hopes as I reached his table. 'So, how have you been keeping? You're looking cheery.'

'Yes, it's all good,' I replied, looking down and patting Poppy to hide my dismay.

Abandoning me, Poppy trotted over to Toby and rolled over for him to pat her tummy, which she loved.

'She likes you,' I told him.

I didn't add that she liked anyone who made a fuss of her.

'I've always wanted a dog,' he admitted, with a smile.

It was tempting to ask him to take Poppy home with him, but I wanted to keep Rosecroft. If my great aunt's dog was given away, I wasn't sure who would find out, and how that might impact on my ownership of Rosecroft. Besides, I liked having her in the house with me at night. Although she was bound to roll over for an intruder to tickle her tummy, she would at least bark and wake me up if anyone broke in during the night. I had lived by myself before, and knowing she was in the house made me feel safe.

'The trouble is, I'm out at work all day, and my mother's allergic to dogs,' Toby went on.

'That's a shame.'

He nodded. 'Just one of those things. Hannah told me you're working at the tea shop. So how's that going?'

I took a seat. 'I can't say working as a waitress was exactly a lifelong dream of mine, but it's not too bad.'

'You could look for another job if you don't like it at the tea shop.'

'I know, but it's not so easy to find jobs these days, especially in Ashton Mead.'

'Swindon's not that far away.'

'I wouldn't want to leave Poppy alone all day. She's still only a puppy. And besides, it's fun working with Hannah.'

'She's a great girl,' he agreed enthusiastically.

Not for the first time, I wondered about Toby's relationship with Hannah. She had assured me they were just friends, but sometimes Toby gave me the impression he would have liked something more than that.

'How long have you known Hannah?' I asked him.

Straightening up from petting Poppy, he smiled. 'Oh, forever. We used to go out, you know, way back.'

'What happened?' I asked, doing my best not to look dashed by his words.

'The same as what happens to most relationships between a fifteen-year-old girl and a sixteen-year-old boy,' he laughed. 'It was a long time ago and, as I recall, she dumped me for a boy who had a car, or at least could drive and borrow his mother's car. At that age, to have pulling power a boy needed wheels. That seemed to be more important to the girls than anything else.'

I nodded. I could still remember the first girl at my school whose boyfriend had a car. With a mixture of admiration and envy, the rest of us had hung around outside the school gate to watch her being picked up.

'What about now?' I asked. 'Is there a spark of romance between you?' Smiling to conceal how important this was to me, I hoped he wouldn't find my question intrusive, but it was too late to take it back. Toby returned my smile but his answer was evasive.

'Hannah and I have been friends for a long time, since we were very young. We know where the bodies are buried. Talking of which,' he went on, still smiling, 'how are you getting on with your investigation into the body Alice has buried on the other side of her fence?'

Lowering my voice, I told him about Poppy's reaction to my neighbour. 'It's strange, isn't it? I mean, she loves people as a rule. I've never seen her behave like that with anyone else. And then there's the fence.'

Toby raised his eyebrows quizzically. 'What fence?'

'Alice's fence. It's metal. That's odd, don't you think? I mean, it looks as though Alice is trying to hide something and I'm pretty sure Poppy is on to her. Poppy doesn't like her. And –' I paused to allow the effect of my words to sink in before continuing in a theatrical whisper, 'Sophie has disappeared.'

Even though Toby's laughter riled me, I liked the sound. Watching little lines crease the skin around his eyes, I felt an unexpected longing to touch his cheek with the tips of my fingers, and wondered how he would react if I flung my arms around his neck. There was something infectious about his laughter. Had he not been laughing at me, I would have joined in.

'I didn't mean to offend you,' he said, seeing my mortification, and brushing a few strands of black hair off his forehead. 'But honestly, Emily, you can't possibly be serious about all this. If the police suspected a crime had been committed every time someone went off travelling, they'd have no time to hunt for real criminals.'

I smiled to hide my confusion. 'Yes, I'm sure you're right,' I said. 'It was just a flight of fancy.'

'You should watch that overactive imagination of yours,' he warned me, suddenly serious. 'Be careful who you go blabbing to. Not everyone would appreciate being accused of murder, and Alice has friends in the village.'

'I thought she lived like a hermit,' I said, surprised by his words. 'What friends does she have?'

'My mother for a start,' he replied promptly, 'and Maud, and a whole gaggle of old dears who may seem perfectly harmless, but who would hound you out of the village if they knew you were making groundless accusations against one of their coven. Worse, they would work their satanic magic against you and send you nightmares.' He grinned. 'Don't look so worried. I'm joking. I don't believe in witches any more than I believe Alice could possibly have done away with Sophie who, by the way, is a sweet young girl who wouldn't say boo to a goose. But you need to forget about your ridiculous notions, Emily, before you start talking to the wrong person and end up making enemies for yourself. Seriously, I advise you to drop this nonsense.'

'I don't appreciate being lectured to like a silly schoolgirl.'

'Don't behave like one then.'

We scowled at one another and I wondered how I could ever have found him attractive.

'You know your dog is digging up Cliff's precious begonias?' Toby said.

I spun round on the bench and my elbow knocked my drink off the table. Luckily the glass didn't break. Poppy stopped scrabbling in the flower bed, spraying earth all around her, as I leapt to my feet and tugged at her lead to pull her back from the begonias. She dashed over to the table and set to work licking the grass, while I tried to pull her away from my spilt beer, and pat the earth surreptitiously back into place around the plants at the same time. When I finished, I sat down again just as Toby stood up and told me he was leaving. Poppy trotted to the other side of the table where he had been sitting, lay down and closed her eyes, as though to express her disapproval of me. It seemed no one felt any sympathy for my concerns.

10

THE NEXT MORNING, ALICE was returning home with her shopping as I was taking Poppy out for her early walk before I went to work. Passing my neighbour on the pavement reminded me of Toby's warning. Hoping Toby would hear that I was not one to engage in malicious gossip, I stopped and offered to listen to some of her daughter's letters, ignoring Poppy's frantic barking. On reflection, I was forced to acknowledge that there was no reason to suspect anything sinister about her, and I bitterly regretted having shared my idle speculation with Toby. Befriending Alice, weird though she was, would hopefully restore my reputation with him.

Fortunately Alice was ignorant of what had taken place between me and Toby. I didn't really relish the prospect of spending time with her, but having offered to listen to her letters, I couldn't change my mind without risking offending her. It had been difficult enough to speak to her in the first place and having succeeded in pinning her down, I had to see it through. So I agreed to visit her that evening.

Tethered in my back garden, Poppy contented herself with snuffling around for worms and licking moss and I went to knock on Alice's door.

A box of letters was waiting for us on the coffee table in her front room. Alice offered me tea or coffee, but I explained that I wouldn't be able to stay long as Poppy was alone at home. Sitting on the sofa with her box of letters in front of her, Alice cleared her throat and began to read.

'This is Sophie's most recent letter,' she said, by way of introduction.

I was relieved to discover the letter was very short.

'Hi Mum

I hope this finds you well. I'm missing you and looking forward to seeing you again, but I'm having a really great time so you don't need to worry about me.

It's very hot here and I'll be pleased to leave and move on, but it's a very interesting place and I'm fine, so you don't need to worry. I've met some great people and am travelling with a really friendly group of girls. We're all on our way East, heading towards Japan, so I'm travelling with them for the time being. Everything I've heard about Japan sounds awesome, and I'm so lucky to be going to see it for myself.

The other girls aren't English, they're Australian. We might not be travelling together for much longer as at some point we'll be going our separate ways, but I'm hoping we'll keep in touch. I've made so many wonderful friends since I started travelling, far more than I ever had back in Ashton Mead. The Australian girls are good company for now and more fun than many of the English people I've met, so I've decided to stick with them for as long as I can.

We've seen some beautiful temples and pagodas and things, and are now just chilling out on the beach for a day before setting off again.

You'd love it here. We must come here together for a holiday one day!

Take care of yourself, and I'll see you soon.

I love you, Mum.

Sophie.'

Alice replaced the letter carefully in the box, and looked at me expectantly. Muttering that it was fascinating, I asked whether Sophie had sent any pictures and Alice shook her head.

'I'm not very good with technology, and in any case some of the places she visits don't have good reception, or we'd be Skyping or chatting on Zoom every day,' she said. 'But she's going to bring thousands of photos with her on her phone, when she comes home.'

'When are you expecting her back?'

Alice laughed as though I had said something amusing. 'Oh, you know how it is,' she replied.

Actually I didn't know what she meant, but I didn't like to say so. When she offered to read another letter, I agreed, just to be polite. She seemed really pleased, and I was glad to bring some small comfort to her in her lonely life.

'Hi Mum

It's me again. I hope I'm not boring you with all these letters,
but I miss you a lot.
We finally set off yesterday and there was a lot of fuss about
where we were going, and how we were going to get there,
but we made it over the border in the end without any
trouble, just a lot of hanging around waiting in long queues.'

'What border was that?' I asked, wondering where
Sophie was. Nothing in her letters had indicated her
location, only that she was hoping to travel to Japan.
Alice put her finger to her lips to tell me to be quiet, and
continued reading.

'It's unbelievably hot here. You wouldn't believe how tanned
I am. We all are. I'm glad you bought me a sunhat before
I left. You remember the one I mean, don't you? It's the
white sunhat with pink and yellow flowers round the brim.
Everyone admires it and asks where I got it and I just say it
was a present from my mum.

The point is that in this heat it's essential to keep your head
covered. Thank you so much for getting it. When it's really
hot I soak my hat in cold water, and it keeps my head cool.
That's a tip I picked up from one of the Australians and it's a
really good idea.

I suppose the weather is quite cool at the moment in the
village, and just thinking that makes me feel homesick!

I miss you and will write again soon.

Love from
Sophie.'

Alice read aloud in a singsong voice that was quite soporific, and after a while Sophie's letters became not merely dull but repetitive. She never seemed to have anything interesting to say, even though she was travelling to far-flung and exotic locations. Perhaps if I had met her, they would have seemed more interesting, but the travels of a stranger were hardly gripping and after listening to Alice droning on for nearly half an hour, I wasn't sure I wanted to hear much more about Sophie's travels.

After a while, something about the letters began to strike me as a bit odd. Saying almost nothing about her surroundings, and the places she visited, Sophie concentrated on tedious details about her everyday life. I said as much to Hannah when we were at work the following day.

'I mean, it's difficult to explain, but they really do seem quite strange because she hardly says anything about where she is, but just writes about herself. And who writes to their mother to say they're missing her?'

As I spoke I remembered that I hadn't called my mother for a couple of weeks and had yet to invite her to Ashton Mead to see my new home. Toby visited his mother whenever he could, but only because she was in a wheelchair and he was afraid she might be struggling. Hannah saw her mother every day, but that was different, because they lived together. Even if they didn't deliberately set out to spend time in each other's company during the day, they were bound to keep bumping into one another while Jane was out walking her dog, or if they were both in Maud's shop or the pub. Jane even came into the tea shop from time to time with a friend.

Perhaps I was the odd one, seeing very little of my mother. Feeling guilty, I resolved to invite her to visit me soon, and to call her more often. We hadn't seen each other for months and now that I had finished sorting through Great Aunt Lorna's boxes, and the house was looking fairly presentable, there was no longer any reason not to invite her to stay.

'I've got a spare room,' I added, when I phoned her that evening. 'It's all ready for you. Come for the weekend. It'll be lovely.' I hesitated. 'There's just one thing I ought to mention. I'm not on my own here.'

'So Ben's come to his senses at last, has he?' she blurted out, ever the diplomat. 'Well, I can't pretend I'm not glad to hear it, even if he has messed you around. He needs firm handling, and you shouldn't be such a shrinking violet when it comes to keeping him in order. Men like to be controlled, you know. It makes them feel safe.'

'No, it's not Ben,' I interrupted her ludicrous relationship advice. 'The thing is, there was a condition to my inheritance. Your aunt Lorna had a puppy, and I had to agree to look after the puppy if I wanted to keep the house.'

'That's ridiculous,' my mother replied. 'No one can force you to keep a dog. Anyway, aunty Lorna's not going to know, is she?'

'No, but –'

'But what?'

'It was in the will that I have to look after her.'

'Is this a problem dog?'

'No, she's lovely.'

'There you are then. You can easily find a nice home for it. Puppies are very popular, you know.'

'No, no, you don't understand,' I protested. 'And please don't refer to my dog as "it". Poppy's a female dog and I like her and I'm keeping her. It's not just that Great Aunt Lorna wanted me to take care of her, I *want* to. She's my dog now.'

'So you're going to keep this animal?'

'Yes, I am.' I was surprised at how fierce my response was.

This was the first time my decision regarding Poppy had been questioned, and the discussion clarified my feelings. My mother carried on chatting, and we arranged for her to visit Ashton Mead the next Saturday. I took the weekend off work and she phoned me when she boarded the bus from Swindon. Poppy and I walked down to meet her at the bus stop. I was surprised how excited I felt about seeing my mother again after nearly four months, and as for my mother, she couldn't stop grinning. Her blue eyes seemed to glow, and her blonde curls were so neat, she could have just stepped out of a hair salon. I was touched to think she had taken so much care to look her best just for me. A heavy shower had fallen early that morning, but by the time my mother arrived, the sun was shining and the village looked beautiful in the clean sharp light after the rain.

We had a pleasant walk home through the village, with my mother admiring everything she saw, from the picturesque river with its quaint bridge, to the soft yellow brick buildings and majestic trees. She gasped when she saw Rosecroft. Admittedly the house looked beautiful, its yellow stonework appearing to glow softly in the early afternoon sunlight.

'It's lovely,' my mother cried out as soon as she saw it. 'Whoever would have thought Lorna had such an enchanting house?'

I felt ready to burst with pride, gazing at Rosecroft. Wisteria was in bloom, growing up two narrow trellises on either side of the white front door, and curling over the top to frame it in sprays of delicate purple flowers. Brilliantly coloured pansies bordered the cracked and crooked path, and patches of grass on either side of the path were dotted with daisies and glossy buttercups.

With proprietorial pride I showed my mother around the house, and was gratified by her expressions of delight. She actually clapped her hands when she saw the kitchen, and I was really pleased I had devoted so much time and effort to making it look presentable. After our tour of Rosecroft, I took her to The Plough for supper. Cliff greeted her like an old friend and we sat in the garden on a pleasant summer evening, with Poppy lying peacefully under the table. I tried not to wish I was sitting there with Toby.

'To be honest, I was starting to worry about you,' my mother confessed, as she was finishing her third gin and tonic. She grinned tipsily.

Instantly defensive, I asked her what she was talking about, although I knew exactly what she meant.

'A woman needs some security,' she said, correcting herself quickly to say, 'a person needs some security. With Rosecroft you will never be destitute, even if you never find a partner and end up having to depend on yourself for the rest of your life.'

Before I could retort that I had never been dependent on a partner, nor would that prospect ever appeal to me,

Tess brought our food, and my flash of anger passed. Back at Rosecroft, we sat over a mug of cocoa, and my mother continued with her account of the gossip from around the family. We spent a comfortable evening chatting about nothing in particular. Sitting with Poppy snuggled up beside me on the settee, I was only half-listening to my mother prattling, when something she said caught my attention.

'Apparently he's absolutely bonkers about stamp collecting, which seems like a harmless enough pastime for a young boy. He could be doing far worse things than collecting stamps, if you ask me. Far worse. Teenagers these days are out of control and being cooped up at home for so long didn't do most of them any good.'

I sat forward, and Poppy stirred without opening her eyes.

'Who's collecting stamps?' I interrupted my mother.

'Joel. I just told you. Don't you listen to anything I say?'

I hadn't seen my sister's son for nearly two years, since before the first lockdown. The last time we met he had been ten. I had no idea he collected stamps and guessed this was a new hobby.

'My next door neighbour receives letters from all over the world,' I said. 'Her daughter's away, travelling. I don't know where she is right now, but somewhere in the Far East, I think. If I ask my neighbour, she'll probably be able to give me lots of stamps for Joel.'

My mother beamed. 'That would be wonderful. I'm sure Joel will be thrilled, and Susie would really appreciate it.'

'How is Susie?' I asked. 'I haven't heard from her in ages.'

'She said exactly the same thing,' my mother replied sharply. 'She said you never call her.'

I wasn't convinced my sister had actually said that, but I let it pass. My mother could hardly be blamed for wanting me and Susie to speak to each other more regularly. I resolved to call Susie after my mother's visit and catch up with her news.

11

MY MOTHER'S VISIT PASSED off very pleasantly and she left, promising to return soon. I didn't see my next door neighbour again for a week or so, but one day I spotted her coming out of the village shop. Seeing her reminded me of my nephew's hobby. Alice was laden down with shopping, but there was no time to offer to help her carry her bags as I was on my way to work. Poppy began tugging at my trousers and growling, as I explained why I couldn't help Alice with her shopping. Before we parted, I mentioned my nephew, the youthful philatelist.

'Philatelist?' Alice repeated, looking baffled.

'He collects stamps.'

'Yes, yes, I know what philately is,' she replied. 'That's very nice for him. I'm sure it's an interesting hobby.'

'I was hoping you might give me some stamps from your daughter's letters.'

Alice smiled warily. 'Oh, ah, I don't think I can do that,' she muttered, looking unexpectedly apprehensive.

'Why not? Just a few would be great. He's very enthusiastic and he's only twelve.'

'I don't keep stamps from letters. I throw all the envelopes away. I have no use for them. They're just envelopes. And now I really need to get this shopping home.'

'What a pity,' I said. 'Maybe you could save them for me in future?'

A faint scowl crossed Alice's face and she shuffled a few steps backwards. Muttering that she would see what she could do, she turned and hurried away, leaving me standing thoughtfully on the street. My suspicions rekindled, I made my way to the café and blurted out what was on my mind.

'Oh for goodness' sake, you're not banging on about that again,' Hannah snapped. 'Really, Emily, what is your problem?'

'It's not a problem, just a hunch,' I replied, annoyed that she refused to listen to my concerns.

But it wasn't just me. Poppy knew there was something wrong with Alice. I refrained from mentioning that to Hannah, who was unlikely to accept Poppy as a reliable witness. Hannah would just say that Poppy was responding to my unease, when in fact the opposite was true.

'If you ask me, it's a good thing that Sophie has finally managed to escape,' Hannah said.

'What do you mean, "escape"?'

'What I mean is, Alice was always a complete control freak. Everyone knew. Maybe it was because it was only ever the two of them, but Sophie couldn't move without her mother breathing down her neck. She wasn't even allowed to go up to town with the other kids her age when we were teenagers. She was going to have to break free of her mother one day, and it sounds like she's gone about as far away as she can. I can't say I blame her. And before you ask me, I don't feel in the slightest bit sorry for Alice.

She brought it on herself. You can't control someone else's life like that, you know? Eventually they're going to rebel. I think Sophie's done it in a very nice way, actually. She's been far kinder than Alice deserved.'

I thought about this. 'What happened to Sophie's father?'

Hannah shook her head. 'I don't know. They arrived here without him and I never heard Sophie mention him. I'm not sure she even knew him. There was talk at one time about him having disappeared without trace, or something along those lines, but honestly I can't remember. I was only about eight or nine when Sophie and Alice arrived in Ashton Mead, and she was even younger. It was all a long time ago, and I was never close to Sophie. I don't think any of the children in the village were. You'd have to ask my mother if you want to know about Sophie's father. She might remember the gossip.'

I made a mental note to do just that. Listening to Hannah talking about Sophie's father made me recall the cryptic comments in my great aunt's journal, starting with 'No sign of S'. I told Hannah about it, but she was preoccupied with lifting a tray of scones from the oven.

'What's that you said?'

'It said, "No sign of S",' I repeated, 'and then she wrote that she was concerned about it. No, not concerned, she said she was worried, worried about S. Don't you see? If "S" referred to Sophie, then that means my great aunt was worried about her and that could have been because she disappeared. There was no sign of her. That's what my great aunt said. She was worried because there was no sign of S.'

Hannah put her tray down and wiped the back of her hand across her forehead, leaving a floury white streak.

'Well, your great aunt's "S" can't be Sophie, because she went off travelling, so obviously there would be no sign of her. And your great aunt would have known about Sophie going away. Everyone knew about it. Sophie never stopped talking about it before she left.'

'Did anyone actually see Sophie leave?' I asked, a horrible suspicion reawakening in my mind. 'And has anyone heard from Sophie since she went away?'

'You just told me that Alice gets letters from her regularly.'

I let the subject drop for the moment, but Alice's reaction to my request for stamps continued to trouble me, and I determined to find out more. After work, I walked home with Hannah to see her mother. Poppy trotted happily along in front of me, stopping to sniff at the grass verges and bark at the occasional bird that flew by overhead.

When we arrived, I didn't like to launch straight into the subject that was on my mind in case it appeared that I had gone there only to quiz Jane about Sophie's father. Jane was a curvaceous woman, who looked like an older version of her daughter. I wondered if Hannah found it strange, looking at an image of herself in thirty years. Hannah had brought some cakes and scones home from the tea shop, and we sat in the garden, chatting over a cup of tea, while Poppy and Jane's dog sat on the grass together.

'Do you think Holly likes Poppy?' I asked, watching as my puppy tried to play with Jane's dog, who steadfastly ignored her.

Jane shrugged. 'Holly's too old and lazy to play. She just wants to sit in the sun and doze. I gave up trying to work out what my dog was thinking a long time ago.

Basically dogs need sleep, food and water, and it's that simple.'

'What about affection?' I asked, looking at Poppy who had given up trying to entice Holly to respond and was now lying comfortably sprawled out on the grass. 'Don't they need to feel loved?'

Jane laughed. 'What better way can there be to show you love a dog than to make sure it's well fed and warm and comfortable, and gets the exercise it needs?'

When Hannah went indoors to put the kettle on, I turned to Jane and broached the subject that was on my mind.

'You want to know about Alice's husband?' she repeated. 'My, that's going back a few years.'

'What happened to him?'

Jane shook her head. 'Alice introduced herself to us as a widow when she arrived in Ashton Mead.'

'What had happened to her husband?'

'There was a rumour going round that he had died in so-called suspicious circumstances. Some people said that was why Alice had moved here, to get away from the publicity.'

'What did people think had happened to him?' I asked, eager to hear confirmation that Alice had been suspected of committing at least one murder before her arrival in Ashton Mead. 'Did you suspect foul play?'

'Oh, I don't think anyone thought he'd really come to a sticky end, or anything like that,' she laughed. 'It was just a silly rumour. When a newcomer arrives in a small village like Ashton Mead, people like to invent stories about them. It helps us pass the time.'

Jane laughed, and I wasn't sure whether she was being serious or pulling my leg. After all, I was a recent arrival in the village myself. But I refused to be distracted by rumours that might have circulated about me.

'What were the rumours about Alice?'

'Some people didn't believe she was really a widow, as she claimed.'

'If you didn't believe she was a widow, what did you think had happened to Sophie's father?'

Jane sighed. 'There were people who thought she never had been married at all,' she explained. 'Some people assumed she was a single mother when she arrived in the village with a small child. It sounds ridiculous in this day and age, but some of the older villagers thought she was embarrassed to admit to being single, so she invented a husband who had died. Mostly we believed that she was a widow because, really, why would anyone lie about it?'

'Did you believe her?'

Jane shrugged. 'It's a long time ago. I really can't remember.'

'What about my great aunt?' I ventured.

'Poor Lorna,' Jane replied. 'What about her?'

'Did she ever have a boyfriend? You know, a relationship with a man?'

'If she did, she kept it very quiet.'

Hannah came out with a tray of tea and cakes. Glancing regretfully at my expanding waistline, I took the smallest cake on the plate, and the conversation moved on.

That evening I retrieved my great aunt's diary from the back of a drawer, and read right the way through it again, from cover to cover. As I flicked through shopping lists and reminders to pay various bills, I wondered whether Alice had remembered to save any stamps for me. I resolved to march straight up to her front door when I had some time to spare, and knock until she answered. If there was nothing scandalous going on, she shouldn't have too much trouble in persuading me I was mistaken, but I was determined not to be fobbed off. When I took Poppy out into the garden before bed, I stared at the metal fence glowing softly in the moonlight, and wondered what secrets lay hidden on the other side.

12

THE FINE WEATHER GAVE way to a rainy period and the flow of customers became sporadic. We were still busy serving morning coffees, and had periods of hectic activity around teatime, but otherwise we were fairly quiet. By midday the café was usually empty. If Poppy wasn't at Jane's house, I would take her for a walk before sitting with Hannah over a mug of steaming hot chocolate, while my little dog dozed in the corner. During my chats with Hannah, I kept quiet about my suspicions of Alice and her letters, instead focusing on more mundane matters. I really wanted to ask Hannah about Toby, but I was chary of mentioning him in case she also liked him, and since I didn't dare mention Sophie again, I sat back and let my friend direct the conversation.

She had plenty to talk about, like the state of the tables and chairs, and whether the walls needed redecorating. The wood on several chairs was showing through the yellow paint, and one of the tables had rickety legs. In addition to that, there was the question of my scones, which were still nowhere near as light and tasty as Hannah's. She was keen to share the baking with me but, despite my continuing efforts, my scones were not yet good enough to sell to customers. Hannah's protestations that it just took practice were beginning to sound plaintive. Talking about Hannah and the tea shop were safe topics, and we nattered companionably for a while. When I asked her whether she had always lived in Ashton Mead, she told me about her time at university on the south coast, and I listened without comment. Hannah was entertaining and it was a relief for me to sit quietly, enjoying my chocolate, letting her talk. In the end, she ran out of anecdotes about her student days and it was she who brought up one of the subjects that was uppermost on my mind.

'I saw Toby the other day,' she said, glancing at me from under lowered brows.

Keeping my eyes fixed on the table I felt my face turning red and cursed my tendency to blush. It had started when I was a teenager, and I hadn't managed to grow out of it yet. I cleared my throat before replying as nonchalantly as possible. 'Oh, I remember Toby.'

That was a stupid thing to say. I could hardly have forgotten him, but Hannah didn't remark on my awkward response.

'How is he?' I enquired, trying to sound blasé.

'Yes, he seems fine. He was asking after you. He said he hasn't seen you for a while and wondered if you're all right.'

I took a sip of my drink before answering. 'Did he really ask about me? What exactly did he say?'

Hannah stared at me and I had a feeling she could see right through my affectation of indifference. I kept my head lowered as she told me that she had met Toby for a drink, and he had made a point of enquiring about me.

'He said he hasn't seen you at The Plough for a while and wondered where you've been hiding and what you've been up to.'

'What did you tell him?'

'I said that your mother's been visiting you.'

I nodded and thanked her and the conversation reverted to the tea shop, and Hannah's plans for the future. I let her ramble on, while I turned over in my mind what she had told me about Toby. Snippets of her conversation reached me and I gathered she was hoping to save up enough money for a deposit for an extension at the back of the tea shop.

'The yard is basically wasted space,' she said. 'All we use the area for is dogs, but that's not exactly productive. Poppy's adorable but she's not a paying customer.' She laughed, before returning to her serious proposal.

In a corner of the room, I saw Poppy's ears prick up at the mention of her name, but she didn't deign to open her eyes.

'If we can afford to extend into the yard, we could shift the kitchen further back and have room to seat another four customers, or maybe even six. And that would increase revenue in the summer.' Hannah launched into figures, estimating the increased profit we could expect from an additional six customers. 'But first we have to make enough money to do the extension,' she concluded.

'No point in counting your chickens before they're hatched,' I advised her, but she dismissed my caution with a wave of her hand.

'You can't stand still in life,' she said. 'Either you're moving forward or you're going backwards. I'm thinking of taking out a mortgage. But I need to be sure of getting a return on the investment. It will mean no pay rise for you for the foreseeable future.'

She carried on scheming, but I wasn't really paying attention. Apart from the fact that listening to her figures was boring, I was still mulling over what she had said about Toby.

After that, I started hanging out at The Plough again whenever I was free, and a couple of days later I saw Toby in the bar. He nodded at me with a friendly smile. Encouraged by what Hannah had told me, I joined him. It had started drizzling outside so we sat indoors in a corner of the bar, with Poppy lying quietly under the table. Cliff didn't object to well-behaved dogs in the pub. All the same, I did my best to keep her out of sight and hopefully out of trouble. There were few distractions for her under the table and, once comfortably stowed there, she tended to fall asleep, unless I was eating in which case she would sit perfectly still, staring at me.

'Anyone would think she's starving,' I laughed one evening as she watched me eat. 'She turned her nose up at a second helping of her supper less than half an hour ago. But if I drop one crumb off my plate she leaps at it as though I never feed her.'

Toby and I chatted politely about the weather, and work, avoiding any controversial topics. Our conversation was slightly strained, but that was preferable to falling out. I recounted the details of my mother's visit, and he told me about his own mother.

'The sad thing is that she used to be so active,' he told me. 'She was a PE teacher when she was younger, and now she can't even walk. I mean, she couldn't have done more to keep herself fit and healthy. It's ironic, really, but, as she says, we have no control over what happens to us, only over how we deal with it. She never complains, but she must find it frustrating.'

'What happened to her?'

'I thought you knew. She was paralysed in a car accident. She has good days and bad days, but she'll never walk again.'

'She must love it that you're living near Ashton Mead.'

'Yes. That's the least I can do. My dad died a couple of years ago, and soon after that my mother was injured, so within the space of a year she lost my dad and the use of her legs. I couldn't leave Swindon, not after all she's gone through. She has carers who come in to help her, so I could move away, but I want to stick around. I'm all she's got now.'

He seemed to be about to say more, but he looked away and fell silent. His words reminded me of something Hannah had told me about Sophie and *her* mother, and I felt a tremor of guilt at my suspicions of Alice.

'You don't have any brothers or sisters?' I enquired, determined to stick to polite topics.

'No, it's just me.'

I told him about my sister who lived in Colchester, and rarely came to see me or my parents. Moving to Ashton Mead was the furthest I had moved away from London where my parents lived.

'Although with all the lockdowns, none of us saw much of each other for ages anyway. I mean, I get on really well with my sister, but we just don't get to see much of each other.'

He nodded and started telling me about his work as a chemistry teacher in a secondary school in Swindon. With his amusing stories about his pupils, and my anecdotes about Poppy, the time passed pleasantly. Too soon, Toby said he had to go, but we exchanged a casual promise to meet for a drink again soon. After he left, Poppy whimpered softly under the table as if she knew I was feeling bereft now that he had gone. I tried to convince myself that I was indifferent to him, but in my daydreams he invited me out for a romantic candlelit dinner, after which he would come back to Rosecroft with me...

Snapping myself out of my reverie, I went home with Poppy.

'It's just you and me,' I told her and she wagged her tail.

Eating a microwaved macaroni cheese in front of the television, I watched a rerun of *Bridget Jones's Diary*, which I had seen a few times before. Previously, I had always fancied the actor playing Darcy, but this time instead of Colin Firth, I imagined Toby playing the role of Darcy to my Bridget. As though she sensed my loneliness, Poppy leapt up on the sofa beside me when I had finished my supper, and nuzzled my arm with her nose.

'I'm not really alone, am I?' I whispered, tickling the back of her neck. 'What would I do without you?' I asked her, and she licked my hand.

13

MY MOTHER GAVE A disapproving sniff when I admitted that my neighbour hadn't given me any stamps.

'I'm disappointed in you, Emily, really I am,' she said. 'You're always telling me how I ought to be more careful with my carbon footprint, and your neighbour just gave you a perfect opportunity to do some recycling, and you did nothing about it. And now all those stamps have been thrown away. What a waste.'

Uncomfortable with her disapproval, I lied stupidly. 'Oh no, they haven't been thrown away.'

'Why don't you ask her to give them to you, then?' my mother asked sharply.

Unable to extricate myself from my story, I blundered on. 'Because she hasn't got them any more. She's given them away. She told me she gives them to a charity. So they didn't go to waste. They just didn't come to me, although I did ask her for them, for Joel's collection.'

'Oh? What charity does she give them to?'

My mother sounded genuinely interested, but I suspected she might be testing my story.

'I don't know,' I replied, 'she didn't say.'

'Oh well, never mind. They're gone now.'

Hurriedly I assured her that I had asked my neighbour to keep any interesting foreign stamps for me in future, and my mother seemed mollified. I wasn't a habitual liar, and felt uncomfortable about my pathetic fiction. Somehow my mother had caught me off guard, and I had panicked. It didn't help that I had forgotten my nephew's last birthday, an oversight that still rankled with my mother, because she hadn't tired of reminding me about it for months afterwards. Now I had an opportunity to put things right.

It was only seven in the evening so, fired with enthusiasm, I went next door to remind Alice about the stamps. It was possible she had received another letter since we last spoke, in which case she might have a stamp that I could send to my nephew straight away. One stamp was better than none, and there would be the promise of more. I was sure Alice would help me, once she understood my situation. There was no reason why she would refuse.

Alice came to the door and smiled warily at me.

'I was just taking my dog out,' I said.

Poppy growled, and tried to grab my trousers with her teeth and drag me away. Doing my best to ignore Poppy's freakishly unsociable behaviour, I smiled at Alice.

'I was wondering if you'd heard from Sophie again?' I enquired, approaching the problem head on, while Poppy turned and strained at her leash, in a vain attempt to pull me away from Alice's front doorstep.

'Yes, as it happens I had a letter just this morning,' Alice replied with a flicker of a smile. 'I haven't had a chance to open it yet. Why don't you come over this evening and I can read it to you?'

'That would be great,' I said, trying to sound enthusiastic. 'Can I have the stamp?'

'The stamp?' Alice looked surprised.

'Yes, you remember, you said you might let me have the stamps from your letters, for my nephew. He collects stamps. He's only twelve, and I promised my mother I'd send him some of your stamps.' I paused, sensing her reluctance. 'I wouldn't have offered them to him without asking you first, but we did talk about it. Please. My mother's annoyed with me for forgetting his birthday, and I'm sure a few foreign stamps would help.'

Still tugging on Poppy's lead, I tried to explain the deceit I had stupidly practised on my mother, while Poppy continued straining to pull me away from Alice's door.

'The trouble is,' I concluded lamely, 'I don't think she believed me, so I would really appreciate it if you could let me have a few stamps from your letters- ' I broke off as Alice drew back, shaking her head and looking alarmed.

'I don't have any stamps to give you. I'm sorry if you promised them to your nephew, but I've already agreed to give them to someone else. I forgot, when you asked me, that I'd already said I would give all the stamps to the school, that is, to someone at a school, not the local school. So I'm sorry, but I have nothing to give you.'

She didn't add that it was not her problem if I had lied to my mother, but she might as well have done. With that, she closed the door.

'Do you think she's lying about her stupid stamps?' I asked Poppy, who wagged her tail and looked smug.

'I swear that dog understands every word I say,' I grumbled to Hannah the following day.

'You're in a good mood,' she remarked cheerily. 'You look like you lost a pound and found a penny.'

Making no attempt to control my irritation, I began ranting about Alice's stamps. 'So now I have to explain to my mother why I can't send any stamps to my nephew after all. The thing is, Alice knew perfectly well that I wanted those stamps. She could have at least saved me one or two. She hears from Sophie every week. Would it be such an imposition to pass one of her stamps on to me once in a while? Joel's only twelve and if I can help in a small way to keep him innocently occupied in playing with stamps that can only be a good thing. After all the shit kids have been through over the past two years, it's the least I can do. Only now I can't even do that, because Alice has suddenly remembered that she's promised all her stamps to someone else. She knew I wanted those stamps. First she agreed to save them for me, and now she's saying she's promised them to someone else. Something doesn't ring true. She's lying and I don't know why, but I intend to find out.'

'Oh for goodness' sake,' Hannah replied, 'she just changed her mind, that's all. Do you have to go looking for conspiracies everywhere? When did you become so paranoid? It's obvious Alice wants to keep them herself in case they're worth something. She didn't like to say so, because she was afraid it would make her look stingy. Anyway, they're her letters, and her stamps. It's nothing to do with you what she decides to do with them. She must have found someone else who wants them. She's probably selling them. And if she wants to throw them away, that's her business. Now can we stop talking about Alice's stamps? You're turning into a real bore. They're stamps, for goodness' sake, not the crown jewels. And they're not yours. Get over it. Your nephew's probably moved on to another hobby anyway. Now school kids are allowed to mix again, he'll be outside kicking a football around with his mates, not sitting at home sticking stamps in a stamp album. He's twelve!'

Hannah was right, of course, but that didn't help me to convince my mother that I hadn't forgotten her request. I wondered what she had told my sister, and whether they were talking about me behind my back. The thought made me feel uncomfortable. I was fond of my sister. Mainly to please her, I had planned to send Joel an impressive donation of stamps for his collection to compensate for having forgotten his birthday, but now that was not going to happen and I had let him down again, thanks to Alice. In my own defence, Joel had turned twelve shortly after Ben walked out on me, and I had been a bit preoccupied, but that was no excuse in my mother's eyes. Recalling Great Aunt Lorna, and the tenuous relationship I had experienced with her, I wondered what my nephew would remember about me when he grew up. Probably not much, the way things were going.

On the way home, Poppy trotted eagerly in front of me, stopping now and again to sniff the ground before scampering off again, so that I had to jog to keep up with her. It was a beautiful evening, and walking with Poppy distracted me from dwelling on my problems with different members of my family. By the time we were nearly home, I was feeling cheerful, and thinking about going to the pub after supper. As we turned off the main thoroughfare into our own street, Poppy stopped abruptly. Raising her head, she sniffed the air, pricked up her ears, and let out a low rumbling growl. I nearly lost my grip on her lead when she unexpectedly twisted round and ran a few steps back the way we had come, barking with unaccustomed ferocity.

'Stop barking, Poppy,' I cried out. 'Come here. Heel. Heel!'

I hadn't heard anyone behind us but looking back, I caught a glimpse of a figure sprinting away from us and disappearing around the corner. I didn't see them clearly enough to distinguish who it was, but I had the impression they were wearing a long dark coat that flapped around their legs as they ran. I retraced my steps as far as the corner and looked up and down the main street. There was no sign of a figure in a long coat. Beside me, Poppy continued barking frantically. The whole incident had a strange, dreamlike quality, not least because the person I had glimpsed had inexplicably vanished. They were clearly keen to avoid being seen, which suggested they were up to something underhand. Unnerved, I went home and nearly stayed in that evening. But by the time I had eaten, Poppy was ready to go out, so we went to the pub as usual. We saw no suspicious-looking characters on the way, although I kept a lookout.

'Is there much crime in the village?' I asked Hannah and Toby that evening in the pub.

Hannah looked surprised. 'This isn't London,' she said. 'Everyone here knows everyone else and outsiders don't stay long. Ashton Mead is just a picturesque stopover for travellers on their way to somewhere else, not a destination.'

'The village certainly isn't a mecca for thieves, if that's what you're worried about,' Toby said, smiling. 'But I wouldn't leave Poppy outside unattended. She's very cute, and you don't want someone walking off with her.'

Hearing her name, Poppy peered out from under the table where she was busy demolishing one of her chew toys, and wagged her tail.

'What about muggings on the street?' I asked.

Toby shrugged. 'Among the kids from time to time,' he said. 'Nothing you need to worry about. It's not as if you carry the crown jewels around with you. In fact, with what Hannah pays you, any self-respecting mugger ought to give you money.'

Hannah laughed.

Despite the reassurances from my friends, walking home in the dark I stayed more alert than usual, and was relieved to get home.

14

A FEW DAYS LATER, I bumped into Pete the postman outside my house. There were only two properties in Mill Lane, and neither my neighbour nor I received very many letters, so he didn't come along the lane every day. Sometimes as much as a week could go by without my seeing him, but he always greeted me like an old friend. Petting Poppy, he commented on how much she had grown. It was true. Since she had first come to live with me, she had grown visibly sturdier. Her coat looked fluffy and glossy, and her eyes were lively and bright. As Pete was remarking on the improvement in her appearance, it occurred to me that I might enlist his help in my mission to acquire some foreign stamps for my nephew. In a roundabout way, I explained my problem.

'My mother still hasn't forgiven me for forgetting my nephew's birthday, and I thought I could go some way to redeeming myself if I sent him some foreign stamps for his collection. So I was wondering if you could tip me off any time Alice receives a letter. If you could let me know just before you deliver her post, if I'm at home, then I could knock on her door straight away and she wouldn't be able to say no, would she? Not every time. I'd be really grateful,' I added, seeing Pete's perplexed expression.

'Explain to me again why you want to know when I'm about to deliver your neighbour's post,' he said, straightening up from stooping to pet Poppy.

'It's just the foreign stamps I'm interested in,' I said, explaining all over again about my nephew's stamp collecting. 'I forgot his birthday, so this would be a way for me to make it up to him.'

'Yes, I see,' Pete conceded. 'But why the interest in Alice's post specifically?'

It was my turn to be slightly puzzled, but I guessed Pete was so inured to delivering letters that he didn't even notice where they originated. I explained it was the stamps on letters from Sophie that were my objective.

'I know she writes to Alice every week or so, sending letters from abroad, and those stamps would be perfect.'

Poppy rolled over onto her back for him to stroke her tummy and he shook his head, with a tolerant smile. 'Alice doesn't receive letters from overseas, as far as I'm aware,' he told me, looking down at Poppy. 'I'm not bending over for you again, even if you do look at me like that.'

His words surprised me. All at once my earlier suspicions resurfaced, but I hid my confusion. There must be a logical explanation for this situation. Alice had read some of Sophie's letters aloud to me yet, according to Pete, he hadn't delivered those letters. For some reason, Alice must have arranged to collect them from the main post office in Swindon herself. Perhaps she was afraid her letters might get lost if she trusted to the normal delivery.

Somehow I was determined to get to the bottom of this mystery. Mumbling that I must have misunderstood what Alice had told me, I thanked Pete and hurried away. I had a lot to think about, and was not sure it would be wise to share my thoughts with anyone else. Hannah and Toby already thought I was weirdly obsessed with Alice and Sophie, and they were probably right. I didn't want to make a fool of myself in front of my friends again. But I knew that I couldn't let this rest until I had discovered the truth, and somehow I was going to get hold of those missing stamps.

All that afternoon, I wondered what to do. Taking Poppy out in the back garden and tethering her in the long grass, I laid my plans. First of all, I was going to acquire a lawnmower and tidy up my garden. Having cut the grass, I would set to work weeding the flowerbed that ran alongside Alice's fence. There might be a hole under the fence that I could manage to peer through in the course of my gardening. It was useless trying to inspect it from my upstairs windows, as the next door garden was shielded by trees and tall thick laurel hedges on the other side of the metal fence. On the face of it, the fence and the bushes were perfectly innocent, but combined with my unease about Sophie's letters, they were beginning to take on a sinister meaning. All the time I was plotting, I knew that my concerns were probably ridiculous. But even if I was being foolish, there was no downside to tidying my overgrown garden. Only Poppy appeared to share my suspicion of Alice.

'And you're just a dog,' I told her, kneeling down to stroke her head.

Instead of wagging her tail at my attention, Poppy put her head on one side and gazed up at me keenly, as if to challenge what I had said.

There was no need to study Great Aunt Lorna's diary again, as I knew the references to 'S' by heart. It was clear that something had happened to arouse my great aunt's suspicions. Perhaps she had deliberately left her diary behind for me to read, hoping that I would investigate what had happened to the mysterious 'S'. It was quite likely that 'S' didn't mean Sophie at all, and I wondered if my great aunt had ever conducted a romance in secret. My family had lost touch with her for years, during which time anything could have happened. Jane seemed to think Lorna had lived a single life, but my great aunt could have had her reasons for keeping quiet about a relationship. Perhaps she had an affair with a married man, or she might have been involved with a woman at a time when such liaisons were still frowned on.

The other aspect of my great aunt's history that troubled me was that she had suffered a fatal accident very shortly after she acquired Poppy. I couldn't help wondering if that had been a coincidence. If Alice had been present when my great aunt fell down the stairs, that might explain Poppy's hostility towards my neighbour. Perhaps she had even pushed Lorna down the stairs. My great aunt might have stumbled on a terrible secret, after which Alice decided she had to be silenced. It seemed highly unlikely but it was possible, and it would certainly account for Poppy's behaviour. So far Alice was the only person my dog seemed to have taken against, with a hostility that was unmistakable. There had to be a reason.

'If only you could talk,' I said to Poppy, and she whimpered softly, as though she understood that I was disappointed in her.

One way or another, I needed to investigate the circumstances of my great aunt's death. Hannah and her mother didn't seem to know anything, so I decided to visit Lorna's friend, Catherine, and question her about the fatal accident.

'I'm probably being silly,' I said to Poppy. 'What do you think? I'm so confused.'

For answer, Poppy just stared at me, her head on one side.

'Shall we go and see Catherine?'

Poppy wagged her tail.

'Does that mean you think I ought to look into what happened to Great Aunt Lorna? Or do you just want to go and see your friends? Do you think it's daft to suspect there's some mystery about her death?'

Poppy laid her head down on her front paws and closed her eyes.

'Well, you're no help, are you?' I chided her affectionately, scratching the back of her neck gently. 'Even you're getting bored of hearing me wittering on about Alice.'

Poppy opened her eyes and growled before settling down to sleep. Watching her sides move in and out almost imperceptibly, I smiled, grateful for her company.

Maud told me Catherine lived with her sister in a cottage called The Haven, in a tiny hamlet five miles away. Armed with detailed instructions, I set off. Poppy trotted eagerly ahead of me, blithely ignoring my instructions to walk to heel. Jane had advised me to make sure my puppy walked just behind me whenever we went out.

'If you let her lead the way, you'll make her feel she's in charge,' she explained.

Try as I might, my efforts to train Poppy to walk at my heels failed miserably. It didn't bother me. We got along fine, and I wasn't interested in engaging in some kind of battle for mastery. Poppy seemed to enjoy the bus ride and sat quietly on my lap with her chin resting on the window sill, watching streets and fields trundling past. Once, when we were stationary, a fox emerged from a hedge and strolled across the road. Poppy sat up, barking excitedly. The fox took no notice, but a woman seated across the aisle made a tutting noise. Before I could explain, we moved on and Poppy settled back down on my lap.

The hamlet where Catherine lived was no more than a handful of cottages stretched out along the main street between an old church and a tiny pub. Poppy and I alighted from the bus. As I set off one way, Poppy dragged me in the opposite direction. I followed her. It was a beautiful day in late June. The summer heat had not yet turned fierce and it was lovely weather for a walk, but my quest was frustrating. None of the cottages were numbered, and not all of their names were visible from the road. I was trying to look at each sign in turn, hoping by some random chance to spot the one we wanted, when Poppy suddenly darted towards a narrow terraced cottage situated in a row of little houses that opened directly onto the pavement.

Catherine made no attempt to conceal her surprise at seeing me, but she welcomed me warmly and was clearly delighted to see Poppy again.

'You should have called me,' she murmured. 'There's no cake.'

Poppy was ecstatic at being reunited with the old lady who had taken care of her when my great aunt died. Once Catherine was reassured that Poppy was happy living with me and I did not intend to return her, she showed me her little fish which was now swimming around in a large rectangular tank and clearly thriving. Having established that we were both well, we agreed that it was fortunate Poppy was well-behaved, because she was too adorable to discipline. I was secretly relieved to learn that the fish had come to no harm while I had been looking after it. With all of that settled, we made ourselves comfortable in plush armchairs in the living room, where every surface was crammed with ornaments and knick-knacks.

'Most of this is my sister's clutter,' Catherine explained, waving a gnarled hand around the room. 'She's gone into Swindon today. She'll be sorry to have missed Poppy. I wish you'd called to let us know you were coming. I would have baked a cake. We have so few visitors these days. But it's lovely to see you,' she added quickly. 'You're welcome to drop in on us any time. Now, I'll put the kettle on and then you can tell me what you've been up to. I'm sure Poppy's been keeping you on your toes, haven't you, little rascal?'

After making a fuss of Poppy, Catherine went off to make tea. Listening to the faint sounds of her clattering about in the kitchen, I leaned back against a lace antimacassar and studied my surroundings. There was a faint cloying scent of lavender and soap, and a film of fine dust had settled on the small occasional table beside my chair. Everywhere I looked, ornate china animals stared back at me, while the only other living creature in the room curled up on an armchair, yawned, and fell asleep. The room was warm and airless and I almost dozed off. It seemed to take a long time but finally Catherine returned, clutching a tray with matching china teapot, jug, and teacups and saucers, and a plate of biscuits.

'I would have baked a cake if only I'd known you were coming,' Catherine repeated mournfully.

At the mention of cake, Poppy opened her eyes and let out a hopeful whimper.

'Oh well,' Catherine went on, brightening up, 'we have biscuits. I hope you like shortbread? Let's have tea, and then you can tell me everything.'

15

Sipping my tea, I broached the subject of my great aunt's death.

'I know she went into hospital after falling down the stairs, but no one's told me what happened in any kind of detail. I mean, I know she died, but what did she actually die of?'

Catherine's eyes narrowed and the lines on her face seemed to deepen, highlighting the pale pink dusting of powder on her withered cheeks. For the first time since we met, she looked terribly frail. She set her cup down carefully on its saucer, and I noticed her fingers were trembling.

'What makes you ask?' she countered.

Her words seemed innocuous, but I had the impression she was frightened and she kept her head lowered, unable to meet my gaze.

'It just seemed rather sudden,' I replied.

Since I hadn't been in contact with my great aunt, I had no grounds for supposing there had been anything unexpected about her death, but Catherine nodded in agreement.

'It was all very sudden, just as you say,' she murmured, still staring at the carpet. 'Denise and I were in Ashton

Mead just a week before Lorna passed, and she was fine then. Fit as a fiddle. She'd only recently taken Poppy home and was really excited to introduce her to us. She'd always owned dogs, you see, and her previous dog had died not long before. He'd been her faithful companion for many years, and we thought she'd never get over losing him. She was inconsolable when he had to be put down.'

Taking a tiny lacy handkerchief from her sleeve, she dabbed at the corners of her eyes. It wasn't clear if she was distressed about her friend's death, or about her friend's grief at losing her dog. Either way, she seemed to be doing her best to dodge my question. I decided to follow her lead for a moment.

'What did the dog die of?'

'Nothing dramatic, just old age.'

It occurred to me that my great aunt's old dog could be the 'S' of her diary.

'What was the dog's name?'

Catherine smiled. 'She called him Penguin, because he was black and white, and she said he waddled when he walked. Anyway, we were pleased she'd acquired Poppy. She seemed fine at first, but we could tell there was something wrong. Finally, she confided to us that she was in trouble.'

'What kind of trouble?'

Catherine glanced around the room as though worried someone might be listening. 'No, not trouble. That wasn't the word she used. She told us her life was in danger. You see, Lorna had a premonition she was going to die. She pleaded with us to take care of her new puppy. "This is it," she told us. "It could be the end for me." Well, we tried to cheer her up and told her it was just the bad weather making her feel melancholy. She said she wasn't ill but she was afraid she was going to die and she made us promise that if anything happened to her, we would take her puppy home with us until you arrived. "If my great niece won't stay around to look after Poppy," she said, "promise me you'll find a good home for my little puppy. I've left a spare key to the house at the local shop. Promise me you'll come and collect Poppy." She was desperate to know that the puppy would be safe and well cared for, so we agreed. We thought something had spooked her and she was overreacting and would feel better soon. She was usually such a level headed woman.' She sighed. 'Neither of us took her fear seriously.' Catherine paused and gazed past my shoulder, lost in memories. 'We didn't know it then, but we were giving our word to a woman who would soon be dead. The day after that conversation we heard she had fallen down the stairs and suffered a fatal injury. She was rushed to hospital, but she was already dead when they found her. I can't tell you how shocked we were.'

Taking her handkerchief out again, she sniffed and dabbed at her eyes.

'What was she afraid of?'

Catherine shrugged. 'I don't know. She didn't say, and I don't think we even asked. We didn't take it seriously, you see. It wasn't until the next day that the postman heard Poppy barking and barking and called the police. If he hadn't chanced to come along when he did, I dread to think what might have happened to the poor little puppy.' She shuddered and wiped her eyes again. 'The postman thought something was wrong and of course he was right, because when the police broke in they found poor Lorna

116

lying stone cold dead at the foot of the stairs. She had left a note about our arrangement, in case anything happened to her. So we went and collected Poppy, like we had promised Lorna we would, and we were wondering how on earth we were going to manage when we heard you'd turned up, like an angel sent from heaven.'

'Weren't the police suspicious?'

'Suspicious?'

'About how she died.'

'Oh there was an postmortem at the time and they recorded a verdict of accidental death. She fell and hit her head and that's what killed her. It was terrible.' She shook her head. 'She had a premonition it was going to happen. I don't think anyone could have prevented it.'

'How could she have known she was going to die?'

Catherine shrugged her shoulders. 'All I can tell you is that she knew.'

'What exactly did she say to you?' I sat forward in my chair, desperate to understand what Catherine was talking about.

'Lorna knew she was going to die,' she repeated.

'What do you mean? Was she sick? Or depressed?'

'No, no, it was nothing like that.'

'What then? What *was* it like?'

'She had a premonition she was going to die just before it happened. She knew. She was expecting it.'

'Do you think someone was threatening her?' My tongue could scarcely form my next words. 'Is it possible my great aunt was murdered?'

Catherine pressed her thin lips together as though afraid words might escape from her mouth against her will.

'Catherine, tell me what happened to my great aunt.'

'No, no, I've already said too much. You shouldn't have come here asking questions about what happened. It's no good asking me to say any more, because we can't talk about it. We just can't. I've told you everything I know.' Her voice shook, and I saw tears in her eyes. 'Poor Lorna,' she whispered. 'She was a good woman. A good friend to us. A very good friend. If anyone – whoever – we never meant –'

She broke off because the front door slammed, startling us both. Poppy sprang up, wagging her tail, as a slightly younger version of Catherine entered the room. She had the same white hair scraped back into a bun at the nape of her neck, and the same heavily powdered face. She greeted Poppy enthusiastically. When she had exchanged greetings with me, and Poppy had calmed down, I brought up the subject of my great aunt's death.

'No.' Denise glared a warning at her sister. 'We don't talk about poor Lorna. She was a very good friend to us,' she went on, turning to me, 'and that's how we like to remember her. We don't have anything more to say about her, do we, Catherine?' It sounded like an order, not a question.

'No, Denise,' Catherine answered, lowering her head submissively.

'Before you came home, your sister mentioned something –' I began.

'Oh, Catherine,' Denise interrupted me. 'You haven't been indiscreet, have you?'

'No, no,' Catherine protested anxiously. 'I didn't say anything.' She threw me a beseeching glance before lowering her eyes again.

'It's been lovely seeing Poppy again,' Denise said, changing the subject with an air of finality. 'She certainly appears to be doing well. We found her –' She paused, searching for the right words. 'She's a bit of a handful, isn't she? But that's only to be expected from a puppy,' she added quickly. 'You must be very experienced looking after dogs. Have you had many of your own? I take it you grew up with dogs?'

We chatted about Poppy, and dogs, but every time I tried to speak about my great aunt, Denise cut me off. For such a diminutive woman, she was surprisingly forceful. After some stilted conversation she smiled at me, and asked me the time of my bus home. A glance at my watch confirmed that it was only fifteen minutes before the last bus back to Ashton Mead. Summoning Poppy, I clipped on her lead, thanked Catherine for tea, and said goodbye. Denise accompanied me to the hall.

'Please don't talk about Lorna in front of my sister again,' she murmured softly. 'Poor Catherine finds the subject very distressing. What happened to Lorna was most unfortunate, and we don't like to talk about it. Catherine finds it very upsetting. We both do. We were very fond of her.' She shook her head. 'It was a tragedy, the way she died. After her grief at losing her faithful dog, she was so happy with her new puppy, and then –'

'We hated seeing her so unhappy,' Catherine interjected, joining us in the hall. 'We were both so fond of Lorna.'

'That's enough, Catherine,' Denise interrupted her sister, with more than a hint of reproof in her voice. 'Why don't you go back inside and sit down?'

Catherine obediently turned away, but not before I caught a glimpse of her face. There was no doubt she was afraid. I had the impression the sisters had discussed my great aunt's death before. If there was any disagreement over what they were prepared to share, there was little doubt in my mind which of them would have won the argument.

Before I had a chance to call out to Catherine, Denise spoke up.

'We'd hate you to miss your bus,' she announced firmly.

Catherine shuffled back into the living room without another word, leaving Denise to see me out. Although she made a fuss of Poppy, and told me she hoped we would come and see them again, I had the impression she was relieved to see me go.

'My sister has a very active imagination,' was the last thing Denise said to me before she closed her front door. I remembered Toby accusing me of the same trait, and wondered if I had imagined that Catherine appeared to be hiding something.

We didn't have long to wait for the bus, and were soon on our way back to Ashton Mead. Staring out of the window at the fields and villages bowling past, I thought about everything Catherine and Denise had said about my great aunt. I had gone to see them looking for an explanation, and had come away with more unanswered questions than before. But I was convinced the two sisters knew more than they had been willing to admit, and I was determined to unravel the threads of the mystery surrounding my great aunt's death.

16

I HAD TO WAIT a few days to see my great aunt's doctor. Having registered at the practice myself soon after deciding to settle in the village, I knew where the surgery was. There were two GPs working part-time at the practice, and I was careful to book an appointment to see the particular doctor with whom my great aunt had been registered. Dr Bruton was a stout middle-aged woman with iron grey hair, a florid complexion, and a forthright air. She raised a quizzical eyebrow on hearing that I had not come to see her with a medical problem.

'Lorna Lafferty was your great aunt, and you are her next of kin?' she repeated, having listened to my enquiry.

'Yes, that is to say, I'm her heir. She left me her house in her will.'

Strictly speaking, I suspected my mother might have been named as my great aunt's next of kin, but she wasn't investigating her relative's death. I was.

'Yes, Lorna Lafferty was a patient of mine, and you want to know how she died?'

I nodded, holding my breath, hoping the doctor wouldn't refuse to share any information with me.

'I'm very sorry to confirm what you must already have been told. Lorna Lafferty fell down stairs at her home and was pronounced dead at the hospital where she was taken. It was recorded as an accidental death,' she added, looking faintly worried. 'If you want to know more you'll have to enquire at the hospital. I wasn't there when the accident happened, nor was I present when she died.'

'But how exactly did she die?'

'She hit her head.'

'When she fell down the stairs?'

The doctor frowned impatiently. 'Yes, exactly. The postmortem showed a deep bleed in her brain, caused by striking her head. By the time the police found her, I'm afraid they were too late to save her. There was nothing anyone could have done for her by then. She had already been dead for at least twenty-four hours, according to the doctor who examined her. The paramedics who were first on the scene made an attempt to resuscitate her, but everyone could see it was hopeless. I'm very sorry.'

I shuddered. Catherine had told me the postman had alerted the police because he heard Poppy barking. By then, my great aunt had been lying dead at the foot of the stairs for more than twenty-four hours.

'If she'd been found earlier, do you think they could have saved her?' I asked.

'That's extremely unlikely. Given the severity of her head injury, she would probably have been dead within minutes of the impact.'

'How did she injure herself so badly?'

Dr Bruton shook her head. Instead of answering my question, she glanced at her watch.

'I'm sorry, but there's nothing more I can tell you. It's

not unusual for serious head injuries to prove fatal. Once again, please accept my condolences on the loss of your great aunt. Now, was there anything else?'

'Could it have been deliberate? I mean, is it possible her death wasn't an accident?'

The doctor's eyebrows rose above the top of her glasses and she stared at me without answering.

'What I mean is, could someone else have been there with her?'

Dr Bruton spoke briskly. 'The police found nothing to suggest there was any question of wrongdoing. There was no mention of it at the time, nor has anyone raised any suspicion of it since.'

Until now, I thought, but gave no voice to what I was thinking. That was the end of my consultation with my great aunt's doctor, but I wasn't exactly reassured. Collecting Poppy from Jane's house later that day, I studied my little dog and wondered whether there had actually been a witness present when Lorna fell to her death.

'Did you see what happened?' I asked her. 'You were there the whole time, weren't you? But was there someone else there with you? If only you could talk.'

Poppy lay down with her head on her paws and gazed forlornly at me as though she shared my regret.

My next task was to apply for a copy of my great aunt's death certificate. That turned out to be easier than I had anticipated, since it was a matter of public record. According to the official document, the death had been accidental, caused by her fall on the stairs at Rosecroft. On the face of it, that seemed straightforward, and it told me nothing new. Yet my great aunt had been convinced she was going to die before the accident occurred. I wondered what had really been going on, and whether there was more to my great aunt's death than anyone else realised. Only her elderly friends seemed to share my unease, but they were too frightened to talk about Lorna's death. It was down to me to investigate what had happened, since no one else would.

Next I decided to make some enquiries at the hospital in Swindon, where my great aunt's body had been examined. Hannah sounded annoyed when I requested a second morning off, but she accepted that I was upset about my great aunt's death. Having managed on her own in the tea shop before, she could hardly claim that she was unable to cope without me for a few hours. Leaving Poppy with Hannah's mother again, I set off on the bus. Finding someone to question at the hospital took nearly an hour. After hanging around in endless grey corridors, I eventually found my way to the mortuary where a squat, dour-faced woman asked if she could help me. It was a polite way of demanding the reason for my unexpected visit. Hearing my explanation, her pasty features reorganised themselves into a sympathetic smile, and she introduced herself to me as an anatomical pathology technologist.

She led me into a small office and, having checked the records, confirmed that she had been on duty the day my great aunt's body was brought in for examination.

'I recognised the name at once,' she said. 'I just wanted to double check that I was here that day. I'm very sorry for your loss,' she concluded gently. 'The police were first on the scene. They did everything they could for her, but your great aunt was already dead when they found her. We examined her before she was finally laid to rest, and her body was treated with every possible care.'

'That was never in question,' I replied, careful to avoid any suggestion that I was there to accuse the mortuary staff of negligence. 'I have no doubt you did everything you could for her. I want to thank everyone here for taking care of her.'

The woman softened visibly. Her raised shoulders dropped, and a smile flickered across her taut lips.

'Is that everything?' she asked, her voice gruff with relief. 'Only I have a job to do.'

'You must be very busy,' I said quickly, eager to detain her. 'I just wanted to ask you how my great aunt's body seemed to you. I mean, was there anything about her injuries that suggested there might be something unusual or puzzling about the cause of her death?'

'Like what?' she asked, wary again.

I wondered how many complaints the hospital staff received from distraught relatives of people who died and were examined in the mortuary.

'She was dead before she was found,' she reiterated, with a defensive scowl. 'The postmortem confirmed a deep bleed in her brain, caused by striking her head. Even if she had survived the impact, she would have been severely brain-damaged. But by the time she was found, it was too late to save her. There was absolutely nothing anyone could have done.' Seeing my evident dismay, her expression softened with a return of sympathy. 'When she fell, I don't think she would have had any idea what was happening. It would all have been over very quickly. It was a tragic death, but she wouldn't have known anything about it. She wouldn't have suffered.'

I hoped she was right.

17

Worn out after spending a morning trekking around investigating, followed by an afternoon serving teas, I was pleased when Poppy seemed ecstatic to see me again. She leapt around my feet, licking my ankles and nuzzling my legs. Happy with her affectionate welcome, I gathered her up in my arms and she snuggled into the crook of my elbow and lay there at peace, warm and furry. I had never felt so grateful to have her companionship as in that moment, when I was feeling isolated with my fears. Having thanked Jane for taking care of my puppy, I went home and Poppy trotted along happily, intermittently stopping to sniff at the grass verges or running on ahead, pulling eagerly at her lead.

That evening I phoned my mother. After we had exchanged our usual greetings, and she had spent ten minutes complaining that my sister never phoned or visited her, I brought up the real reason for my call.

'You never told me about Great Aunt Lorna's funeral,' I began.

She interrupted me before I could say any more. 'That's because I didn't know about it until afterwards. No one told me anything. I didn't know she was dead until shortly before you informed me she had left you her house in her will. I'm always the last to know what's going on in my own family. I'm always the last to know anything. I have no relationship with my own grandson. I know we were in lockdown for months and months, but would it be too much trouble for him to pick up the phone once in a while?'

My mother's sharp tone was not directed at me, so I let that pass. She didn't know anything about my great aunt's worries that her life was in danger, or about the circumstances of her death, apart from what was officially recorded. Our conversation moved on. Feeling awkward that I so rarely phoned her, I invited her to stay again, for a weekend. She launched into a convoluted account of her week, explaining that she was just too busy to get away but would come and see me again as soon as she could, all of which was fine with me.

Once again, my enquiries into my great aunt's death had revealed nothing new, and I still didn't know why she had been convinced she was about to die. Determined to solve the mystery, I fell asleep still puzzling over it. There had to be a perfectly reasonable explanation, but I couldn't for the life of me think what it might be. That night, I dreamt that Poppy could talk.

'Tell me what happened to my aunt,' I begged her, but she just wagged her tail and refused to answer me. 'I know you were there. You saw what happened. Why won't you tell me?'

'You have to find the answer for yourself,' my dog replied in my dream where, disconcertingly, she spoke in my mother's voice.

Unable to come up with an explanation for my great aunt's premonition, I slept badly. After I had given a customer the wrong order, and completely forgotten another one, Hannah marched me into the kitchen and spoke sternly.

'Honestly, Emily,' she said, 'what the hell's going on with you? There have only been six tables today, and you've messed up two of them. How are we supposed to stay open if you can't even remember a simple order of tea and raisin buns? Do you want this job or not? Only I can't keep paying you if you're going to be so sloppy, friend or no friend.'

Ignoring the insult, I caved in and told her what was on my mind.

'I didn't want to bore you with it,' I ended my recital. 'But it doesn't make sense.'

My friend laughed at my perplexity. Hannah was like that, always laughing. It was one of the things I liked most about her, but sometimes her lighthearted attitude was irritating.

'This is serious,' I protested. 'It's no laughing matter if someone is going around killing people. Any one of us could be next.'

I didn't add that if my next door neighbour had murdered the previous owner of Rosecroft, I might be her next victim.

'Oh for goodness' sake,' Hannah replied, still grinning. 'Do you have to be so melodramatic about everything? People have accidents at home all the time. If you ask me, it's a miracle more people didn't have fatal accidents at home during the lockdowns. Did you know more accidents happen in the home than anywhere else? I don't want to sound unsympathetic, and I'm sorry for your loss, really I am,' she went on, suddenly earnest, 'but is there really any great mystery about an old woman tripping over and falling down stairs? And as for her so-called premonition, don't you think she was just worried she had done the wrong thing in taking on the responsibility for a puppy at her age? She must have been concerned about what would happen to Poppy if anything happened to her. She wasn't a young woman.'

'She wasn't that old,' I muttered.

But Hannah had come up with a rational explanation for my great aunt's premonition, and I felt as though a weight had lifted from my shoulders. Just then, the bell above the door rang as a couple of women came in for lunch. Feeling relieved, I hurried out of the kitchen to take their order. Watching their two grey heads bent over the table, nattering, reminded me of the two sisters I had visited in a neighbouring village. Catherine had seemed scared to talk freely, especially once Denise had joined us. The more I thought about it, the more convinced I was that they were hiding something. Of the two, Catherine was more likely to crack under questioning, but she might be too twitchy to come up with a coherent answer.

On balance, I decided Catherine probably wasn't capable of aggression anyway. She would have been far too nervous to push my great aunt down the stairs. It was more likely to have been Denise who had threatened Lorna's life, and possibly even ended it. That would explain why she had been so tight-lipped with me, and so worried about Catherine blabbing, because she had been afraid the truth would come out. But I failed to see what possible motive they could have had for attacking their friend. Besides, if they were responsible for what had happened, it seemed unlikely that Catherine would have hinted to me that Lorna's death was no accident. I wondered if that was her uneasy conscience trying to guide me to the truth. Perhaps she was secretly desperate to confess, but too cowardly to admit the truth unprompted.

That evening I discussed what little I had learned with Hannah and Toby. Hannah stuck to her theory, but Toby agreed it was strange that my great aunt had felt her life was in danger shortly before she died. I wondered if the two sisters had been led to believe they were named in Lorna's will as her beneficiaries.

'But if, as you suspect, Catherine and Denise had anything to do with your aunt's fall, whether deliberately or not, surely Catherine would be the last person to tell you Lorna was feeling threatened,' Toby said. 'And in any case, what could they possibly stand to gain from her death?'

I agreed that my suspicions didn't make sense.

'Even if they were hoping to inherit Rosecroft, it's a bit of a stretch to think they killed your aunt. They hardly sound like murderers.' Hannah smiled.

Toby and Hannah exchanged a glance, and I had the impression they both thought my accusations were crazy. Perhaps they were right. First I had suspected Alice of attacking my great aunt, and now I was suggesting Catherine and Denise were murderers. It was no wonder my friends thought I was overreacting and seeing imaginary villains. But recalling Catherine's uneasiness, and how keen Denise had been to be rid of me, I was certain the two sisters were hiding a guilty secret. The thought of what might have happened made me feel sick.

I needed to speak to Catherine again, and without Denise present. I owed it to my great aunt to discover the truth, even if that truth turned out to be more horrific than anyone else suspected.

18

As the season progressed, we had a flurry of customers in the tea shop during the week. The village was at its most picturesque in the early summer sunshine. The air was pleasantly warm, and everywhere there was a sense of the changing season, filled with unspoken promise, reminiscent of glorious childhood summers and school holidays.

'It must be funny living in a climate where there are no seasons,' I said to Hannah one day, in a quiet moment.

The sky had grown increasingly overcast throughout the morning until, at around two o'clock, it began to rain steadily, putting paid to our hopes of a busy teatime.

Hannah scowled, looking out of the window at the torrential rain. 'As opposed to a climate where the season can change several times in one day. It was lovely and sunny this morning and now look at it. No one's going out in this if they don't have to.'

The weather brightened up by Saturday but, other than walking to and from the café, I saw little of the blue sky, because we were working hard all weekend. By Sunday evening I was ready to collapse. Even my comfortable flat shoes felt tight.

'If it carries on like this, you'll have to recruit more staff,' I said. 'It's too much for two people.'

'There's no room for anyone else to work here,' Hannah replied firmly. 'Apart from the additional wage bill, we'd be taking up space needed for customers, or else we'd be squashed together like sardines in the kitchen with no room to move. I know we're busy, but there's no point in asking for a pay rise, because I'm saving up for a deposit on an extension. When we have room to employ more staff, you'll be promoted to head waitress.' She smiled. 'That's a promise.'

I daydreamed about Toby joining us, although he already had a job and was hardly going to abandon a sensible career in teaching to serve teas and coffees and cakes with us. Still, it was a pleasant fantasy.

In contrast to my weary grumbling, Hannah was jubilant at the upturn in custom. 'If it carries on like this, we'll be building an extension next year,' she crowed.

She continued her scheming when we sat in the pub that evening, drawing complicated little diagrams on a paper napkin, while Poppy obligingly lay under our table and fell asleep.

'What are these strange hieroglyphics?' Toby asked when he joined us. 'Hidden messages from beyond the grave?'

He and Hannah chuckled and I looked away to hide my annoyance. Toby picked up one of the squiggles and studied it with a perplexed expression. Hannah explained she was designing the new layout for the café, for when she had saved enough money to expand.

'One swallow doesn't make a summer,' I warned her, still sour from being the butt of Toby's joke. 'One busy weekend and you're planning to build an extension.'

'I've been planning this for a long time,' she protested. 'Ever since I bought the lease. It's the obvious thing to do.'

'Unless you decide to open a second café,' Toby said. 'Getting builders in can be a nightmare.' He proceeded to complain about how long it had taken to have his mother's house adapted when she was confined to a wheelchair.

We argued for a while about whether Hannah would be better advised to build on her existing site or look for another premises. The discussion grew all the more heated because it was hypothetical. In reality, she wouldn't be able to afford to do either for quite some time, if ever. But it was fun to argue about it, knowing that nothing hung on her decision and we could be as outrageous as we wanted in our advice. The longer we sat drinking, the bolder our suggestions became, until between us we had Hannah running a chain of cafés stretching all the way from Ashton Mead to London. Toby and I were particularly exercised by inventing names for these fictitious tea shops, while Hannah sat and laughed until tears were pouring down her cheeks. 'Hannah's Hungry Haven' was one of our favourites, although Hannah pointed out it sounded as though people would be hungry at the tea shop. Other favourites included 'Here and Scone' and 'The Cake Hole', and 'Hannah's Hole'.

'Stop it, you two,' she cried out. 'I can't laugh any more. It hurts.'

Toby was easy to talk to, and I could have sat there chatting with him all night, but eventually he said he had to go. I was tempted to invite him home with me but had nothing to offer him for supper and, besides, I could hardly invite him and not Hannah, so we said goodbye outside the pub and parted. On my way home, I naturally walked past my next door neighbour's house, where I noticed a light on in the front room. I wanted to ask her if she had seen Catherine and Denise visiting my great aunt on the day she died, but it was probably too late to knock on her door and, besides, I wasn't sure how to pose my questions.

Having put off speaking to Alice for several days, I decided that the next morning, on my way to work, I would make one final attempt to persuade her to give me her stamps in future. It was a daft request, but I thought I would make one final attempt, just to please my mother. While I was speaking to her, I would slip in my question about Catherine and Denise. Alice had obviously been embarrassed about forgetting to save her stamps for me after I had asked, and had invented a poor excuse for no longer having them, but we could try again. I knew it would please my mother. Reaching my front door, I glanced around and noticed a shadowy figure almost concealed by the net curtain at the window next door. As I watched, Alice pulled the heavy drapes across, blocking my blurry view into her front room. Beside me, Poppy whimpered and I shivered.

'Come on,' I said, in as cheery a tone as I could muster, 'it's time for supper.'

We went inside and had a peaceful evening in front of the television, and I tried not to think how lovely it would be if Toby was there with us.

'It's not that I don't love you to bits, Poppy,' I explained to her as she snuggled next to me on the sofa. 'Your happiness means the world to me. But it's not the same, is it? I mean, I can't have a conversation with you, can I? And we can't share a joke.'

Poppy wriggled away from me, leapt down from the sofa, and curled up by the door with her back to me.

We were both tired so when I took her out before bed, instead of going for a walk we went out in the back garden where she darted straight over to the metal fence and began scrabbling at the earth and whimpering as though something had rattled her. Remembering how Alice had closed her curtains next door when we had walked past, I stood for a few moments, staring at the fence. It was too high for me to see over, and the tall hedge that grew up behind it seemed to glare back at me, black and threatening in the darkness. Recalling my earlier suspicions, I had an eerie sensation that something evil was lurking in my neighbour's garden, on the other side of that metal fence.

'Come on, Poppy,' I called. 'Let's go inside.'

For once, Poppy didn't protest but trotted submissively at my side as we went back indoors. It was my turn to close my curtains, and I checked that all my windows and doors were securely locked before going upstairs to bed. Somehow even Poppy's presence in my bedroom was no longer enough to make me feel safe.

19

IN THE BRIGHT LIGHT of morning everything looked different, and I felt foolish for having been unnerved the previous evening. My neighbour was just a lonely woman, who missed her daughter. There was no reason to believe that Lorna's cryptic references to 'S' were in any way related to Alice's daughter. The fact that Alice was by nature introverted didn't mean there was anything sinister about her. Far from being nervous, I should feel sorry for her. If anything, she was the one who ought to be feeling upset that I had stopped asking her to read Sophie's letters to me. On reflection, that had been rather rude of me, and I resolved to put matters right as soon as possible.

We were busy again that day in the café, and I had no time to contemplate my neighbour's reclusive behaviour, or to muse over whether my aunt's friends could actually have pushed her down the stairs. Occupied with taking orders and serving tea and scones, I felt myself jolt back into reality and realised that my conjectures were in fact absurd. Somehow, since Ben had left me, I had become chary of trusting anyone, but it wasn't healthy to be so paranoid. I had to rein in my unfounded suspicions before they grew into an obsession.

When I knocked at Alice's door that evening, she gazed at me warily from her front doorstep without inviting me in.

'Yes?' she muttered. 'What do you want?'

'I was hoping to hear more of your letters from Sophie,' I replied with what was intended to be an eager smile. 'I've left Poppy at home.'

Alice's surly expression relaxed and she thanked me politely for my interest. Explaining that she had her dinner in the oven, she invited me to return in a couple of hours to hear the next instalment of Sophie's adventures. I went home and fed Poppy. With a little time to kill, on a whim I called my sister.

'Well, this is a surprise,' she blurted out.

'A pleasant one, I hope.'

'Of course. It's lovely to hear from you. How are you? And how's life in your village?'

We exchanged news and then I asked her whether Joel was still interested in stamps.

'Stamps?' she laughed. 'He gave that one up as soon as he went back to school. It was just a passing fad. You know how it is with kids. He's back with his football squad now and he's forgotten all about his stamp collection. He never got very far with it.' She laughed. 'How on earth did you get to hear about it?'

We chatted about our mother and her interfering ways, and agreed that she meant well. It was typical of her to get hold of the wrong end of the stick. My motive for acquiring stamps had disappeared, but I still had to honour my commitment to visit Alice. This time she was waiting for me. She opened the door as soon as I knocked, and invited me in straight away. We sat on her soft armchairs with the floral window drapes closed, a box of letters by her feet. Slowly she withdrew one, unfolded it and began to read aloud in a soporific monotone.

'Hi Mum,

I hope you're well. I'm missing you and looking forward to seeing you again before too long.

It's very hot here and in some ways I'll be pleased to leave, but it's an interesting place.

I'm fine, so don't worry. I'm still travelling with the same group of friends. We're on our way East, heading towards Japan, so I'm going to carry on travelling with them for now. I've been fine but one of the girls was quite sick and we all took care of her, because we look out for each other, so you don't need to worry about me. There are six of us and we've become really good friends. They're much more fun than anyone I knew at school, and we all get on really well.

We've seen lots of temples and pagodas and some of them are really beautiful. We're now chilling out on the beach for a few days before setting off again, because it's just so nice here. Seriously, you'd love it. We really must come here together for a holiday one day! Although you might not like the heat.

I love you, and I'll see you soon.

Sophie.'

'That's lovely,' I fibbed.
Actually I thought the letter was dull and generic, like

all the others Alice had read out to me. Either Sophie lacked any talent for describing the places she visited or, more likely, her letters were no more than a perfunctory note jotted down with minimum effort. She couldn't really have wanted to spend her travelling time writing letters home, and was doing so just to appease her mother, perhaps prompted by guilt at having gone away.

'There are more,' Alice said, with pathetic eagerness.

I didn't have the heart to refuse to listen to yet another tedious, but thankfully brief, letter. There was something poignant about the poor woman deriving comfort from such cursory notes from her absent daughter. While I sympathised with Sophie's desire to break free from an overprotective mother, and find her own way in life, I found Alice's solitude almost unbearably sad, and was glad my own mother wasn't alone.

'I'd love to hear more,' I lied, with as much enthusiasm as I could muster, and was rewarded with a smile from my neighbour before she cleared her throat and began.

'Hi Mum,

I hope my letters are reaching you okay, and finding you well. I'm glad to see from the news that life in England is beginning to return to something like normal, after the chaos caused by the pandemic.

I miss you a lot and am looking forward to seeing you again before too long.

It's still really hot here but I'm actually getting used to it and anyway we'll be leaving soon. We visited some more temples yesterday, and are preparing to set off on the next stage of our journey. It's very exciting! They have working elephants here, which are used to cart stuff around, and we saw some of them hauling logs yesterday.

I think it might be too hot for you here, but don't worry, I'm being careful and, like I said, I'm getting used to the heat.

I hope you're having a nice summer with plenty of sunshine.

With lots of love,
Sophie.'

After sitting through ten of these boring and repetitive letters, I had heard enough.

'That's quite all right,' Alice replied when I said it was time to return home to Poppy. 'There is something else I wanted to mention to you before you go.' She paused and eyed me with a calculating expression. 'It's about your friend, Toby.'

I was instantly attentive, although I did my best to conceal my interest. 'You know he wanted to see my daughter?' she went on.

'See her?'

'Yes, yes, you know what I mean. He asked her to be his girlfriend.'

'Toby and Sophie?'

Alice nodded.

'When was that?'

'Does it matter? It was when he had just finished school.'

According to Hannah, Sophie was about four years younger than Toby, but it was nothing unusual for an eighteen-year-old boy to go out with a fourteen-year-old girl.

'The point is he wanted to be her boyfriend.' Alice said impatiently, her face twisted in a curious expression. 'I'm only telling you this because I've seen you with him, and I think you ought to know what he's like. You've been very kind to me, and I'd hate to see you get hurt, knowing I could have prevented it.'

'I didn't know he had a relationship with Sophie, but we're not close friends so there's no reason why he would have mentioned it, especially now she's left the village.'

'Temporarily,' Alice interjected swiftly. 'She's gone temporarily.'

'Yes, of course.'

Privately I thought there was a strong chance Sophie might never return to her mother's home. Ashton Mead might seem very quiet and dull to her now she had travelled around the world, but I didn't say that to Alice.

'Anyway, there was never actually any relationship,' Alice said. 'Toby wanted to go out with her but she wasn't interested in him. Why would she be? Sophie's a beautiful girl. She could have any boy she wanted. What I want you to know is that Toby wasn't happy about being rejected. He took to stalking her and became obsessed with her.'

'He stalked her?'

My disbelief must have shown in my face, because Alice's scowl deepened.

'Yes,' she spat. 'You may not want to hear this, but he behaved very badly towards her. Very badly indeed.'

'It was a long time ago, and they were teenagers,' I pointed out.

'People's natures don't change,' she said. 'Once a thug, always a thug.'

Toby had never struck me as thuggish, and I told her so.

'Yes, he's a thug,' she insisted, her eyes bright with suppressed fury. 'I don't use such words lightly. He gave my poor daughter a terrible scare. She thought he was going to do her some real harm. Anyway, she got herself away from him. She's not as feeble as she looks.' She added with a complacent nod. 'He never lifted a finger against her after she warned him that she would go straight to the police if he ever tried to go near her again. After that he left her alone. I'm telling you this for your own good, Emily. I'd hate to see you get hurt. You need to be careful around that man. He has a vicious temper and will stop at nothing if he's crossed. If you take my advice, you'll stay well away from him in future.'

'What did he do to her?' I asked, struggling to take her accusation seriously.

'He terrified her with vile threats. You don't need to know the details, but if you want my advice, you'll stay well away from that man. After the way he treated Sophie, you should give him a wide berth.'

It was hard to believe what Alice had told me about Toby, but the longer I lived in Ashton Mead, the more menacing everyone around me seemed.

'Tell me honestly, is it just me being paranoid?' I asked Poppy, who lay on the sofa and gazed at me mournfully. 'And now I'm talking to my dog,' I added. 'No wonder Toby thinks I'm crazy.'

Poppy jumped down from the sofa and left the room without looking back.

20

THE VILLAGERS WERE PREPARING for an annual summer solstice celebration on the weekend closest to the longest day, which occurred towards the end of June every year. Everyone I met was keen to tell me that the previous year had been the first time in living memory that the event had been cancelled, due to the lockdown. There was understandable excitement in the village at its resumption this year. The whole village seemed to be involved. Hannah was kept busy preparing cold food to accompany the barbecue which the butcher was organising. I was left to run the tea shop virtually single-handedly while she dashed between the shop and her mother's house, baking trays of sausage rolls, buns and cakes.

On the streets, children of all ages seemed to materialise from nowhere, dressed in various outlandish costumes, begging for coins. Some of the outfits were shamefully half-hearted affairs, no more than a yellow hat or scarf thrown on over their own clothes, but others were really quite complicated, with faces drawn on yellow papier-mâché heads and old coats painted in all different shades of yellow and orange. It wasn't immediately clear how their dressing up was connected to the summer solstice.

'It's just a bit of fun for the kids,' was the general response, although a few villagers explained that the children were dressing up to honour the sun.

'It's for the summer solstice,' they said, as though that explained everything.

'It's just an excuse to throw a party and have a good time,' Hannah told me, which seemed to be a good enough explanation for the excited preparations.

Toby came along to the tea shop and offered to lend a hand. Remembering Alice's warning, I was cautious about accepting his help too readily. In any case, he had no inkling that I was attracted to him, and had given me no firm reason to believe he reciprocated my feelings. It was best if I didn't grow too close to him and risk rejection or possibly worse. In a small village like Ashton Mead, where rumours spread quickly, it would be wise to keep my feelings to myself.

'I'm not sure Hannah would agree,' I muttered awkwardly, refusing to meet his gaze. 'I don't think it's a good idea. I mean, I'd need her permission.'

If Toby was surprised at my rebuff, he didn't show it.

'I've helped her out before,' he assured me. 'But if you've got it all under control, that's great. I'll pop over to the house and give her a hand there.'

With that, he was gone, leaving me decidedly disgruntled, having missed out on an opportunity to spend time alone with him. But there was no doubt my neighbour's intentions had been kind when she had warned me about the darker side of Toby's nature. All things considered, it was better that I had not welcomed an opportunity to spend time with him in a hot small kitchen where it would have been impossible to avoid some physical contact.

I soon realised that, not only had I missed out on an opportunity to spend time alone with Toby, but I now had to cope in the café by myself. As luck would have it, two groups of customers arrived at the same time, and I had to prepare their order, and serve them, all on my own. At least I had left Poppy with Jane that day, and didn't have to worry about abandoning her for hours.

At last Hannah returned to the tea shop, flushed and excited, with Toby in tow. Seeing how attractive she looked, I felt a stab of jealousy, but squashed it fiercely. Toby and I were not together, and there was unlikely to be any hint of romance between us. As soon as the opportunity presented itself, I intended to pass Alice's warning on to Hannah, and tell her there was no smoke without fire. Rumours had to start somewhere.

'We're ready,' she gushed. 'I never could have done it without Toby. He's a gem.'

Toby looked faintly embarrassed.

'He even took over and carried all the trays to the green so I could shower and get ready for the party this evening,' she added, tossing her blonde curls and grinning at him. 'I feel like a million dollars.'

She was wearing a sparkly T-shirt and figure-hugging chinos, and her glamorous make-up shimmered when she moved her head.

'You look great,' I stammered.

My own jeans were spattered with milk and tea, and smeared with jam where I had carelessly wiped my fingers. My shoes were flat, ugly and heavy. Since I was on my feet all day at work, they were chosen purely for comfort. When I removed my apron, my shapeless grey sweatshirt bunched around my waist so that I resembled a grey version of the Michelin man. Hannah went into the kitchen to fetch a few last minute items, leaving Toby and me alone together in the café.

'You look lovely too,' he murmured, leaning towards me with an appreciative smile. 'You don't have to make an effort.'

Had any other attractive man whispered those words to me, I would have been gratified. As it was, I turned away abruptly and began furiously wiping tables. Much as I desperately wanted Toby to like me, I couldn't risk having my feelings hurt again, not after what had happened with Ben. By pushing him away, I was doing what was necessary to protect myself from further pain, although part of me cried out against being sensible and longed to risk encouraging Toby.

'Leave all that,' Hannah cried out, returning from the kitchen.

She frowned at Toby who shrugged, and I wondered what private message they had exchanged, and when would be a good time to tell her what I had learned about Toby.

Together the three of us walked down to the river, where the party was being held. Smells from the barbecue reached us on the breeze before we arrived, along with the noise of loud excited voices. On our approach, we saw children racing around, largely ignored by groups of adults. Trestle tables set up for the food were covered in plates of barbecued sausages, beefburgers none the less appetising for being slightly burned at the edges, lamb koftas, drumsticks and all sort of other mouth-watering meats. Alongside them were platters of cakes and scones freshly baked in Hannah's oven.

She disappeared in the crowd, leaving me with Toby who offered to fetch me a drink. It was hard to believe his polite good-natured façade concealed a vicious nature, but Alice could have no motive for vilifying him without good reason. Grateful though I was for her warning, I could not help feeling bitterly disappointed. With so much that had happened, it felt like a long time since I had last had a boyfriend, and I could really have fallen for Toby. With a sigh, I left him and went to mingle in the crowd, determined to avoid him. At one point I caught a glimpse of Hannah and Toby together. He was standing in front of her with a hangdog expression, while she gesticulated wildly and seemed very animated. He hardly looked as though he could ever be aggressive, and I almost went to join them. But then Alice's words rang in my head and I moved away out of sight, too afraid of being hurt to risk responding to his tentative advances. He was probably just being friendly, in any case.

Shortly before the fireworks began, I hurried home to take Poppy indoors and reassure her that we had nothing to fear from the loud noises and flashes. As we were waiting for the fireworks to begin, my phone rang. Hoping it was Toby trying to find me, I saw my sister's name on the screen. In spite of my disappointment, I was pleased to hear from her. We chatted until the noise of fireworks disturbed Poppy, who began barking at the window. I explained to Susie that I had to end the call, and reassure Poppy that there was nothing to worry about.

'Bloody fireworks,' my sister sympathised. 'They're a menace if you've got pets. I hope they don't go on too late.'

Witnessing the display from my bedroom window, I gazed at showers of brilliant sparks illuminating the darkening sky in flashes and flecks of scarlet, green, blue and yellow. Poppy was trembling in my arms, and I held her close, trying not to think about Toby and Hannah standing together in the crowd. The whole village was out watching the magical fireworks in a throng of tipsy adults and overexcited children, up long after their normal bedtime.

'It should have been me,' I whispered to Poppy, even though I was afraid Toby had an ugly temper, and Alice had been right to warn me. 'I know he's a bad lot. Oh, why can't I meet someone normal and nice?'

Poppy's black eyes stared up at me.

'At least I have you,' I said, and she stretched up and licked my cheek apologetically, whimpering softly.

It was doubtless the noise from the fireworks that disturbed her, but it seemed she knew her company would never be enough to make me happy. In silence we shared a moment of sorrow, each of us weighed down by our unfulfilled longings.

21

As we were sitting watching through the window, Poppy started squirming so I stood up to take her outside. When I opened the bedroom door, she ran back to the window and crouched beneath it, whimpering. She didn't want to go out after all. Closing the door, I went to sit down again, and did my best to dispel her fears, assuring her that the fireworks could not hurt her, and the noise was all outside. She calmed down for a moment but then grew increasingly unsettled and leapt from my lap once again. This time she dashed over to the door, barking furiously.

'It's all right, Poppy,' I reassured her. 'It's just fireworks. Come over here and I'll hold you up so you can see for yourself what all the fuss is about. Poppy, here, Poppy, come!'

Gathering her up in my arms, I carried her over to the window. Before sitting down again, I noticed a figure pass through my gate and hurry away along the street towards the party. It could only have been Hannah coming to find out where I was. Clearly she had thought better of it, because she hadn't knocked on the door. That irritated me, but there was no time to think about her inconsistent behaviour because Poppy scrambled out of my grasp, ran across the room, and resumed her barking, scratching furiously at the door.

'Come on, then,' I said, heaving myself off my chair again. 'There's no need to destroy the paintwork.'

I went over and opened the door for her. Instead of running downstairs, she hung back, clinging to the hem of my trousers with her teeth to prevent me from leaving the room. There was a faint smell of burning from the fireworks outside.

'Well, do you need to go out or not?' I demanded crossly. 'That's the second time you've got me up and I'd like to watch the display, if you don't mind.'

I returned to my seat at the window. The smell of burning grew stronger, and Poppy seemed genuinely distressed. Refusing to come and sit with me, she stood in the doorway, yelping as though she was in pain, or very frightened. This time when I went over to fetch her, I noticed she was shaking, and the smell had grown markedly stronger. I ventured out of the room to look down the stairs, and felt my breath catch in my throat. Behind me, Poppy's whining had grown frantic.

As I stood transfixed, a thread of smoke rose into the air from a rocket lying on the hall carpet. Poppy barked. Galvanised into action, I rushed down the stairs. By the time I reached the hall, one end of the firework was glowing brightly and had singed a hole in the carpet. Within seconds the smoke grew thicker, twirling upwards in multiple delicate tendrils, while a tiny flame flickered, a tongue licking the air to test it. In a panic, I dashed forward, grabbed my coat that was hanging on the wall, and smothered the nascent fire before it could take hold. If Poppy had not been there to warn me, I would still have been sitting upstairs, watching fireworks outside my window, oblivious to the one that had landed right inside my house.

Shaking at the danger we had so narrowly escaped, I picked Poppy up and went into the kitchen to make myself a cup of tea. Although I never usually sweetened it, on this occasion I added a hefty spoonful of sugar which was supposed to counter the physical effects of shock. Like Poppy, I was trembling. Having sat down to drink my tea and console Poppy with treats and cuddles, I returned to the hall to inspect the extent of the damage. The carpet had been in the house when I moved in. It was old but still serviceable, and I could cover the scorched patch with a rug until it was eventually replaced. My coat was another matter. That was completely ruined, and there was no point in even attempting to mend it. In addition to black soot marks, the fire had singed a large ragged hole in the middle of the back.

But the state of the carpet and my ruined coat were insignificant in comparison to the danger Poppy and I had so narrowly escaped. Having spotted a figure running off, I knew someone had been to my house, but I had no idea who it could have been. It was such a dangerous attack, not even drunk teenagers could have found it amusing to send a lighted rocket through my letterbox. I wondered whether to report the incident to the police but, without any evidence, there was not much they could do.

This could only have been a deliberate attack, and I desperately wanted to know who had been responsible for shoving a lighted rocket through my letterbox. But the culprit had presumably been wearing gloves, and had no doubt been careful not to breathe all over the rocket, so there would be little chance of identifying them. In any case, just because someone had handled a firework was no proof that they had posted it through my letterbox. There was nothing to be done, other than be vigilant from now on. It appeared that I had an enemy in Ashton Mead, an enemy who would not hesitate to endanger my life. The thought that someone wanted to kill me was horrible, and I was glad that I had Poppy with me.

'I'm going to have to rely on you to protect me from now on,' I told her and then felt a stab of real fear, realising how small and helpless she truly was.

I was the one who ought to be protecting her, and it seemed I was doing a poor job of it. That night I struggled to get to sleep. Every time I managed to doze off I was woken with a start by a suffocating feeling. Once I dreamed that Rosecroft was ablaze, with Poppy inside, and all I could do was stand and watch.

'I have to rescue her,' I shouted in my dream, and woke myself up.

On the floor beside the bed, Poppy stirred on the bundle of clothes she had adopted as her bed. I was glad of her presence in the room, even though the responsibility of caring for her weighed heavily on me, even disturbing my dreams.

Eventually, exhausted, I fell into a deep sleep. By the time I woke up in the morning my terror had abated. Apart from a faint stench of singed fabric, and a hole in my hall carpet, nothing remained to remind me of the previous night's trouble. My coat was missing, of course. I had thrown it away, along with the offending rocket. There was no point in holding on to them. Neither could prove that a crime had been committed.

In daylight, the incident seemed altogether less disturbing, although just as hazardous. The rocket could have been intended as a practical joke by passing kids who had no idea someone was actually in the house at the time. It might just as easily have been a stray rocket that flew off course and by some unlikely chance hit against my letterbox and entered the house. Rockets could fly with some speed and force.

Unlikely though it was that a firework had entered my house by chance, even that was more credible than the idea that someone had deliberately posted a lit rocket through my letterbox. If someone actually wanted me dead, there must surely be more reliable ways of killing me. With that thought offering an uneasy kind of comfort, I set off for the tea shop. Poppy trotted and frisked beside me, clearly none the worse for her scare the previous evening, and as the sun came out, I felt my spirits lift. We were back to life as normal, and any dark fears that I was being targeted by a killer receded further with every step I took.

'Everything's okay,' I told Poppy, who was too busy sniffing at the roots of an old tree to pay any attention to what I was saying. 'We're going to be okay. I'll take care of you.'

22

'WHAT HAPPENED TO YOU last night?' Hannah demanded when I arrived at the tea shop. 'We looked everywhere for you.'

I explained that I had gone home to look after Poppy who had been frightened by the loud fireworks.

'You could have brought her with you,' she said. 'As long as you were holding her, she'd have been okay. It's not as if she's very heavy. You missed a stonking display. Everyone was there. It was absolutely awesome.'

'Yes, well, I watched it through the window.'

I had arrived at work early, eager to tell her about the rocket in my hall, but Hannah seemed cross with me and was clearly in no mood to chat. Ever since I had shared my suspicion that Alice had buried her daughter in her garden, Hannah had regarded me as a drama queen. No doubt she would dismiss my story about a lighted rocket flying through my letterbox as just another fantasy.

'Let me get this straight,' I could imagine Hannah saying, her hands on her hips and a sceptical expression on her face. 'You think someone tried to murder you by putting a lighted rocket through your letterbox?'

It did sound absurd, and I decided not to say anything about it.

'Toby missed you,' Hannah went on, throwing me a sly glance to gauge my reaction.

'Well, I didn't miss him,' I replied tersely.

Hannah scowled at me. 'Emily,' she said sternly, 'what has got into you?'

I turned away to straighten the condiments on a table.

'You must know how much he likes you,' she added. 'He's been a good friend to you.'

'I don't know what you're getting at.'

Hannah actually stamped her foot. 'Oh come on. You deliberately went out of your way to give him the impression that you like him. He took it seriously. If you're just messing him around, you need to be honest with him before he gets even more hurt.'

'I don't dislike him,' I replied, feeling my face turn hot with embarrassment. 'It's just that I'm not ready for a relationship. Not after what happened last time.'

Hannah nodded. 'You have to let go of the past,' she commented before she went to the kitchen to light the oven. 'Toby's a great guy and you shouldn't mess with his feelings. It's not fair on him.'

Work was a welcome distraction from my problems. Hannah had known Toby for years, but clearly she had no idea how aggressive he could be when he was thwarted. It was my duty to warn my friend, and it had to be done soon. There was a danger Hannah might start dating Toby. If that happened, she would be bound to dismiss anything negative I said, in the belief that I was jealous. In a way I was, but I had to put such thoughts out of my mind, and I had to tackle Hannah at once and put her straight about Toby. Hard though it was to believe Toby could have stalked Sophie, it was impossible that Alice could have been mistaken, or fabricated the story.

As well as worrying about Hannah and Toby, I was concerned that Denise and Catherine knew how my great aunt had fallen down the stairs, and had conspired together to conceal the truth. That was another problem I had to deal with, and it was difficult to see what could be done about it. Perhaps, in the end, my only viable course of action was to do nothing at all about anything. Sophie's issues with Toby were history, and Lorna was dead. There was no point in stirring up old troubles. But I knew that I could not ignore my responsibility to my friend, or to my dead relative. One way or another, the truth had to be brought out into the open.

I turned around from serving a couple of elderly women and saw a man had entered the café. He was standing with his back to me, looking out of the window, but I recognised him instantly. You cannot live with another person for six months and fail to know what they look like from behind. When he turned and grinned at my astonishment, I felt lightheaded, seeing his familiar face smiling at me.

'How did you know where to find me?' I stammered as he came towards me.

'It wasn't difficult. Your mother told me you were hiding out in this quiet backwater. I hope you don't mind that I came looking for you, but I've been so miserable without you, babes. I'm telling you, my life hasn't been worth living since we split up.'

He flung his arms around me and kissed me ardently. Ignoring the faint tutting from my elderly customers, I responded. It was a while since I had felt a man's arms around me. Remembering how much fun we used to have together, I held him close, savouring the familiar scent of his aftershave, mingled with a faint whiff of sweat. It was like coming home.

'I can't wait to get you into bed,' he murmured softly. 'I missed you so much.'

Something in the back of my mind warned me to be careful and I pulled back from his embrace just as Hannah appeared from the kitchen.

'Emily,' she called and stopped, catching sight of me in a stranger's arms.

I disentangled myself from Ben and frowned at him.

'What are you doing here?' I demanded in a fierce whisper.

'For Christ's sake, Emily, why do you think I'm here? I miss you. Have you forgotten how good we were together?'

He was right. Until lockdown our relationship had been strong. I had thought it was for keeps.

'Emily,' Hannah interrupted my thoughts. 'Are you working today or not? Only there are customers waiting to be served.'

It was disappointing that she sounded so vexed, when she should have been overjoyed for me, but we were busy so I let that pass.

'Who is this stunning woman?' Ben asked, turning his smile on Hannah, who accepted his compliment with an uneasy nod.

'Hannah,' I said proudly, 'this is Ben.'

Attempting to smooth down her hair and inadvertently leaving streaks of flour in it, she repeated that we had customers waiting to be served. I gave Ben my keys, with instructions where to go, and promised to be home as soon as possible.

'I'll be waiting,' he whispered, kissing me again. 'I can't bear to be apart from you, even for a moment.'

Having finished with my customers, I requested the afternoon off. Hannah looked worried. Dragging me into the kitchen, she held on to my arm.

'How can you trust your ex after what he did to you? How do you know he's not going to hurt you all over again?'

'Don't be daft. He wouldn't have come back if he wasn't serious about me. Don't look so worried. It's fine. He missed me, that's all. He's been miserable without me.'

Too happy to be offended by her scepticism, I batted away her concerns.

'He walked out on you once,' she reminded me. 'He could do it again.'

'He walked out, but don't you get it? He's come back,' I replied. 'He was just unsettled by the lockdown. It happened to a lot of couples. But he's back now and everything's going to be fine. I know it is. He can't bear us being apart.' I hesitated, before mumbling, 'And neither can I.'

Hannah looked closely at me as though she was trying to read my expression.

'Have you really been that lonely?' she asked. 'You could have- ' She broke off, fidgeting with her apron. 'You know I'm always here for you. And- ' She hesitated. 'Toby likes you a lot.'

'You and your precious Toby. Why don't you go out with him if you think he's so wonderful? But you might need to take a course in self-defence first.'

Hannah looked mystified. 'What on earth are you talking about? Have you lost your mind?'

I didn't have time to convince her that Toby was hiding his vicious temper from her. Ben was waiting for me at Rosecroft.

'You'd better see to your customers,' I said coldly, and marched off.

Halfway down the street, I remembered that in my irritation with Hannah I had left Poppy in the yard outside the tea shop. Cursing under my breath, I raced back.

'It's all right,' Hannah greeted me as I dashed breathlessly into the café. 'I'll take Poppy to the pub after work and you can pick her up from there if you like. If you're sure this is what you want,' she added. 'You don't have to do this, you know.'

Thanking her, I left and ran all the way home. Sweaty and breathless, I fell into Ben's arms and he insisted on carrying me upstairs to bed.

'When did you get to be so romantic?' I asked him, laughing.

'When I realised that I missed you and I can't live without you,' he replied and I felt as though I would burst with happiness.

A little voice whispered in my head, warning me that he had walked out on me before; I wished Hannah hadn't brought that up. But Ben was back in my life, and I was confident everything would be fine from now on. In any case, I couldn't live the rest of my life fearing the worst. There were times when it made sense to be optimistic, and this was definitely one of them.

'I missed you too,' I replied, 'and I never want to live without you again.'

23

BEN AND I HAD a passionate reunion, but something had changed in his lovemaking. He seemed to be trying too hard to please me, and that made me uncomfortable. At last he rolled out of bed and reached for his jeans, talking all the while about our dinner plans. Remembering that Hannah was waiting for me at The Plough with Poppy, I told Ben about the food at the pub and he grinned and said it sounded good.

'I don't suppose there's much choice out here, anyway,' he said. Seeing my face fall, he added quickly, 'But there's nothing like good pub grub. Come on, I'm starving.'

After a quick change, I went downstairs and found Ben pacing across the living room. He looked round, startled by my entrance.

'I didn't hear you coming down the stairs.'

'What are you doing?' I asked.

'Nothing at all. That is, I was waiting for you. Come on, I'm famished. Where's this pub you were talking about?'

Hannah was at the bar chatting to Tess who, for once, was looking cheerful, giggling at something Hannah was saying. There was no sign of Poppy. Tess gave a surly nod in my direction and Hannah turned and came hurrying

161

over to us. She told us Poppy was in the garden with Toby, and we went out to join them. Poppy seemed strangely guarded when I arrived, merely flicking her ears at me and closing her eyes again, while Toby was taciturn, and Hannah seemed tetchy. She had never struck me as bad-tempered before, and I wondered how I had spent so much time in her company without noticing how crabby she could be.

Within the claustrophobic community of Ashton Mead, Hannah and Toby had seemed like brilliant companions. It only took a few hours with Ben to show them up for what they really were: parochial and desperately dull. Dismissing the idea that it would be foolish to discard the two people who had recently befriended me when I was struggling with my life, I smiled at Ben. His charisma had exposed how boring my new acquaintances really were. He was now the focus of my attention, and I was in love with him all over again.

By contrast to Hannah and Toby, Ben was in an expansive mood and seemed completely relaxed, chatting as he sampled the local ale. He was something of a connoisseur of beers, and used to insist on drinking at pubs recommended by CAMRA.

'What's that?' Hannah asked.

Ben raised his eyebrows at her question. 'I would have thought you'd know all about it, seeing as you work in the hospitality industry. It's the Campaign for Real Ale.' He launched into a detailed description of the work of CAMRA, together with an explanation of why he preferred not to drink at pubs that didn't subscribe to the organisation. 'They all would if they could, but CAMRA is exclusive and only accepts pubs that serve proper beer.

It's just a way of ensuring quality,' he explained. 'To be honest, I feel the same way about the wines I buy. No supermarket plonk for us, eh Emily?'

'You prefer to support independent off-licences?' Hannah asked politely.

Ben laughed. 'No way. You never know what you're getting if you shop just anywhere. No, it's the Wine Society for me. You might think it sounds extravagant, but they do some fantastic offers for people who can afford to join, and you always know what you're drinking is class.'

'Because someone else tells you it's good?' Hannah murmured.

'So what do you think of the beer here?' Toby asked.

Ben shrugged. 'It's good enough. I'll have another one if you're going to the bar. Cheers.'

As he drank, Ben talked about his experience during the lockdowns. 'One thing I won't be doing is go back to that shitty job,' he announced, after talking about how his boss had refused to allow him to continue working from home full-time after the lockdown ended.

I was faintly puzzled, having always believed he worked for himself, but I wasn't going to challenge him in front of my friends.

'It's not as if I wasn't getting the job done from home. He was just trying to assert his authority. Well, he can stuff that as far as I'm concerned. I told him exactly where he could go. "You might pay me a whopping great salary," I told him, "but you don't own me." Stupid prick. Who did he think he was, talking to me like that.'

'What are you going to do?' Hannah asked politely.

'Well, you won't catch me working in a café.' He laughed.

Hannah looked upset and I giggled uncomfortably in a feeble attempt to pass Ben's comment off as a joke. Toby looked away and stayed silent.

'I think Ben's a bit drunk,' I said by way of an excuse.

Hannah muttered darkly about there being no justification for bad manners and I was dismayed to discover that, for once, she seemed to have lost her sense of humour. Ben put his arm around me and I grinned with relief. At least he was cheerful company. It was difficult to know what to say, with Hannah being so huffy and Toby ignoring us all. I wasn't sorry when Hannah said she was tired and going home. Ben banged his fist on the table, making Poppy start. She opened her eyes lazily, looked at me and turned away again.

'One more drink,' Ben announced loudly. 'Emily will get them, won't you, babe?'

'Of course,' I agreed, standing up.

'Not for me,' Hannah said. 'I've had enough.'

'You've only had two pints,' Ben replied. 'Lightweight.'

As Hannah walked away, I stood up and Ben slapped me on my backside. 'Off you trot, then,' he said cheerfully, and I thought I saw Toby flinch.

When I returned with a tray of glasses, across the garden I saw Toby leaning down, gently scratching Poppy's neck, while Ben appeared to be playing a game on his phone. Ben appreciated people listening to him when he was talking, and Toby was being even less responsive than usual that evening. His behaviour bordered on rudeness.

'You have to agree, it is nice here,' I said brightly, putting the tray down on the table. 'I mean, Ashton Mead is beautiful, isn't it?

'It's all right,' Ben replied. 'If you like living in the middle of nowhere.'

Toby seized his glass and gulped his pint as though he had been thirsty for a long time, while Ben talked about his plans for the future. It wasn't altogether clear how he was proposing to fund his scheme, but he assured us he was going to make a lot of money importing grains from overseas, and his confidence was contagious.

'Where will you be importing the grains from?' Toby asked, seemingly genuinely interested at last in what Ben had to say.

Ben waved his arms in the air, narrowly missing knocking my glass off the table.

'Oh, that's not the point,' he replied. 'The thing is, there's a market for it here and where there's a market there's money to be made.' He grinned.

I wished Hannah had stayed on to hear what Ben said about investing for the future and watching his funds grow. It sounded very impressive and I certainly had no objection to having a wealthy boyfriend.

'Well, I'm off,' Toby said when Ben paused for breath. Leaving his pint half-drunk he stood up. 'I have to be up early tomorrow. Good night.'

Ben and I finished our drinks in silence as he was studying his phone again. He told me he was checking the price of grain.

'The beeps from your phone sound just like you're playing a game,' I told him.

'Yes, well, that's what it does,' he replied.

'Come on, Poppy,' I said, standing up when we had finished, and unhooking my puppy's lead from beneath the leg of a chair.

Ben's eyebrows shot up. 'Don't tell me you're taking that dog home with us?'

'Of course. Poppy's my dog.'

'Okay, whatever.'

Usually Poppy trotted eagerly in front of me, but this evening as we walked back to Rosecroft, she dragged behind me. When we entered the hall, she growled at Ben, who didn't seem to notice. I put it down to her being unfamiliar with him, and perhaps a little jealous. She was used to having me to herself at home.

'Just make a bit of a fuss of her and she'll be fine,' I told him. 'She likes attention. If you play with her, you'll soon make friends.'

Murmuring in my ear that he would rather play with me, Ben led me upstairs, closing the bedroom door behind us. I was momentarily distracted by hearing Poppy whimpering outside the door.

'Never mind about that,' Ben said, opening a bottle of wine. 'Look what I found in the kitchen.'

'I didn't see you bring that upstairs,' I protested, laughing. 'Haven't we had enough to drink for one night?'

'We're celebrating,' he replied, pouring a generous amount into two glasses.

'What are we celebrating?'

'I'm back with the most beautiful girl in the world, and if that's not worth celebrating, I don't know what is.'

Flattered, I gave in to his blandishments. I had been living alone for too long and, in any case, Poppy had already been outside for hours that evening and could hardly be desperate to go out.

'Get over here and kiss me,' Ben said, dragging me towards the bed.

I was more than happy to comply.

24

THE NEXT MORNING, I overslept and woke up with a pounding headache.

'Cheer up, babes,' Ben said. 'Let's go out for breakfast. How about going to that café your friend works at? I'm sure she'll do us mates' rates, and there's nothing like a good fry-up when you're feeling delicate.'

'Oh shit,' I burst out. 'The café.' I looked at my phone in a panic. 'I'm due at work in ten minutes!'

I sat up but Ben pulled me back down on the pillows. 'Take the day off,' he said softly. 'You deserve some time to yourself. You can't work all the time, not at something as physical as waiting at tables. You don't want to wear yourself out.'

He started to kiss me. With an effort, I pushed him away, insisting that I had to get to work. I dressed as quickly as I could, yanked a brush through my tangled hair, splashed cold water on my face, and almost tripped over Poppy who was waiting patiently on the other side of the bedroom door. She leapt up at me, barking and rubbing her head against my legs.

'Poppy, did you think I'd forgotten you?' I crooned.

Actually, I had overlooked her in my excitement at

167

spending the night with Ben, but she seemed to harbour no resentment and set to work licking my shoes. I hesitated for only an instant before gathering her up in my arms. It would hardly be fair to expect Ben to take care of her without any discussion and there was no time to tell him when to feed her, or how to tell if she needed to go outside. They would soon get used to one another but in the meantime, she was my responsibility and if I was going to work, she would have to come with me. Grabbing a bag of her food, I shouted out to Ben that I was leaving, and hurried to the café.

'No Ben?' Hannah asked as I arrived, hot and flustered from rushing. 'I say, Emily, are you all right? You look terrible.'

'Well, since you ask, I feel pretty sick. Ben opened a bottle of plonk after we got back from the pub.'

'Plonk? I thought he only drank expensive wine?'

I was too tired to argue and went outside to tether Poppy and give her breakfast.

'I take it Ben wasn't happy to be left in charge of Poppy?' Hannah enquired when I went inside.

Pouring myself a mug of coffee I sat down and propped my chin on my hands. Somehow it was too much effort to hold my aching head up without support. Hannah looked concerned.

'Are you sure you're all right? You really do look terrible. Can I get you anything?'

I started to shake my head but had to stop because the movement set off a hammer inside my skull. It drummed against the side of my head, just above my right ear, making me nauseous. Muttering that I would be okay, I took a swig of coffee and scalded my tongue. But somewhere inside me a song was playing, and I was filled with joy, because Ben had returned and I was in love once again. Hannah sat down opposite me and gazed earnestly at me.

'Emily, can I speak freely?'

I groaned but felt too sick to argue.

'I know you haven't been living in the village very long, and I don't want to be presumptuous or intrusive in any way, but I feel like we've become good friends, and I care about you. We've known each other now for over three months, and in that time we've spent just about every day together, ever since you started working here, and –' She broke off as a customer entered. 'You stay here and finish your coffee. I'll deal with them.'

I could have kissed her for that. As it was, I let out a low groan of relief.

Giving me a final concerned look, she went to serve the customer. All through the morning Hannah brought me glasses of water, ordering me to keep drinking, and gradually my headache faded. Finally I was able to swallow a poached egg on toast she insisted on making for me, and I began to feel better. After a couple of hours, the breakfast rush receded and the café emptied.

'Now,' Hannah said, sitting down opposite me. 'We need to talk.'

'Shouldn't we clear up in the kitchen?'

'Five minutes,' she said. 'We need to talk.' She sounded so serious, I had no choice but to comply after she had been so kind to me.

'What's up?' I asked.

Hannah heaved a sigh. 'This is difficult. I want to talk to you about Ben.'

'He's the most wonderful thing that's ever happened to me!' I gushed.

'Emily, you're forgetting he walked out on you.'

'He says that was a mistake. He's come back, hasn't he? He loves me, Hannah. He really does. And I love him.'

'I don't want to be unkind, but I think you should weigh everything up very carefully before letting someone back in your life after they've let you down once. He walked out and now that you've inherited a nice property of your own, he thinks he can just waltz back into your life, and profit from your good fortune. Think about it, Emily. Are you sure his motives are completely disinterested? He seems very acquisitive. He certainly aspires to the finer things in life, and you're a prosperous woman now. Have your forgotten how he walked out on you when you were down on your luck, and had just lost your job? Are you sure he doesn't want you back for the wrong reasons?'

For a moment I was too shocked to speak. I could hear my voice shaking as I told her that she was completely wrong about Ben.

'As for only being interested in me because of Rosecroft, you couldn't be more wrong. He doesn't know I own a house of my own. He knows nothing about Lorna's will. How could he? The question hasn't even come up. Why on earth would he suspect the place belongs to me when I was virtually penniless when we parted? I'm sorry if you don't like him, but you don't know him like I do. You've only just met him. We're in love, and that's all there is to it. If you say one more word against him, I'll walk out of here and never talk to you again.'

'I thought we were friends –' she stammered, looking strained. 'I just wanted to talk about it and make sure you've really thought this through. I'm only thinking of you.'

'Well, I'm perfectly capable of sorting out my own life, thank you very much. You should spend more time worrying about yourself. How's your love life these days?'

With that bitchy comment, I went outside to see Poppy. At least she was pleased to see me for my own sake, and didn't judge how I chose to live my life, unlike Hannah who seemed jealous of my happiness. It was sad to discover how selfish she was, but I now knew who my true friends were. Miserably, I returned to work, where Hannah and I avoided one another for the rest of the morning. What she didn't appreciate was that I was feeling unnerved after being followed on the street, and having a rocket pushed through my letterbox. With Ben at home I felt less vulnerable, especially at night. As I was taking an order that afternoon, he walked in. Looking at his neatly slicked back blond hair, and his chiselled features, I felt my spirits lift. Ben was vain of his looks with good reason. He winked at me as he took a seat. Rushing through the order I was in the middle of taking down, I hurried over to his table.

'What would you like?'

'How about a kiss?' he replied, reaching out and dragging me towards him.

I laughed, and felt my face blush at this public display of affection. But I didn't really mind that everyone in the tea shop, including Hannah, saw that my good-looking boyfriend was besotted with me. In my happiness, I even forgave Hannah for feeling jealous. I could hardly blame her for that.

25

Leaning back in his chair with a proprietorial air, Ben ordered a full English breakfast.

'I'm sorry,' I told him. 'Breakfast stops at midday and it's after one.'

Ben laughed. 'Don't be daft. You work here, don't you? You can serve breakfast any time you want.'

'No, I'm sorry, I really can't,' I insisted, half laughing yet frustrated with him for being awkward. 'Don't be a pain in the neck, Ben.' I broke off anxiously, nervous about upsetting him. 'It says quite clearly on the menu that breakfast is served until midday. Look! Breakfast served until midday. That means it stops at midday.'

'Well, you can just start it again. Are you my girl or not? Consider it a perk of the job that you can keep your fella happy.'

I hesitated, torn between pleasing Ben and following Hannah's rules. 'Oh all right. I'll go and ask in the kitchen.'

Hannah was taking rolls out of the oven. 'You know we stop the fry-up at twelve,' she replied. 'It's says so clearly on the menu. The pans are all washed up, so why are you even asking?'

'It's for Ben,' I told her unhappily.

'He'll understand then. He won't want to make things difficult for you, will he?'

I did my best, but Hannah was intransigent. There was nothing I could say to change her mind. Ben was understandably cross, so in the end I offered to make his fry-up myself.

'And I suppose you'll be paying for it?' Hannah asked me sharply.

'You can take it out of my wages,' I replied miserably.

She turned back to the oven, muttering that I was letting Ben walk all over me. It was obvious that she was fuming, and I wondered if she was right and I was being stupid, giving in to Ben over something so petty. He could have chosen something from the lunch menu. I regretted not having stood up to him, but it was too late to change my mind now. Having prepared a full English breakfast, I took it out to Ben. Seeing him tucking in, people at next table complained.

'I wanted to order a full English but I was told it wasn't available,' a stout man bellowed. 'The menu says it stopped at midday and it's after one now.' He looked pointedly at his watch.

'I'm sorry, sir,' I told him, 'that was the last breakfast order.'

'We were here before him,' the man pointed out, not unreasonably.

'Yes, we were here before him,' the stout man's wife bleated shrilly. 'Why were we told we were too late?'

Flustered, I tried to defend the preferential treatment Ben had received. Just then, Hannah emerged from the kitchen with a tray of tea and buns.

'Look, we were here first, and were told breakfast

173

was finished before he was served,' the man insisted.

Ben put his fork down and turned round to address the other customer. 'Don't sweat it, mate. This fry-up's not that great. Look – the yolk's hard, this sausage is burnt and the tea's weak as piss.'

I felt my face turning red. Ignoring Ben, Hannah offered the other customer complimentary teacakes, as compensation for their disappointment.

'What about my disappointment?' Ben demanded.

Although I felt sorry for Hannah, I had to agree Ben had a point. He hadn't been offered free food.

'You're not paying for what you had,' Hannah snapped at him. 'You let your girlfriend pay for you.' With that, she stalked back to the kitchen.

Ben finished his breakfast in silence and stood up to leave.

'Aren't you taking Poppy for a walk?' Hannah asked him, looking out from the kitchen. 'She's in the yard.'

Ignoring her, Ben left. Hannah was frosty with me for the rest of the day. Working with her used to be fun but had now become uncomfortable, and by the end of the day I could no longer bear it. I decided there was nothing else to do but hand in my notice. Since I had not taken a single day's holiday since starting to work at the tea shop, Hannah agreed to let me leave without working out my notice. I wanted to thank her for giving me the job, but it seemed inappropriate given the bad feeling that had arisen between us. It was the end of a chapter in my life when I had believed myself happy. Now that Ben had returned and reminded me what true happiness felt like, I realised that I had just been surviving without him. We were together again and I was determined that this time our relationship would succeed.

That evening, Ben wanted to go out. I was reluctant to go to the pub, where we were likely to bump into Hannah or Toby, if not both of them, so I was relieved when Ben made it clear he had other plans.

'We can do better than that shit pub,' he said. 'Let's go into the nearest town. I'll call an Uber and we'll find somewhere to eat in Swindon. Go on, get yourself tarted up and I'll have a look online and book a restaurant. What do you fancy? Indian? Chinese? It would be great to go into London, but that's a bit too far for an evening, isn't it? There must be some night life in Swindon, surely.'

I felt a stab of guilt leaving Poppy on her own at home while we went out enjoying ourselves, but Ben had arranged an evening out, and I did not want to upset him so soon after he had returned. He booked a car to take us into town, and a slap-up meal in a Chinese restaurant. The food was superb, but the price was extortionate, compared to a supper at the pub. Over dinner, Ben plied me with wine. I protested when he ordered a third bottle, not least because I was paying for it and had just lost my job, but Ben insisted we celebrate our reunion. It was, as he kept insisting, something special, the start of a whole new life for us.

I had no intention of talking about my great aunt's death on such a happy occasion, but the wine made me indiscreet. Provoked by Ben's dismissal of Ashton Mead as boring, and intent on sounding dramatic and mysterious, I revealed my suspicion that my great aunt had been murdered.

'Murdered?' Ben scoffed. 'You're not serious, are you?'

Regretting my indiscretion, yet stung by his scepticism, I nodded. Yielding to his entreaties, in the end I confessed my suspicions about Denise and Catherine and the part they had played in my great aunt's death. As I was talking, Ben's expression changed. Glancing around to make sure no one could overhear our conversation, he leaned forward and listened closely to every word I said. The more I talked about my theory, the more far-fetched it sounded. All the same, I was pleased by Ben's rapt attention. Aware that my voice sounded slurred, I enunciated my words with care.

'They were hiding something,' I concluded. 'There's no doubt about it. Not in my mind at any rate. Catherine hardly dared raise her eyes to look at me, and Denise seemed determined to stop her sister talking to me. Every time Catherine opened her mouth, Denise jumped in. In the end she sent Catherine packing.'

'Sent her packing?'

'Yes, well, sent her into another room.'

Ben looked grave. 'Do they know you're on to them?'

'I think Denise realised I suspected they were involved in my great aunt's death, yes.'

'Then this is serious,' Ben said solemnly. 'We can't sit around doing nothing. We have to take the initiative. We'll go and see them first thing tomorrow. No, don't try to put me off. You can leave all the talking to me. If we handle this properly, it could be just the break we've been waiting for. But only if we convince them we're serious.'

When I remonstrated, Ben insisted.

'We have to frighten them or we'll never get anywhere,' he said.

'So you think we should go to the police?'

'No, no, absolutely no police. We don't want to cause any trouble, do we?' He grinned at me. 'Listen, once they know you're not alone, they'll agree to our demands. If they aren't frightened, there's no point in pursuing it. But as long as they take us seriously, I'm sure we can make this work.'

'I've no idea what you're talking about. Why do you want to threaten them, and what about?'

I was beginning to feel uneasy, but decided that was probably down to the alcohol. Ben's next words reassured me.

'Don't worry,' he replied, his eyes shining. 'You did the right thing, bringing this to me. I'm going to look after everything and I'm going to look after you.'

'I still don't understand what you're getting at.'

While I was keen to know what he meant, I was pleased he was taking control of the situation because I really didn't know what to do.

'Listen, babes, we have to deal with them or they could come after you next, to silence you.'

I shuddered, but it was hard to believe Catherine or Denise could pose any threat, and I wasn't keen on confronting them. It wasn't Ben's place to interfere, and I told him so. But he must have seen that I was wavering.

'It is absolutely my place to protect you from any danger,' he replied firmly.

Despite my disquiet, it was gratifying to know that Ben cared about me enough to feel protective. He made me feel safe. Groggily I watched him fill his wine glass. It was just as well neither of us was driving back to Ashton Mead that evening.

'Here's to us,' Ben announced, raising his glass. 'And our glorious future together. Let no one come between us, ever.' He hiccupped and spilt his wine.

I began to giggle uncontrollably as I raised my glass. Our night out might be proving expensive, but it was certainly more exciting than going to the pub for pie and mash and, as Ben had pointed out, our reunion was something to celebrate. Life seemed suddenly full of possibilities and excitement and it was hard to believe I had ever thought myself happy without Ben. In the morning, I would talk him out of going to see Catherine and Denise but, in the meantime, we were having fun together and I was happier than I had been in a long time.

'This is better than the pub,' he announced, filling his glass again and waving at the waiter to bring another bottle. 'Come on, let's have some fun.'

Staggering out of the restaurant, we were unable to find anywhere else to go in Swindon, where most of the clubs were still closed after the last lockdown, so in the end we took an Uber home. Ben grumbled about cutting the night short all the way back to Ashton Mead, but I was quiet. The motion of the car was making me nauseous. As soon as we left the cab, I threw up on the pavement.

'Lucky it wasn't in the house,' Ben said before he stumbled up the path, leaving me to stumble after him.

It was an ignominious ending to our celebrations.

26

THE FOLLOWING MORNING I left Ben in bed when I took Poppy out for her first walk of the day. Kissing me goodbye, he made a sleepy promise to get up and make breakfast, by which time I would be home.

'Sounds good to me!' I said. 'But don't rush. It's still early.'

The fresh air revived me a little, but I was still feeling groggy from the previous evening's drinking as I followed Poppy across the wide patch of grass that ran from across the lane down to the river. She amused herself pursuing a curious zigzag path, picking up scents that were concealed from me. She was happily scampering and sniffing around, when all at once she froze, her ears pricked up, and she began tugging me towards a hooded figure that was walking rapidly across the grass towards us. Unable to see who was approaching, it crossed my mind that Denise could be stalking me. Having realised I had stumbled on her secret, she might have come to silence me. Ben had warned me that might happen. We were out in a public space, but it was early, and there was no one else around. As I tensed to defend myself, I recognised Hannah peering out from beneath her hood, and let out a sigh of relief.

'Emily,' she greeted me with a worried expression as she drew near. 'Please, don't walk away without hearing what I have to say. I really want to talk to you.'

'Okay, go on then, talk.'

Poppy was frolicking between us, alternately nuzzling my ankles and jumping up at Hannah hoping to be petted.

'First of all, if you want to come back to work –' Hannah hesitated, seeing me scowl, and bent down to tickle Poppy under her chin. 'You're always... that is, there will always be a place for you at the tea shop.'

'I won't be coming back to work, and I won't be visiting the tea shop as a customer,' I replied coldly. 'Was there anything else? I take it you didn't follow me here just to say that?'

'You're right, I did follow you. I knew you'd be taking Poppy for a walk so I waited outside your house because I guessed this was going to be the only time I could get you on your own.'

I didn't answer but resumed my walk towards the river.

'Emily,' she went on, words hurtling out of her now she had started, 'I just wanted to ask you not to rush into anything with your ex. I'm worried about you. I'm worried you're going to get hurt again.'

'You don't understand,' I replied, pulling Poppy away from her and walking faster. 'I love Ben and I intend to spend the rest of my life with him.'

'You thought that once before and look what happened then. He walked out on you as soon as you lost your job. Think about it, Emily. What made him come back now? I mean, are you sure he didn't come back just because he heard you now own a house? How can you be sure he's come back just for you and not for your money?'

I paused in my walk to glare at her. 'He came back because he loves me. And I've already told you he doesn't know the house is mine, so that's got nothing to do with it. And that's a really horrible thing to say. You make it sound as though he couldn't possibly be interested in me for myself. Some friend you are!'

Hannah sighed. 'I'm only saying all this because I care about you, and I'm really afraid this won't end well. I don't understand why you would take him back, when you must realise he's only going to end up hurting you again. And he does know you own Rosecroft. He boasted about it to Toby the other evening at the pub, when you were at the bar ordering a round.'

'No, he didn't. He can't have, because he doesn't know Rosecroft is mine. Unless you or Toby told him,' I added in what I hoped was a menacing tone.

'Of course neither of us told him. But he knows all the same. He said he bet Toby was sorry he was too slow to get his hands on you and your house when he had the chance, but now it was too late.'

'I don't believe you,' I replied, angry that she would spread a story like that.

'It's true, Toby told me.'

'Like you can trust a word he says.'

'What are you talking about? I've known Toby all my life and he's never lied to me. Of course I trust him. Emily, look at me. What are you doing back with Ben? It's obvious he's just sponging off you.'

'No he's not,' I protested, nearly in tears. 'I don't like living alone. It suits some people, but it's just not for me.'

'You've got me, and you've got Poppy. You weren't alone

before Ben came back, and you were happy then, weren't you?'

'That's not the same as living with someone. I thought I was happy, but I wasn't. And I don't want to be alone for the rest of my life.'

'There are other men,' she pointed out.

'Well, if there are, I haven't noticed a queue of them beating a path to my door.'

Hannah glanced at me and looked away. 'Toby likes you,' she said in a low voice.

'So you keep saying. Well, he's never said anything about it to me and anyway, even if he does like me it's too late now because I'm with Ben and nothing's going to change that. We're in love.'

'Emily, have you forgotten how betrayed you felt when he left you? He just walked out and broke your heart. That's not the action of someone who genuinely loves you.'

'Yes, he left, and he came back because he loves me,' I answered irritably. 'I told you, he only left because he was freaked out by the lockdown. It was a difficult time for everyone. It's not your place to judge him for what he did. I've forgiven him, and that's what matters. He's admitted he made a mistake. Everyone makes mistakes. I dare say you're not so perfect yourself. Anyway, it's my life we're talking about. Why should I care what you think?'

Hannah gazed at me sadly. 'You've changed,' she said.

'I'm happy now,' I replied, suppressing a crazy impulse to tell her I missed her company and the laughter we used to share.

'Just ask yourself one thing. Would you have taken him back if he wasn't so attractive? I mean, is it really his character you're in love with, or his looks? Just because you fancy someone doesn't mean you're in love with them. Don't be blinded by Ben's prowess in bed, Emily. There's more to a successful relationship than sex.'

'Like you're suddenly an expert on relationships,' I muttered crossly.

My love life was none of Hannah's business. Just because we had been friends for a while, and had worked together, that did not give her the right to criticise my choices in life, and I told her so.

'Listen, why don't you just piss off and stop trying to run my life for me? What makes you think you know what I want better than I do? I had enough of that from my mother.'

Whether it was my tone of voice, or because she wanted to explore the grass some more, Poppy began to whimper.

'Now you've gone and upset my dog!' I snapped, losing my temper. 'Leave me alone. What makes you think you have any right to hound me like this?'

'Just remember that I'll be here for you if you ever do need me again,' she replied sadly before she turned and walked away.

'The cheek of it,' I fumed to Ben when I went home and told him what had happened.

'She must have been waiting for you,' he replied. 'Watching outside and waiting for you to go out alone so she could pounce and try to turn you against me.'

'Why would she do that?'

'Isn't it obvious? She was worried I'd open your eyes to the shameful way she's been exploiting you.'

'What do you mean?'

'You just don't get it, do you? Ask yourself how useful you've been to Hannah, working in her shitty little café for next to nothing. I don't understand why you let her use you like that. She's afraid she's going to lose you, now I'm here to tell you what's going on. As for criticising our relationship, that's outrageous. Who the hell does she think she is, telling you how you should live your life? I've half a mind to go and tell her exactly what I think of her and her pathetic attempt to come between us. As if anything could ever break us up!'

He kissed me and I soon forgot all about Hannah and her insinuations. As for the idea that I might ever have become romantically entangled with Toby, I no longer even considered him a friend and was going to avoid him from now on, whatever else happened. I felt guilty about having failed to warn Hannah about him when we were still talking to one another. A man who had behaved badly once could turn nasty again. People didn't change. Realising that was exactly what Hannah had been telling me about Ben, I drew away from his embrace.

'What is now?' he asked, pulling me back into his arms.

'I'm just worried about Hannah,' I admitted.

'Hannah is no friend of yours. And she can look after herself. She runs a café, doesn't she?'

Hannah would never believe me if I passed on Alice's warning now. It was time to accept that she was no longer my friend. In the meantime, Ben was back to protect me, and I was determined to do everything in my power to make sure he never left me again.

'You're right,' I replied, and returned his kiss.

27

BEN WAS KEEN TO discuss my suspicions of Catherine and Denise. Reluctant to dwell on my great aunt's death, I regretted having shared my idle speculation with him.

'It was an accident,' I insisted. 'We know that. There was an autopsy, and that's what they concluded. It had nothing to do with Catherine or her sister.'

I could hardly admit that I had just been trying to sound fascinating when I had told him my theory that my great aunt had been murdered. But Ben refused to be satisfied.

'No one else was there,' he pointed out. 'We can't be sure it wasn't murder.'

He grew quite animated and insisted we had to 'warn the old bitches off', as he put it. Now that we were both sober, I was keen to let the whole idea drop. Ben did his best to convince me that my own life might be in danger if we did nothing. If the sisters had killed once, he said they might do so again. Disturbed by Ben's warnings, I resolved to share my suspicions with the police. If the situation really was as serious as Ben thought, then we couldn't deal with it by ourselves. But Ben shook his head.

'The police won't be interested unless we can give them evidence, and at the moment it's just an impression you have, isn't it?'

I nodded. 'It's a daft idea, when you think about it. They had no reason to want their friend dead. Honestly, I was horribly drunk the other night or I never would have mentioned it to you. I'm sure they've done nothing wrong.'

'You don't know that. And as long as we keep quiet, you're going to be in danger now they know you suspect them.'

'But they don't know that.'

Ben shrugged off my protest. 'Remember, if what you suspect is true, one or both of these women have already been responsible for at least one murder. Come on, Emily, wake up. People who have killed once aren't going to hesitate to kill again if they see you as a threat.'

But I had been thinking about what happened, and it didn't add up.

'It just doesn't make sense,' I said. 'Let's forget it, please. What possible motive could they have had for wanting to kill my great aunt?'

Ben kissed me. 'You poor sweet innocent. There could be all sorts of reasons, when you think about it. They might have been expecting to get their hands on Rosecroft. The old woman had trusted them to look after her dog, hadn't she? So they must have been good friends. With her out of the way, they might have thought the house would be theirs. Perhaps it was left to them in an earlier will and once they discovered she was planning to leave everything to you, they decided to kill her before she could change her will. One of them might have lost her temper when she found out they were too late and the will had already been altered, and pushed her down the stairs in a fit of pique.'

'Some pique!' I muttered.

His hypothesis sounded as far-fetched as my own suspicions, but I had to admit it was possible.

'Are you saying you think they planned to kill Great Aunt Lorna for her house?'

'I've no idea what their reason might have been, but yes, that's a pretty powerful motive if you ask me. You'd be surprised what people will be prepared to do to get their hands on a valuable property. And don't underestimate the anger some people might feel if they think they've been cheated out of something they expected to inherit. But that's all beside the point. The fact is, I'm not going to let you live with this danger hanging over you. If they want to threaten you, they'll have me to deal with. I'm not prepared to see you put at risk. I just won't have it.' He kissed me again. 'You're too important to me.'

Catherine and Denise hadn't actually threatened me, but Ben was set on going to see them. In the end, I agreed, partly because he was so adamant, but also to put my own mind at rest about my suspicions concerning my great aunt's death. I felt it was the least I could do after she had given me Rosecroft. And someone had posted a lighted rocket through my letterbox and almost succeeded in setting fire to Rosecroft. Ben didn't know about that, but I seemed to have an enemy who was prepared to put my life in danger.

After lunch we took the bus to the hamlet where the two sisters lived. Once again I knocked at their door. Poppy was excited and jumped around, while Ben stood, poker-faced, as we waited on the doorstep. I had almost given up and decided that Denise and Catherine were not in, when the door opened and a wizened face peered out at us. If Ben was surprised at how feeble Catherine was, he didn't show it. Seeing me and Poppy, the old woman's expression altered and she smiled with what appeared to be genuine pleasure.

'Emily! And Poppy!' she cried out. 'What a delightful surprise. Come in, come in, and your young friend too. Come in. Denise has just put the kettle on. I'll tell her to set out another two cups. And we'll find you a water bowl,' she added, reaching down to pat Poppy on the head with a gnarled hand, and straightening up with a groan.

Chattering excitedly, she led us down the hallway to the front room and hurried off to the kitchen to announce our arrival to her sister. Ben and I sat down to wait, with Poppy curled up at my feet. Ben gazed around the room, taking in the ornaments and fussy furniture.

'What a load of crap,' he muttered.

I hushed him, embarrassed in case our hostesses overheard his criticism of what was probably a lifetime's collection of treasured knick-knacks.

'Now,' Denise said, coming in and setting down the tray of tea things, while Catherine followed her in with the matching teapot. 'Introduce us to this young man.'

She smiled eagerly at Ben and I felt a spasm of doubt about the reason for our visit. Ben glanced at me, waiting for me to begin, but I hung my head. Two such gentle old ladies were hardly likely to be murderers, but I had watched many crime dramas on television and knew that evil comes in many guises. Still I hesitated. Ben had no such qualms and launched straight into the accusation.

'We're here to tell you that Emily knows what you did.'
Having convinced myself that the two sisters would
have no clue what Ben was talking about, I was surprised
at the effect his words had on them. Catherine's hands
fluttered to her lips and she stared at me with a frightened
expression in her eyes, while Denise glared angrily at us.

'How did you find out?' Denise whispered at last. 'We
were so careful.'

For an instant I was too stunned to speak. There could
no longer be any doubt that Catherine and Denise had
been responsible for my great aunt's death.

'Which one of you was it? Which of you?' I stammered,
scarcely able to speak.

'Well, we both agreed –' Catherine said and burst into
tears.

'Now, now,' Denise interrupted her. 'Don't go upsetting
yourself, Catherine. We only did what we thought was
best for her. We agreed at the time it was necessary.'

'Best for her? Necessary? Which one of you did it?' I
cried out, my temper suddenly getting the better of me.
'Who was it?'

'Both of us,' Denise said with a return of her usual
firmness. 'We talked it over and decided it was best for
everyone.'

'But who did it?' I repeated. 'I need to know the truth.
Which of you pushed Lorna down the stairs?'

Catherine and Denise stared at me as though I had
dropped into their living room from another planet.
The teapot fell from Catherine's grasp, and landed on its
side. Tea dribbled from the spout but for a moment no
one moved. I lunged forward and put the teapot on the
table, while Catherine stared in dismay at a dark patch

glistening on the carpet. Only Poppy seemed energised by the accident. I had to cling to her collar to stop her running over to lick the spilt tea which was probably still hot.

'Have you taken leave of your senses?' Denise demanded in ringing tones, standing up and raising herself to her full height, which was still barely taller than I was sitting down. 'What are you talking about, Emily? Poor Lorna might have been disappointed in us, but I hardly think our actions would have upset her. If anything, she would have been pleased, or at least she would have understood why we did it. Our intentions were kind.' She sat down. 'As for anyone pushing her down the stairs, let us have no more of these melodramatic accusations. We understand you are distressed at losing your great aunt so suddenly, and we share your grief. Lorna was very dear to us, very dear.' She broke off, her voice cracking with emotion. 'We are all upset. But there's no call to make such wild statements.'

'Which one of you was it?' I repeated.

Ben took over. 'We know one of you pushed Lorna down the stairs and you've been concealing the truth from everyone. Unless you want us to call the police and tell them everything, we want you to tell us why you did it. Emily deserves to hear it from you.'

Catherine and Denise couldn't have looked more astonished if Ben had told them he was an alien and had suddenly sprouted tentacles.

'Listen, we understand you could be in serious trouble,' he went on in a gentler tone, 'but let's not be hasty. The police have accepted the old woman's death was an accident, so there's no need for anyone else to find out what you did. Now, let's stay calm and discuss our terms for keeping this between us. Emily's great aunt is dead and nothing can alter that, so there's nothing to be gained from telling the police the truth. We're willing to be reasonable. You must have some savings put by. We don't want to leave you short. We're just asking for a modest payment in exchange for our silence.'

Denise rose to her feet again. This time her eyes were blazing with fury. 'Enough!' she cried out. 'Yes, we concealed the truth, but only because we were ashamed. Lorna entrusted Poppy to our care, and we passed on that responsibility. But Poppy was better off for it and we stand by our decision. Lorna would have understood. More, she would have approved of our decision. As for the ridiculous notion that someone pushed her down the stairs – ' She broke off, unable to speak.

'We couldn't keep up with Poppy,' Catherine confessed. 'She's too lively for us. We're not young any more. So we paid a dog walker to exercise her every day. It's not what Lorna asked us to do, but we thought it was best...' She spoke in a low voice, tears glistening in her eyes. 'We never intended to let her down. We didn't think it would matter, but perhaps we should have tried harder. It was the last thing poor Lorna asked of us. The last favour –'

'*That's* the secret we were hiding,' Denise said. 'And now, we'd like you to leave before *we* call the police and have you arrested for malicious slander.'

'Don't be too harsh on her,' Catherine said. 'The poor girl is grieving for Lorna, and grief can make you think and say the most outlandish things that wouldn't normally even cross your mind.'

But Denise was not so easily mollified. 'Emily,' she said

sternly, 'your great aunt would be ashamed of you for attempting to blackmail us. You're a wicked girl.'

'That's okay,' Ben said breezily, snatching up a biscuit. 'Emily didn't know her great aunt anyway, did you, babes?'

28

BEN AND I DID not exchange a single word on the way back to the bus stop. For once Poppy behaved like a model dog and trotted obediently behind me. Our walk through the picturesque hamlet would have been very pleasant, were it not for the knowledge that we had just attempted to blackmail two old ladies for a terrible crime they had not committed. The more I thought about what we had done, the guiltier I felt. Catherine and Denise were probably in tears, smarting from being accused of murdering their friend. We had almost reached the bus stop when I halted. My great aunt's friends had been doing their best to take care of Poppy, and did not deserve such defamation. But when I suggested we return and apologise, Ben shook his head.

'No way are we going back there,' he said. 'Come on, cheer up, the bus will be here soon. Look, you made a mistake, that's all. You got it wrong. But there's no harm done. Those two old biddies are probably too senile to remember what happened. Who would believe them anyway? There's no point in going back and stirring it all up again for them. They won't want to be reminded about it. They're probably sitting down now having a nice cup of tea. The kindest thing we can do is walk away and leave them in peace.'

So that's what we did. Not long after we reached our decision the bus arrived, and we were soon travelling back to Ashton Mead, away from the scene of our embarrassing debacle.

'You won't tell anyone what just happened, will you?' I asked Ben.

He put his arm around me and kissed my hair. 'I won't say a word,' he assured me. 'What is there to say anyway? Nothing happened, did it?'

There remained the possibility that someone had murdered my great aunt and if it wasn't Catherine or her sister, then it must have been someone else, but after the mortifying scene that afternoon, I decided it would be best to let the matter drop. Lorna Lafferty was dead, and nothing could bring her back. But the circumstances of her death continued to plague me and in the end I decided to return to the hospital to ask some more questions. I told Ben I had a routine doctor's appointment, which was not exactly true, and asked him to look after Poppy while I was gone. Walking down the front path, I heard her barking for me, but ignored her even as her yelping grew more frantic. She and Ben would have to start getting used to one another.

I tracked down the anatomical pathology technologist who had spoken to me before but had to wait for an hour until her shift ended. She recognised me and was reluctant to talk, telling me she had finished work and was going home. Even though my funds were running low, I offered to buy her whatever she wanted in the canteen if she would only agree to talk to me for a few moments. With a sigh, she agreed.

'It's hard to let go when someone you are close to dies,' she conceded kindly.

Once we were sitting down with hot drinks and toasted teacakes, I touched on my concerns as delicately as I could.

'So was she already dead by the time she was found?'

'Yes.'

'And how long had she been dead by then?'

'I'm sorry, but it's impossible to give a specific time of death.'

'So there's no way of knowing whether she was alone when she fell down the stairs?'

The woman's eyes narrowed and then she shrugged. 'I'm not sure where you're going with this, but yes, it's possible there was a witness when she fell, perhaps someone who is too scared to come forward because they shouldn't have been there.'

'Or because they pushed her down the stairs?'

She shook her head with a dismissive sniff.

'It's possible, isn't it?' I pressed her.

'Of course it's possible,' she agreed. 'Anything's possible. We can't know what we don't know.'

'Did you say anything about your suspicions at the time?'

She shook her head, with a tired expression. 'No, because I didn't have any such suspicions at the time. To be honest, it didn't even occur to me that she might have been murdered and, if it had, I would have dismissed the idea in the absence of any evidence. Everyone could see what had happened. It was clear that she had fallen. I mean, it is unlikely, isn't it, that someone would have killed her and tried to make it look like an accident. It's the kind of thing that happens in films, but in an English village? I don't think so.' She gave a nervous laugh.

'It's unlikely but it's possible,' I replied.

'Well, it would be a pretty stupid way of committing murder, is all I can say. The chances of someone dying from such a fall are probably not that high. She could have just broken a few bones.'

I had to admit that my hypotheses were not always grounded in fact. My suspicions of Denise and Catherine had proved false, but that was not my fault. They had concealed a secret from me, albeit a perfectly innocent one, and that had set me off on the wrong tack.

'I just think someone's lying, but I don't know who,' I said.

'People do strange things when they're upset,' she murmured, staring at me with a sceptical expression.

She seemed wary of me, and probably thought I was slightly unhinged.

'Well,' I said, drawing back and trying to look calm, 'the fact remains it's possible my great aunt was murdered.'

'Possible, I suppose,' she agreed, 'in the sense that just about anything could be possible.'

'My great aunt told her friend she thought her life was being threatened,' I whispered. 'And then she had a fatal accident, when no one could see what was happening.'

'If she was feeling threatened, she should have told the police.'

The technologist left soon after that, giving the impression she was eager to get away from me. Clearly she did not give any credence to my suspicion that my great aunt had been murdered. I no longer believed that Catherine or Denise had been lying to me about Lorna's death. They had innocently wanted to make sure Poppy was well cared for. On reflection, it was looking increasingly likely that my great aunt's death had been nothing more than an unfortunate accident. Nevertheless, there remained the question of why Lorna had claimed her life was in danger.

I decided not to discuss my findings with Ben. Apart from anything else, he had no idea I had gone to the hospital to speak to the anatomical pathology technologist who had been on duty the day my great aunt's body was examined. It was ironic, but in some ways I felt more alone with Ben than I had been before his return. This was a problem I could have discussed with Hannah, and I missed her practical common sense. She would have dismissed my speculation as histrionic, and I was beginning to agree with her. Even Ben had only gone along with my suspicions of Catherine and her sister because he had hoped to profit from their guilt. I didn't entirely blame him. We were running short of money. At the same time, I was disturbed by his behaviour.

Still, if no one else took my suspicions seriously, perhaps there was a reason for that. By the time I reached the bus stop, I had abandoned my conviction that my great aunt had been murdered. Like my concerns about Alice and her daughter, it was my overactive imagination that had put such a crazy idea into my head. I felt embarrassed at having shared my thoughts with anyone else, and angry with myself for discussing my concerns with Ben. Resolved to disregard all such fanciful notions from now on, I made my way home.

Scurrying through a sudden downpour, I hurried indoors and found Ben sprawled on the sofa watching television, several empty cans of beer on the table beside him.

'You look comfortable,' I said.

'More comfortable now,' he replied, pulling me down next to him. 'Give us a kiss.'

From far away, I heard a dog barking.

'Where's Poppy?' I asked, withdrawing from Ben's embrace.

'That bloody animal has not stopped whimpering since you left,' he replied with a flash of irritation. 'I had to put her outside just to get some peace. Come on, give us a kiss. And then you can get us another can of beer.'

'Not until I've seen to Poppy.' A thought struck me. 'You haven't left her out in the rain?'

He shrugged. 'Is it raining? Well, she's a dog, isn't she? Dogs don't mind a bit of rain. Getting a bit wet is natural for them, isn't it?'

With a sigh, I went to find Poppy who leapt for joy on seeing me and nearly strangled herself with her lead which had somehow become tangled around her feet.

'You poor little thing,' I crooned. 'Did Ben leave you all on your own out here to get wet?'

Poppy shook herself and raced inside ahead of me. I put down a towel for her to roll around on and helped her to dry herself. She was shivering so I held her close to my chest and she settled there. Meanwhile, from the living room, I heard Ben calling for another can of beer.

'Really,' I muttered to Poppy, 'he is a lazy old sod, isn't he? But we love him, don't we? Anyway, you're going to have to get used to him.'

Poppy let out a low growl, and then closed her eyes. Not for the first time, I wondered what she would say about my great aunt's death if she could talk. She seemed to be making her feelings about Ben quite clear and, for once,

I couldn't blame her. Clearly it was going to take longer than I had anticipated for the two of them to become friends. I wondered if I was being naive in thinking that would ever happen, but firmly dismissed that negative thought. In time, Ben would learn to love Poppy. I just had to be patient with him.

29

THE FOLLOWING AFTERNOON THE weather brightened up. Ben made no objection to being left alone again for the afternoon, so I took the opportunity to go into Swindon to do some shopping. This time, I took Poppy with me. I spent a long time choosing a shirt for Ben, as well as new underwear for me. Arriving home with my shopping bags, I saw a car parked outside Rosecroft. Either a neighbour was being cheeky, or Ben had decided to surprise me. Entering the house, I heard voices, and found Ben chatting with a stranger. Dressed in a suit, with neatly trimmed hair, the visitor looked exactly like a car salesman and I grinned in anticipation. But instead of proudly announcing that he had bought a car, Ben hurriedly showed the man out without introducing him.

'Who was that?' I asked, peeved at being ignored. 'You could have introduced me. I do live here.'

'It was no one,' Ben replied. 'Just an old friend of mine.' He paused. 'He was admiring our home. It is a lovely old house, and have you considered there's scope to extend at the back? With only one neighbour, no one's likely to object. It really is a fantastic property, with oodles of potential.'

I smiled, pleased at the praise and thrilled that Ben seemed to have long-term plans for Rosecroft. Clearly he had come round to thinking we had a future together in Ashton Mead. I was not too keen on the idea of extending the house, but in any case there was no question we could ever afford it, at least not in the foreseeable future. Ben had shown no interest in offering to share living expenses, and I had said nothing to him about my arrangements. I had yet to reveal to him that not only did the house belong to me, but it was mortgage-free.

Hannah had suggested he might already know I owned Rosecroft, but that was idle and malicious speculation. She was probably jealous of my good fortune. Secretly I had resolved to wait until Ben asked me to marry him before sharing the news. He had already dropped a few hints about our future together, and I expected him to propose any day. His plans for the house felt like a very positive sign and I could not stop smiling as I showed him the shirt I had bought him.

'Nice,' he said, glancing at the shirt and tossing it on to a chair. 'Yes,' he went on thoughtfully. 'I must say Rosecroft is a decent little house. It must be worth a bit,' he added speculatively.

'I dare say,' I agreed, 'but it's not for sale.'

'I was just saying,' he replied airily. 'Must be worth a bit, even if it is out here in the middle of nowhere.'

'Ashton Mead is hardly the middle of nowhere,' I protested.

'No, of course not,' he conceded agreeably.

It struck me that Ben had changed a lot. He was far more amenable than when we had been together before.

In those days, he used to lay down the law all the time and dig his heels in whenever I tried to challenge him. But I had changed too. When we first met I was barely twenty and not very sure of myself. Now, four years on, I was older and more secure in my life. He was probably responding to my newfound confidence. He didn't yet know it, but I was a home owner now, and he was living in his girlfriend's house. The balance of power between us had shifted subtly and I was pleased to think that we had the basis for a successful long-term relationship.

After supper that evening, Ben finally brought up the subject of our future together.

'We need to decide where to live,' he added.

'Here,' I replied without thinking. 'We live here.'

'Yes,' he said, 'but we have to make big decisions like that together. I'm looking for another job, and that'll be in London. You can't expect me to live out here in the sticks indefinitely.'

As sternly as I could, I pointed out that trains ran regularly from Swindon to London. The journey only took an hour.

Ben stared at me. 'Are you joking? Why on earth would you want to carry on living here?'

'Well, I do, and that's that.'

'Come here,' he said. 'I'll change your mind for you.'

Ben knew exactly how to get round me, but as he kissed me, Hannah's words rang in my head. 'Is it his character you're in love with or his looks? Fancying him doesn't mean you're in love with him. There's more to a successful relationship than sex.'

The next day I arrived home from taking Poppy for a walk to find Ben deep in discussion with another stranger. This time the visitor introduced himself before Ben could escort him to the door, and I was taken aback to discover that Ben had invited an estate agent to view Rosecroft.

'I was just curious,' Ben explained to me after the stranger had gone. 'I mean, you seem really set on staying in Ashton Mead and I wondered if we could ever afford a place of our own here.'

'It's bound to be a lot cheaper than London,' I pointed out sharply.

'You're not going to believe what this place is worth,' Ben said. 'Not that the value of Rosecroft is of any particular interest to us, but you're not going to believe it.'

He was curiously excited and I almost told him that I owned the property, but something held me back.

'I don't want to move,' I said.

Ben leaned down and kissed me on the lips. 'We won't do anything you don't want to do.'

That evening we strolled down to The Plough for a pint before supper and saw Hannah and Toby in the garden. Poppy was pleased to see them and tugged at her lead, eager to run over and say hello. Toby bought a round and so we sat with them for a pint.

'We're thinking of moving,' Ben announced, quite unprompted.

Hannah scowled and Toby looked gutted. I was annoyed with Ben for speaking on my behalf like that, especially after I had made it clear I had no intention of moving away from Ashton Mead, but I kept quiet, embarrassed to contradict Ben in public. Hannah watched me closely and I smiled brightly at her.

'Yes, we're thinking of moving back to London, aren't

we, babes?' Ben went on, putting his arm round me. 'Fresh start and all that. We'll find a little flat like we had before, but this time it'll be a place of our own. Just something small to start with. We don't need anything fancy, do we? Just a bedroom.' He laughed and Toby looked away as Ben leaned over and kissed me on the lips.

'You'll need a garden,' Hannah pointed out, glancing at Poppy who was sleeping at her feet.

'No way,' Ben replied. 'Far too much work,' he added, by way of explanation.

'But you'll need somewhere for Poppy to run around,' Hannah said, 'especially if you're both working.'

'We'll sell the dog,' Ben replied airily. 'We can probably get something for her, and that'll pay for a few things while we get ourselves set up.'

'Sell Poppy?' I blurted out, too shocked to remain silent. 'I'm not selling Poppy!'

This no longer had anything to do with worrying about moving from Rosecroft. Poppy was my dog and I loved her.

'Whatever you say, gorgeous,' Ben replied. 'We can give the dog away if you like, although that seems a waste. It must be worth something, don't you think? Now, let's get going. The dinner should be ready by now.'

It was a shock to discover that Ben had been quietly making plans of his own, without consulting me. But I was ready for him, and as we walked home I worked out exactly what to say to him, should the subject of our moving crop up again. Once dinner was on the table, and Ben was eating, I couldn't restrain myself any longer, and explained very clearly that we were not moving from

Rosecroft, and Poppy was my dog. Nothing was going to change any of that.

'Listen, gorgeous, I've got it all planned,' Ben replied, as though he hadn't heard a word I said. 'We'll find ourselves a place in London and your friend can take care of the dog until someone buys her. You can find a job and I'll get going setting up a business of my own. It's going to be perfect. Just wait till you hear my plans. This time things are really going to work out for us.'

'No,' I burst out so loudly that Poppy barked in surprise. 'You need to listen to me, Ben. There's no way I'm getting rid of Poppy.'

'Well, it looks like you've got no choice. It's me or the animal. So come on, don't cut up rough. It's not that important. What matters is that we're back together again and I love you. We're going to have a ball once we're back in London. I don't know about you, but I can't wait. You know I'm only thinking of you,' he went on in a wheedling tone. 'You're not really happy here. You might kid yourself it's a rural idyll, but how long is that fantasy going to last? It's a boring place, the people are boring, and you're bored. We need more excitement in our lives, you and me. We're not backwater people. Are there any more of your spuds? I'm starving.'

Poppy growled as Ben leaned back and held out his arms with the cheeky grin that always won me over. But this time I shook my head.

'Come on, babes, it's just a dog.'

Gazing into Ben's eyes, I knew what my decision had to be. But when he reached out and pulled me onto his lap, it was like being drawn by an irresistible magnet. As I fell into his embrace, Hannah's words rang inside my head. 'Is it really his character you're in love with, or his looks?' I scarcely noticed when Poppy whimpered and nuzzled my leg gently.

30

THAT WEEK, MY MOTHER phoned to arrange to pay me a visit at the weekend. Looking forward to seeing her again, I wondered how she would react when she found out that Ben had come back to me, and hoped she would be pleased.

'Ben's come back and is living here with me,' I warned her. 'I just thought you'd like to know.'

To my surprise, she told me she knew he had returned. It was not clear how she had found out, but I was pleased she sounded happy about it. When Ben and I had lived together, my mother had been really friendly towards him. I had always suspected it was only her eagerness to see me settled in a relationship that had prompted her to treat him with such warmth, yet when Ben and I split up, she had appeared to be genuinely dismayed. Now that Ben and I were together again, she seemed nearly as pleased as me.

Ben and I walked down to the bus stop, hand in hand, in time to meet the bus. After stooping to pat Poppy on the head, my mother held out her bag to Ben who took it from her with a smile.

'What a gentleman,' she crowed.

'It's my pleasure,' he assured her.

My mother's hair looked even more perfectly coiffured than on her previous visit, with light blonde highlights that worked well with her few streaks of natural white. Her make-up was a touch heavy for my taste, but she looked well and was clearly excited to be visiting us. She made a huge fuss of Ben, and as soon as he was out of earshot she whispered to me, wanting to know how we were getting on together.

'We're fine, mother,' I assured her. 'We're living together.'

'Oh yes, yes, I know, I know,' she said, beaming. 'I mean – ' she lowered her voice. 'Has there been any talk? You know what I mean.'

'No, I don't. What are you talking about?'

'Has Ben proposed to you yet?'

She was obviously disappointed that Ben and I had no plans to marry. When I assured her we were perfectly happy as we were, she heaved a sigh and shook her head, as though I had said something really stupid.

'Yes, yes, you're happy,' she said quickly, before I could remonstrate. 'I can see that you're happy. But how long is that going to last?'

That evening, Ben insisted on cooking and made a sensational beef casserole. It was the first time he had cooked for me in Rosecroft and he managed the kitchen well.

'This man's a keeper,' my mother told me, winking at him. 'He even cooks for you.'

We all drank slightly too much and enjoyed a lovely dinner round the kitchen table. After I had cleared up, my mother and I took Poppy for a walk, leaving Ben watching football on the television. It was a chilly evening and we walked briskly, gazing up at the stars and trying to identify them, without much success. I was feeling relaxed and mellow, when my mother brought up her favourite topic of conversation: my life and what she thought I ought to do with it.

'I'm really very pleased you're not living on your own any more, Emily, but tell me where is this all heading?'

Not wanting to argue, I said nothing.

'He walked out on you before, didn't he?' she persisted. 'So, what kind of security is he offering you now? Having left you once, surely it's fair enough for you to demand a token of his intentions, some guarantee that he means to stay with you this time. I'm only asking because I care about you and I want to see you settled.'

'I am settled,' I assured her. 'Although –'

'Although…?' she prompted me.

I told her of Ben's plans to leave Ashton Mead and return to London, and she nodded knowingly.

'Yes, that makes good sense, and you wouldn't be so far away.'

'I'd be nearer to you, is what you mean.'

'Exactly. And there's nothing wrong with that. Families are important, Emily, especially as you get older. In any case, you must admit that Ben's plans all seem very sensible. I'm very glad he's thinking in the long term, and you should be too. What he has in mind means you could afford to get yourselves on the property ladder in London, and once you're married, if you decide you want a family, I'm sure he'll be able to provide for you. He used to have a well-paid job, didn't he? What kind of job prospects do either of you have here in the village? He can earn good money in London, and with the money you make from this place you'll be well on your way. I think his plan to sell Rosecroft and move back to London is an excellent one, really sensible.'

Her words puzzled me. 'Ben isn't planning to sell Rosecroft,' I corrected her. 'It's Poppy he's talking about selling, not Rosecroft. He doesn't even know I own a house.'

'Of course he does. He knows all about you inheriting Rosecroft.'

'How would he know? I've never told him.' I didn't add that I had been careful to keep that knowledge from him.

'He knows because I told him, you silly thing.'

'What? When?'

She chuckled. 'I thought it might entice him back and it worked, didn't it? He came running as soon as he knew you had inherited a house. He told me he never should have left you, and he was right about that. You've wasted enough time being miserable on your own.'

She continued talking but I was no longer listening. Suddenly everything that had happened since Ben had joined me in Ashton Mead seemed false. I felt as though I was seeing him clearly for the first time. Good-looking, sexy and seductive, he was an opportunist who had won me over again and again with his undoubted charm, and I had been stupid enough to fall for him again and again.

'Hang on, mum, are you saying you told Ben that I had inherited a house before he ever came to find me in Ashton Mead?' I asked her, appalled by what she had told me.

'Yes,' she replied cheerfully. 'You were so much happier when you were with him, and I could see you were too proud to chase after him. So I stepped in and did what I could to induce him to return. It seemed the best way to help you, seeing as you were too stubborn to win him back by yourself.' She drew in a deep breath and beamed at me. 'I can't tell you how pleased I am that it's all worked out for you! It's just wonderful. Susie was furious with me for what she calls interfering, but I know it was the right thing to do. He makes you happy. And after all, Emily, what was the alternative for you? I knew you would never be content to live all alone like my poor Aunt Lorna. It's not natural for a woman to live on her own like that. When it became clear to me that you weren't going to do anything about it, I had to step in to help you get back together with him.'

'Oh mother,' I said softly. 'I know you acted for the best, but please, please, promise me you will never ever try to sort out my problems for me again.'

She laughed. 'Well, I won't need to take care of you any more, will I? It's up to Ben to look after you from now on.'

That evening, my mother and Ben stayed at home while I took Poppy for a walk. Angry with my sister for not telling me about my mother's machinations, I called her to vent my irritation. She told me she had been reluctant to stir things up between me and my mother.

'What you do about Ben is up to you,' she concluded. 'It's none of my business.'

'It's not mum's business either,' I snapped.

Susie gave a kind of grunt. 'You try telling her that. So, what are you going to do about Ben?'

'Like you said, that's none of your business.'

With that, I rang off. I'd had enough of other people meddling in my life. From now on, I was going to make my own decisions, and keep my own counsel.

31

MY MOTHER LEFT US early the following day, promising to return soon. The sun was shining and the foliage on the trees fluttered in a light breeze as we accompanied her into the village and waited with her for the bus, while Poppy darted around my feet, tugging at her lead and sniffing the pavement. A neighbour passed by with a white poodle which stopped to exchange playful growls with Poppy who skipped back and forth in an ecstasy of excitement. On the surface, everything in my life was perfect. At last my mother's bus arrived and we said our goodbyes, after which Ben and I stood for a few moments watching the bus disappear down the road. Although I was annoyed with my mother, I was sorry to see her go, not least because once we were alone again, it would be time for me to confront Ben. I waited until we were back home before telling him what was on my mind. He was flippant at first, making fun of my indignation.

'It's no joking matter. You knew all along that I owned Rosecroft. You lied to me,' I fumed.

'When did I lie to you?' he countered, smiling. 'Do you know how sexy you look when you're angry? Come here and give me a kiss.'

It was true he had never claimed ignorance of my ownership of Rosecroft. It had actually never come up in conversation, because I had been very careful to avoid the subject. As I accused him of deceit, I remembered lying to him about going to see the technologist at the hospital. It seemed we had not been honest with each other. This was a poor basis for a life together, but sex and fun had blinded me to the serious faults in our relationship. Hannah had asked me if I was only staying with Ben because of his good looks. At the time I had found her question insulting. Now I realised that if she asked me again, my answer might be very different.

'Be sensible, Emily,' Ben said, sitting on the sofa and smiling at me in his usual relaxed manner. 'There's nothing for either of us in this godforsaken hole. Why are we even here? There's no reason to stay.' He flicked an invisible crumb from his trouser leg.

'I have friends here,' I replied stiffly, although I was not sure that was true any more.

'These country folk are not your friends.'

'What you mean is, they're not *your* friends. But all of that is beside the point. My friends in Ashton Mead have nothing to do with my decision. How can I live with someone who lies to me repeatedly, and is prepared to consider selling Poppy?'

Lying in the corner, Poppy's ears pricked up at the mention of her name.

Ben gave a derisive snort. 'Don't tell me you're choosing a dog over me? That's the most ridiculous thing I've ever heard. Have you lost your mind?'

'I mean it, Ben. I can't just abandon her. She's my dog and she stays with me whatever else happens.'

'You've only had the animal for a few months. How attached to it can you be? It's just a dog. You're pulling my leg, aren't you? All right, listen, keep it for now, if it means so much to you,' he went on, seeing my glowering expression. 'When all's said and done it's just a dog, so if you want it, you keep it. And if you don't want to leave Ashton Mead, we won't. We can stay here for as long as it takes you to come to your senses.'

'What makes you think I'll change my mind?'

'This place is nowhere. Who's even heard of Ashton Mead? You can't spend the rest of your life stuck in this dreary backwater. You'd die of boredom. It's lucky for you I came back. Emily, we have our future to think of, and it's looking a lot better than we ever dared hope. This house will see us well on our way. You still really have no idea what it's worth, do you? I'm telling you, we could do very nicely out of it.'

He stood up and reached out to me, and the familiar desire to feel his arms around me was overwhelming. Coupled with my reluctance to return to sleeping alone and waking up alone, I felt my resolve weaken. When he drew me into the warmth of his embrace, I yielded to his importunate kisses. My mother had been right all along, and it was pointless to resist; my future lay with Ben.

When Poppy whimpered, I pulled away from Ben's embrace and went to the kitchen, with my little dog trotting eagerly at my heels.

'Where are you going?' Ben asked. 'Come back here.'

I told him Poppy needed feeding.

'The dog can wait,' he replied. Coming up behind me, he put his arms around me and kissed my neck.

'No, stop that,' I said. 'She can't wait, it's already past her breakfast time. It's not fair to make her wait any longer when she's hungry. She's only a puppy. Don't you want me to look after her?'

'What about looking after me? I'm feeling horny,' he grinned. 'The dog can wait.'

I needed to be firm in my resolve.

'No, Ben. She can't wait.'

'But what about me?' he repeated plaintively. 'You don't mind leaving me waiting?'

'Not everything is about you and what you want,' I snapped, losing patience with him. 'You know, this isn't going to work out between us, is it? I think it's time you left.'

'Where do you want me to go?' he asked, giving me a quizzical smile.

'I don't care,' I snapped. 'I just want you out of my house.'

'You're throwing me out?' he asked with an incredulous laugh.

'I'm asking you, very politely, to leave my house.'

'Our house.'

'No, Ben, Rosecroft is *my* house.' I glared at him.

For an answer, he threw himself on the sofa and folded his arms. 'I'm not leaving you again. Look, babes,' he went on, in a wheedling tone, 'what's mine is yours and what's yours is mine. We belong together, you and me. We can't fall out over a bloody dog.'

Poppy ran over to him and growled. Snapping at his ankles, she pulled at the bottom of his trouser leg, as though she was doing her best to force him to follow my instructions and leave. She probably only wanted him to stand up and play, but Ben was irritated by her badgering.

215

'Why does that wretched animal keep attacking me?' he demanded. 'Do you seriously want to throw me out, but keep the dog?' He was on his feet now, red-faced and angry. 'She ought to be put down. She's a menace.'

'Poppy isn't an aggressive dog,' I replied, shocked by his vitriol towards her. 'She's friendly and gentle, and if you made any attempt to get to know her, you'd see how good-natured she is.'

'You know I was going to marry you? We still could. It's not too late to change your mind. I'm offering you what you've always wanted, happy ever after and all that. But you'll have to get rid of that dog first. I mean it, Emily. The dog goes.'

As he spoke, he nudged Poppy with his toe. It was difficult to see whether or not he actually kicked her, but she yelped and sprang back.

'Well?' he demanded. 'Which is it to be? Me or that animal?'

He smiled, confident I wouldn't risk losing him again. Poppy lay quietly on the carpet and looked up at me with a pleading expression in her black eyes, as though she knew Ben was asking me to give her away.

'What makes you think I would ever agree to be your wife?' I replied, strangely calm in my fury.

'Don't be hasty,' he said. The edge had gone from his voice and he had reverted to cajoling me. 'You were right all along. We belong together. Come on, Emily, don't be daft.' He shook his leg, trying to dislodge Poppy who had darted forward and was clinging on to his trousers again. 'Get this wretched animal off me before she tears my jeans!'

'You didn't think we were meant to be together when you walked out on me in London,' I reminded him quietly.

'You didn't think we were meant to be together until you heard about my inheritance. Well, this is my house, Poppy is my dog, and you don't belong here with us.'

If my words were rash, there would be time for regrets later. Right now, it was enough to feel a surge of exhilaration. An invisible trap that had held me for years had suddenly sprung open, and I was free.

'That's it,' he snapped. 'If you're too stupid to know what's good for you, then you can just make do by yourself for the rest of your life, because no one else is ever going to care for you as much as I do. This is it, Emily. If you don't come to your senses right now, then I'm off and this time you won't be able to come crawling back when you realise how much you miss me.'

His words were as effective as pellets bouncing off a bullet proof vest. It was hard to believe I had been taken in by Ben's shallow narcissism for so long, falling for his charm again and again. Certainly he was good-looking and a smooth talker. He dressed well and superficially he was a perfect partner, but that was all he was. Superficial.

'Go and pack your case,' I said, in a voice of command I had practised in my many attempts to train Poppy. 'And give me back your key to my house.'

I held out my hand.

'You're not serious,' Ben stammered, but he could see that I was.

With a snort of anger, he tossed me his key to Rosecroft and stomped upstairs to pack his things. I sat down in the living room, shaking with rage, and too angry to feel wretched. But as soon as the front door slammed behind Ben, I burst into tears. Poppy climbed up on my lap and licked my face.

'This is all your fault,' I told her, even though that wasn't true.

It was Ben's fault for being an unscrupulous narcissist, and mine for being gullible enough to fall for a conman. Because that was what he was. I could see that now. In a way my mother had done me a favour because I was finally going to get over Ben and, once the pain subsided, I would be ready to get on with my life, no longer pining for the ideal man who had existed only in my imagination.

'Come on, let's go for a walk,' I said, and Poppy jumped up and bounded over to the door. 'Mum's not going to be pleased,' I added. 'You know, she'll never believe me when I tell her I threw him out. She'll always be convinced it was the other way round. If only you could talk. You'd put her straight, wouldn't you?'

If Poppy could talk, I wondered what other hidden truths she might tell me.

32

'How about a few cans of beer for that nice young man of yours?' Maud asked when I went to the local shop a few days after Ben's departure. 'I haven't seen him in here for a while. Is he all right?'

'Oh, he left a week ago. He was only in Ashton Mead for a visit,' I replied airily. I hoped she wouldn't see my smile was forced.

That evening there was a knock on my door. For an instant I thought it was Ben, returned to apologise for his callous behaviour towards me and Poppy. Instead, I found Hannah standing on the doorstep. As soon as I saw her, I burst into tears. She came in and put her arms around me, rocking me gently, murmuring that everything would be fine.

'I'm sorry,' I sobbed, 'you were right and I was wrong. I've been an idiot. I should have listened to you all along.'

'Don't be silly.'

She led me to the living room and we sat on the sofa. Poppy jumped up, snuggled down on my lap, and promptly fell asleep.

'You saw through him from the start,' I mumbled through my tears. 'You were right. I was taken in by him. I've been a complete idiot. He's a parasite.'

'You must have really cared for him.' She hesitated before adding, 'And he must have cared for you too. You must have had a good relationship once, and it's hard to let go, isn't it? I should have left my ex ages before I finally managed to walk out. It's not easy to end a relationship, and you were living with Ben for a while.'

'Everything was different when we first met. We were young back then, and all we wanted was to have fun. We didn't really spend much time together just the two of us, we were always working or out with mates. We hardly really knew each other. It was never a basis for a long-term relationship. I see that now.'

'You lived together for six months, which is longer than a lot of marriages last. It can't have been all bad. Don't beat yourself up over it. Sometimes things just don't work out and it's no one's fault.'

'Yes, it suited us both for a while, but not any more. It's over, he's gone, and I'm glad.' I started crying again. 'I shouldn't have let him get round me again. I should have known better.'

'Come on, that's enough self-pity for one day. You're going to upset Poppy if you carry on like this.'

I glanced down at Poppy who was fast asleep and snuffling softly.

'Sort your face out, and we'll go for a drink,' Hannah said briskly.

'I can't believe you're even talking to me after the way I behaved towards you,' I wailed. 'I said some really horrible things.'

'We're friends, aren't we? No, don't start blubbing again. Listen, we can sit here all evening while you wallow in self-pity about the end of your affair with golden boy, or we can go out and get tipsy and have a bit of a laugh. But not if you're going to get all maudlin on me. Well? What do you say?'

I washed my face, put on some make-up in an attempt to conceal my puffy eyes, and we set off. Poppy scampered happily around us as we walked. She had never been so eager to go for a walk with Ben, and I was pleased to see her looking happy again. I had almost forgotten what an energetic little dog she was.

'She's back to her old self,' I told Hannah. 'You know, if it wasn't for Poppy I'd probably still be with Ben.' I explained how Ben's attitude towards Poppy had been the final straw for me.

Hannah looked concerned. 'Don't hold it against her,' she said. 'It's not Poppy's fault.'

'Oh I'm not upset with her,' I assured Hannah. 'Quite the opposite, in fact. I'm grateful to her. She saved me from making a big mistake.'

Our conversation turned to the tea shop, and I agreed to think about returning to work there. I could hardly believe Hannah was being so kind to me and told her so with tears in my eyes.

'Oh for goodness' sake, don't start crying again,' she said. 'We're supposed to be going out to cheer you up! And if you think I'm asking you to come back to work because I feel sorry for you, you couldn't be more wrong. Why wouldn't I want a hard-working waitress who works for peanuts, and is one of the best friends I've got?'

'Does that mean you're offering me a pay rise?' I asked and she laughed.

'Don't push your luck!'

When Toby joined us at the pub, I felt slightly uncomfortable, remembering what Alice and Hannah had told me about him. I had no intention of becoming involved with another problem boyfriend, but he was kind to me, and I decided to remain silent about Alice's warning, at least for the time being. Still feeling emotional about my break-up with Ben, I didn't think I could cope with anything more upsetting than a friendly chat.

'If he was prepared to leave you at the drop of a hat as soon as he didn't get his own way, then you're better off without him,' Toby said. 'Not that it's any of my business, of course.'

'He tried to force her to sell Poppy,' Hannah told him.

I had never seen her looking so angry before. As for Toby, he leaned down and petted Poppy, without further comment. I had noticed he tended to clam up when he was upset about anything, and wondered what he was thinking and whether he would ever flare up in front of me. But Hannah was clearly pleased, and keen to share her feelings with us.

'Aren't you relieved to see the back of that poser?' she prompted Toby, when we had all downed a pint.

He shrugged. 'It doesn't make me happy to see Emily unhappy,' he replied.

'Oh, she'll get over it,' Hannah said breezily. 'She did before. The guy's a tosser.'

'I thought I was in love with him,' I interjected and stopped because my voice was wobbling.

I wondered whether it had been a sensible idea to drink in company in my current emotional state.

'Well, you might have thought so once, but it's time to move on,' Hannah said firmly.

She glared at Toby, who was absorbed in tickling Poppy under her chin while she gazed up at him adoringly.

When Hannah went inside to get the next round, Toby looked up.

'Not all men are like Ben,' he said quietly.

'I will never trust another man,' I replied fiercely. 'I never want to have another relationship with a man as long as I live.'

Much as I liked Toby, what Alice had told me about him rang in my head like a warning bell. It was a pity because I really did like him. He seemed like a genuinely thoughtful and sensitive person, but the gentlest of people could have uncontrollable tempers and I wasn't about to enter into another doomed relationship. Forewarned was forearmed, I told myself. If only I had seen through Ben earlier, I could have saved myself a lot of misery. My experience with Ben was enough to convince me that I was a poor judge of character. Just because I thought Toby seemed kind was no guarantee of his true nature.

I was determined to be far more circumspect in my romantic dalliances in future and if that meant I would end up alone, that was not such a terrible fate. My great aunt had lived happily enough at Rosecroft with a series of dogs, and I would do the same. Like Hannah, I didn't need a man to make me happy. Hannah returned, and glanced at Toby and me before setting the drinks down on the table. She seemed slightly subdued after that, and Toby was characteristically quiet. Only Poppy seemed content as she dozed under the table.

33

MY MOTHER WAS PREDICTABLY cross with me when she heard that Ben had left Ashton Mead.

'You find an eligible man like Ben, and you let him slip through your fingers. You have to go after him,' was her initial response. 'There's no point in being proud. You've already spent years chasing after him. You don't want to waste all that effort. He came back once before which shows he doesn't really want to leave you. At the very least, it means he's in two minds about you. Perhaps he was intimidated by you owning a house? You could offer to put it in both your names, or maybe hint that if you were married you could own it jointly.'

When I explained that I was the one who had ended the relationship, she seemed flummoxed.

'Well, I don't know what you want. Admittedly she is a sweet little dog, and I'm no dog lover, but you can't possibly reject a man like Ben because he doesn't like dogs as much as you do. Perhaps if you got a different dog together, so it could be more his dog? Think about it, he was thrown into a situation where he was living in your house, with your dog. Don't you think he might have felt emasculated? He is the man, after all. Shouldn't you be living on his terms, at least a little? There has to be some compromise in a relationship if you want to make it work. Maybe he'd prefer a bigger dog, or a cat.'

There was a lot more along similar lines, all said with the best of intentions, because she genuinely wanted me to be happy. Knowing that, I couldn't be too angry with her, even though she totally misunderstood me and my circumstances, and was as taken in by Ben as I had been. Above all, she seemed to have a horror of my remaining single, as though marriage was the sole prerequisite for a happy life.

'Maybe I don't want to get married,' I ventured, but she dismissed that idea.

'Don't be silly, Emily,' she snapped. 'Remember how happy you were with Ben. Love is the most wonderful thing. It's what makes life worthwhile.'

'I love Poppy,' I said. 'And I know she loves me.'

'That's not the same thing at all, and you know it,' she replied impatiently.

'If you had a dog, you'd understand.'

'Really, Emily, why do you persist in being so obtuse? Sometimes I wonder what I'm going to do with you, really I do.'

There was no point in mentioning that I was an adult, responsible for my own life, which meant that she had no need to do anything at all with me. I let her talk for a while before telling her I had to go.

'To do what?' she demanded.

'I have to take Poppy for a walk,' I fibbed.

'It's always that dog with you,' she grumbled. 'If it wasn't for that animal attacking him, Ben would never have left you.'

'She never attacked him,' I protested, wondering if Ben had been talking to my mother behind my back.

It would be typical of Ben to try and persuade her to talk me into taking him back. I could see that now. But what Ben chose to do from now on was nothing to do with me, and I didn't even ask my mother if he had been in contact with her. I had to stop thinking about him. With her misguided concern for my happiness, my mother was unhelpful, talking about Ben every time I called her, and nagging me to contact him. She did her best to convince me he would be pleased to hear from me. Perhaps she was right, but I had no intention of testing her theory.

'That ship has sailed,' I told her firmly. 'It's over, and there's no going back. Not this time.'

'Emily, I don't know what you're talking about,' she replied. 'But you need to think carefully about what you're doing. How are you ever going to meet anyone else, living and working in that tiny village? It's very picturesque, I grant you, but there's no one there. You could at least look for a job in Swindon.'

'Working with Hannah suits me, and it's ideal with Poppy.'

'Oh, Poppy, Poppy, you're obsessed with that dog. I'm beginning to see why Ben left you.'

'He didn't leave me. I told you, I ended it. Mum, listen to me. He was never going to make me happy.'

Neither of us wanted to fall out over our differing opinions about Ben, so the conversation moved on to my father and his bunions. I wondered if I could ever have cared so much about Ben's bunions, if he had them.

'You really do love dad, don't you?' I asked her, feeling a little wistful.

226

'Of course.' She sounded surprised. 'Love grows, you know. If you had stayed with Ben, you could have found that out for yourself. Loyalty is a very underrated value.' She sniffed, which was her sign of disapproval.

'Mum,' I sighed. 'Enough about Ben, please. We're never getting back together. It's really over this time. You have to believe me. I just don't love him any more.'

'You don't fall out of love with someone,' she replied. 'Either you love them or you don't.'

'Well, then, we have to agree that I never loved him,' I said.

The conversation ended on cool terms. I resolved to wait a couple of weeks before calling her again, to give her time to recover from her renewed disappointment.

Hannah helped by inviting me to return to work in the café, where she claimed to be run off her feet and struggling to cope without me. We both knew that was not really true. At the height of the summer the tea shop was busy, but Hannah was easily able to cope with her mother helping out on a casual basis. Once I returned, we took to sitting in the café chatting at the end of the working day, while Poppy dozed in a basket in the corner. In those quiet hours, Hannah told me more about her ex-husband. He had many good qualities, generosity with his considerable wealth being one of them. We were both beneficiaries of other people's money, and conscious of our good fortune.

'Maybe our luck has been used up with everything we've been given,' I suggested, 'and we're not destined to be lucky in love as well. We can't expect to have it all.'

'My ex didn't need to give me as much as he did,' she agreed. 'We were only married for two years, and weren't together for one of those, but we parted amicably and he said he wanted to see me settled. He was really fond of me, I think, but he wasn't monogamous. Of course I had no idea what a player he was when we met, but within a year of our marriage he was having an affair. He still wanted me to be his wife, but he was in a relationship with someone else. I took him back once, but when it happened again, and again, that was it. There were probably other flings that I didn't know about. In the end, I'd had enough and he was very decent about it. He said he could understand why I might be upset.' She smiled a little sadly. 'Still, I got this place out of it, and I can't honestly say I'd go back if I could. It's easy to buy into the fantasy, but sooner or later you have to accept what's real. He's married to someone else now, and I dare say he's still having affairs. Maybe his new wife won't mind.' She shrugged. 'It's a funny old world, isn't it? But it's not that bad. I mean, look at us. Shelter from the storm, good company, and an endless supply of cake and hot chocolate. It could be worse.' She laughed.

I glanced at Poppy, sleeping contentedly in her basket, and agreed with my friend. Life could have treated us both a lot worse.

34

WE DIDN'T SEE TOBY in the village for a few weeks, but late one afternoon he came into the tea shop looking uncharacteristically nervous.

'Can I get you anything?' I asked.

'I'd like a couple of fresh scones and a pot of tea for two,' he replied, smiling weakly.

'Do you want to wait until your guest arrives?'

He shook his head. 'No, it's just me.'

'I just thought, when you ordered tea for two...'

'I was hoping you would join me.' He smiled awkwardly. 'At least for a few minutes. I thought you might appreciate the break and it's not busy here.'

Reminding myself that behind his civil façade he had behaved badly on at least one occasion that I knew about, I looked away. Hannah was in the kitchen and although we had other customers, no one else was waiting to be served.

'I'll fetch your order,' I said abruptly and hurried off to the kitchen.

'Another customer,' Hannah beamed. 'Trade is picking up.'

'It's just Toby,' I replied, plonking his tea on a tray. 'And one order is hardly going to make a difference,' I added sourly.

She hurried out of the kitchen to speak to him, and I trudged after her with his tea.

'Sorry I've not been around for a while,' he was saying as I emerged from the kitchen.

'Is everything okay?' Hannah asked him.

'Yes. I was just having car trouble.'

'I don't know why you don't get rid of that old rust heap,' Hannah said. 'If I were you, I'd trade it in and get a newer model. It's not as if you don't have a regular salary.'

Never having owned a car, I said nothing but put the tray down. Toby owned an old blue Ford which rattled and jolted along the country lanes. Ben had sneered at it, but Toby had dismissed my then boyfriend's contempt with a tolerant smile.

Now Toby shrugged off Hannah's suggestion with the same easygoing smile. 'Yes, you're probably right. It's an old boneshaker, it's true, but it gets me about.'

'Clearly,' Hannah replied.

Toby smiled at her sarcasm and she turned back to the kitchen, leaving me to set the table.

'Sit with me,' he repeated his invitation. 'Please, bring another cup. There's more than enough tea here for two, and get yourself a plate to go with it.'

I shook my head, wondering whether to tell him I knew about his abusive behaviour towards Alice's daughter. 'Thank you for the offer, but you can see I'm working.'

'Hannah won't mind. Please, join me just for a moment.'

While I stood hesitating, another customer came in.

'I'm sorry,' I said. 'I have a customer to see to.'

'Please, Emily,' Toby said, reaching out and placing his hand lightly on mine. 'Serve them and then come and sit with me. I've ordered tea for two and I can't possibly manage all this on my own.'

'Hannah's in the kitchen,' I replied, snatching my hand away from the soothing warmth of his touch. 'I'll send her out.'

'I didn't come here to see Hannah,' he said miserably.

Determined to walk away from Toby, I went to speak to the customer who had just come in. While Toby seemed like a decent man, I could not ignore Alice's warning, and I was worried. He had been dropping hints that he was interested in something more than friendship with me, and I was falling for him. Given what I knew about him, this budding relationship could not be allowed to develop any further. While I was taking the other customer's order, Hannah emerged from the kitchen and I saw her muttering to Toby. Both of them glanced in my direction and looked away again quickly; it was obvious they were talking about me. After a few minutes, Hannah passed by and told me to follow her to the kitchen.

'What's wrong with you?' she hissed at me, closing the door.

'Nothing. Why? What do you mean? Why should anything be wrong?'

Hannah put down the tray she was carrying and turned to face me. I had never seen her looking so stressed. She took both of my hands in hers and gazed earnestly at me.

'I'm asking you, Emily, what's wrong?'

Uneasy now, I asked her what she was talking about and she explained that Toby was deeply troubled by my coldness towards him. He had thought we were friends, but now, she said, he complained I hardly spoke to him. I hesitated. The time had finally come for me to share with her what I had learned about Toby. To my surprise, Hannah burst out laughing when I repeated what Alice had told me, without revealing the source of my information or the identity of the girl he had stalked. Hannah dismissed my account as another of my melodramas, while I insisted my information came from a reliable source.

'Either you are a complete fantasist, or your so-called reliable source lied to you,' she replied with an air of finality.

'He stalked this poor girl and terrorised her when she refused to have anything to do with him,' I insisted. 'Someone told me, someone who would have nothing to gain by making up a story like that.'

'Then someone lied to the person who spoke to you,' Hannah said. 'Look, I don't know the "source" that's spreading these malicious lies, but I've known Toby all my life and I can assure you he's the kindest, gentlest person I've ever met.'

'That's not what I've heard.'

'How on earth do you expect anyone to take your nonsense seriously when you won't even say who it is he's supposed to have terrorised?' She giggled. 'That's the silliest thing I've ever heard.'

'Well, all right then, he stalked Sophie Thomas when she rejected him,' I blurted out, determined to persuade her of her mistake. 'And that's the truth.'

'No, no, you've got that the wrong way round,' Hannah said. 'Sophie was mad about him. She wouldn't leave him alone. You don't have to believe me, if you don't want to. Ask anyone who was at school with us. They'll all tell you she was crazy about him and he wasn't interested in her. I don't blame him. She was really full on, you know how girls can be at that age.'

'What age? What do you mean?'

'Oh, it all came to a head around the time Toby and I were leaving school, but I think she was after him for ages before that. I mean it was never going to come to anything. Everyone knew that right from the start, everyone but Sophie, that is. They never went out together or anything. It was all in her head, you know. A schoolgirl crush. She's four years younger than him.'

I was confused. There was no reason for me to doubt Hannah's word, but equally I couldn't understand why Alice would want to lie about Toby. It was time to ask him to his face exactly what had happened between him and Sophie. I went back to the front of the café but he had gone. After work I collected Poppy and went to see him. It was a lovely walk through the village. Trees displayed their autumn foliage like victorious pennants flying from the masts of a conquering armada. There was a light carpeting of russet and gold on the ground, while leaves that had not yet fallen fluttered in the breeze, some as yellow as the awning outside the Sunshine Tea Shoppe.

I hadn't been to Toby's mother's house before. She lived on the outskirts of the village, on the ground floor of a neat detached cottage with a well-tended garden. The woman who opened the door looked far too young to be Toby's mother. As I explained that I was a friend of his, a voice called out, wanting to know who was there. The young woman ushered me in to the front room where a woman in a wheelchair was asking who was at the door. Before I could introduce myself to her, she broke into a smile that lit up her gaunt face and, for an instant, I could see that she had once been quite beautiful. Now, her cheeks were sunken and her limbs looked as though they were awkwardly attached to her thin frame, but she had Toby's soft blue eyes.

'Oh, there's Poppy,' she cried out in obvious delight. 'And you must be Emily. I've been wanting to meet you for such a long time! Do come and sit down.'

'Thank you. It's lovely to meet you too,' I replied politely. 'Actually, I was hoping to talk to Toby.'

'Oh, Toby's gone away,' she told me.

It was lucky I had already sat down, because the room seemed to spin around me.

'What? Where?' I stammered, trying to hide my consternation. 'Where's he gone?'

'Don't worry, he's only gone away for a few days,' she laughed, seemingly gratified by my reaction to her announcement. 'He's gone to Bristol, for a course. He'll be back before you know it. You only just missed him. He popped in to say goodbye about an hour ago.'

'So he'll be back soon?'

'Yes, and in the meantime he's buggered off to Bristol and left me here all alone.' She pulled a sad face and then laughed. 'Now, you will stay for a cup of tea, won't you? Della, put the kettle on before you go, there's a dear. Jenny won't be here for a couple of hours, so I'll be pleased of the company,' she insisted, when I protested that I didn't want to impose on her. 'And Della, can you bring some water for Poppy? And I think Toby has a few dog treats hidden away somewhere. Be good enough to have a look for the bag, will you?'

The young carer nodded and bustled off to the kitchen, while I sat with Naomi.

'Toby's told me so much about you,' she repeated, after she thanked me again for visiting her. 'It's so kind of you to come and see me. I get very few visitors these days. Not that I'm complaining,' she added quickly. 'I'm very lucky, considering, and Toby couldn't do more for me. He's gone off to Bristol, but it's only for a few days, and he knows he's left me in good hands. My carers come in twice a day. It's selfish of me, but I'm going to miss him. I'm used to him popping in to see me every few days. I mean, he can't come to Ashton Mead every day, of course, but I always know he's nearby. Swindon isn't far away, is it? And he likes to come round and just check that everything's all right. As much as it can be,' she added, briefly solemn. 'Still, worse things happen at sea, as my mother used to say. I've been fortunate in many ways, and we're not ones to complain in my family.' She was smiling again.

'I can come and keep you company while Toby's away, if you like,' I offered, without thinking.

'That would be wonderful,' she beamed. 'But I wouldn't want to put you out. He won't be gone for long.'

I assured her it would be no trouble, and she smiled and petted Poppy who licked her hand vigorously.

'She's such a sweet little thing,' Naomi said.

The next day I called in to see Toby's mother again. Nervously, I asked her what had happened between Toby and Sophie.

'Toby and Sophie?' she repeated, looking mystified

'Yes, Sophie Thomas. Alice's daughter.'

'Toby and Sophie Thomas?' Naomi shook her head. 'There's nothing between them, as far as I'm aware. She's gone away travelling, hasn't she? As I understand it, she's been away for quite a while. Poor Alice must miss her terribly.'

'Yes, but before that, before she went away, I mean. Was she ever Toby's girlfriend?'

'Not as far as I know. Between you and me,' she lowered her voice, 'she was very keen on him at one time.' She chuckled at the memory. 'Poor Toby, she pursued him, and he didn't know what to do. He was disconcerted at the thought that he had upset her but, really, she brought it on herself. Still, young girls will be silly, won't they? I know I was at her age. I was madly in love with one of the gardeners at my school, although I would probably have run a mile if he had ever actually spoken to me.'

It was difficult to remain calm and sound uninterested as I listened to her. 'What do you mean, she pursued him?' I wanted to know. 'What happened?'

'Oh, it was all very innocent. They were still at school, just kids, really. It all came to a head when Sophie asked him to invite her to an end of year party. They call it a prom these days, like the Americans, don't they? Toby turned her down. Of course that meant he couldn't go at all, without hurting her feelings, but I don't think he minded missing the party. He told me he didn't really want to go anyway. By all accounts Sophie was very upset. It seems she'd set her heart on going to the prom with him. She'd spent a fortune on a dress, from what I heard, expecting him to invite her. But it was all in her mind. Well, these things matter dreadfully when you're young, don't they? And she was only about fourteen at the time. Can you believe it? I don't suppose there was any bad feeling between them, once she got over it, but I'm not sure he ever saw her again after they left school. She was probably embarrassed at having behaved so stupidly. I don't really know. It was all a long time ago, and he's never mentioned her.'

It seemed that Alice had misinterpreted what had happened between Toby and Sophie. Perhaps Sophie had spun a yarn for her mother, to explain why she wasn't going to the prom with Toby. Several people had given me the impression Sophie was a bit strange. I wished Toby hadn't gone away, but at least he would be back soon. I wanted to talk to him to find out what had really happened between him and Sophie, and I desperately wanted to apologise for having misjudged him. Now that it was clear Alice had been wrong about him, I hoped we could be on good terms again; I missed his friendship.

35

THE WEATHER TURNED COOLER as autumn approached, and we experienced what the weather forecasters called 'a cold snap'. The news was full of reports of icy conditions in the north of Scotland, and we kept the heating turned up in the tea shop, with the street door shut and the kitchen door open. It was too chilly for Poppy to be left tethered outside, and we encouraged her to stay in her basket in the corner of the café. If I hadn't taken her out for walks several times during the day, she would have pestered me or the customers to play with her. As it was, she was generally tired and docile, except when children came into the tea shop. Somehow she seemed to recognise that they too were young, and she tried to enlist them as playmates. Not all of our customers were happy for their children to pet Poppy when they were eating, and I was constantly worried she would eat crumbs of chocolate off the floor which could make her sick. It was a wrench, but in the end I arranged to leave her with Hannah's mother every day, while I was working.

One afternoon, soon after Toby went away to Bristol, I was on my way back from collecting Poppy when I came across Alice returning home with her shopping. She looked quite frail, and was struggling against strong gusts of wind that were blowing the fallen leaves across the pavement. In spite of the accusation she had levelled at Toby, I felt sorry for her. I knew what it was like to be lonely. The tiff between her daughter and Toby had happened many years ago, and no doubt Alice had been very angry with him at the time for upsetting her daughter. Alice had been mistaken, and completely wrong for sharing her misguided opinion with me, but her intention had clearly been to protect me, as she had once wanted to protect Sophie. That was what some mothers did, and I could not hold it against her indefinitely. So as we drew level with each other, I stopped and engaged her in conversation, asking her whether Sophie would be coming home for Christmas, while Poppy hung back, growling.

'Oh no,' she replied. 'Not this year.'

Her breath materialised in little white puffs as she spoke.

'That's a pity,' I said, stamping my feet against the cold while Poppy jumped around, trying to drag me away. 'I expect you'll miss her more than ever over Christmas.'

I hesitated to invite her to spend Christmas with me. It was still three months away, but my parents and sister had agreed to come to Ashton Mead for the day, along with my brother-in-law and my nephew, and Rosecroft was going to be packed, especially as Hannah and her mother had promised to call in for an early evening drink. In any case, I was not sure that Alice would be a congenial guest. She would certainly not be welcomed by Hannah, who insisted she could never forgive Alice for maligning Toby to me. The prospect of Alice offering to read some of her daughter's letters aloud on Christmas day made me shudder. I doubted anyone in my family would be interested in hearing about Sophie's travels, plus the vexed question of Alice's stamps might come up, and that was bound to be uncomfortable. And as if that wasn't enough to make me decide against inviting her to my house on Christmas Day, Poppy didn't like her.

'No, not at all,' Alice was saying, in her curious clipped tones. 'I'm very pleased for her. She's spending Christmas and New Year in Hong Kong with her boyfriend.'

'Her boyfriend? I didn't know Sophie had a boyfriend.'

Alice beamed. 'Oh yes, she met him while she was travelling and now they're inseparable. He sounds absolutely perfect, and she's very happy with him.'

'That sounds wonderful. Where is he from?'

'Why don't you come over later and I'll read you her latest letter? She's told me all about him.' She paused before adding with suppressed excitement that Sophie's boyfriend was a doctor.

A chill wind was agitating the trees above our heads, while dead leaves swirled around our feet. By now Poppy had stopped growling at Alice and was biting the hem of my trousers, in an attempt to pull me away.

'Yes, it's too cold to stand around here talking. I'll come over later and you can tell me Sophie's news then. And don't worry,' I added, 'I won't be asking for any stamps. My nephew's not collecting them any more.'

Lighting the gas hob, I heated up a pan of tomato soup and slipped the matches in my pocket in case I wanted to light the fire in the front room later. Before I had half finished my supper, I was already regretting my offer to visit Alice that evening. It was windy outside, and I wanted to stay indoors in the warm. At least I would have the excuse of needing to get home for Poppy so I wouldn't have to stay out for long. It took ages to put on my outdoor shoes, coat, hat and gloves, before stepping outside, leaving Poppy at home. Even dressed up so warmly I was shivering as I hurried next door.

Alice was pleased to see me and looking at her face made me glad I had made the effort to visit her. If nothing else, it was a good deed. Taking off my coat, hat and gloves, I settled down while Alice read to me. The letters were all very similar. Sophie talked about herself a lot, and said very little about the places she visited, but Alice was obviously thrilled to hear from her. There was no mention of Sophie's boyfriend. When I enquired about him, Alice reproached me for my impatience, saying she was coming to that.

'Dear Mum

I'm going to stay here for a few more months before moving on. I really miss you but it's so interesting here and I've been offered a job teaching English. Basically, as long as you are a native English speaker, they give you a job. It's quite well paid and the people are really nice.

I am very happy here. If it wasn't that I miss you, it would be perfect. I have my own room in a student accommodation block, where we share a kitchen but have our own showers. The other teachers on my corridor are all English or American, and they are interesting and really friendly and the work isn't too hard because they've trained us really well. Everyone says I'm a natural.

I have to go now. I'll write again next week.
Sophie'

'She's obviously having a great time,' I said, struggling not to yawn.

'There are more letters,' Alice said eagerly. 'We haven't got to the part yet where she meets Brett.'

'I'd love to hear about that, but it's getting late and I've left Poppy shut in the house. She'll be needing to go out soon.'

'Won't you at least stay for a glass of something?' she asked, putting the letter back in the box and smiling at me. 'It's so very kind of you to listen to Sophie's letters. It makes me feel as though she's here in the room with me.'

'Oh, I'm enjoying listening to them,' I lied politely.

'Come on then, let's pour that wine, shall we?'

There was something forced about her jollity, as though she was unused to company, and I felt sorry for her. Besides, before I left, I wanted to challenge what she had told me about Toby, so I followed her into the kitchen and waited while she fussed around finding a corkscrew and opening a bottle of wine.

'Just half a glass for me,' I said. 'I really can't stay long. I almost feel as though I know Sophie, from listening to all the letters she's written.'

That was an outright lie, because Sophie had actually shared very little of herself in her letters. No doubt she was doing a lot more than she had admitted to her mother.

'I'm glad she's found a boyfriend,' I added politely.

'Oh yes,' Alice agreed cheerfully. 'Not that it was ever in doubt. She always had boys running after her.'

'Boys like Toby?' I hazarded.

'Toby?'

'I'm not sure if I misunderstood what you said the other day,' I pressed on, now that the subject had come up naturally in conversation.

'Really? What was that?' About to pour the wine, she paused, listening.

'About Toby. You must remember, you told me he became aggressive when Sophie refused to go out with him. You said she had to threaten to call the police before he would leave her alone.'

'Oh yes, that,' she replied vaguely, filling two glasses of wine and handing one to me.

'It's just that Toby seems so nice,' I went on. 'I really want to be sure about what you said. It seems so unlikely.'

'Why are you so suspicious of me?' she demanded, apparently stung by the accusation. 'I don't know what you want. First you keep pestering me to read you Sophie's letters, and now you're calling me a liar. You're always snooping around, coming into my house, interrogating me about Sophie.' Her voice rose to a curious whine, and she seemed strangely agitated.

'I didn't mean to upset you. And now I think it's time I went home,' I said, unnerved by her behaviour. 'You look tired, and I need to get back to Poppy.' I put my wine glass down on the table.

While I was talking, Alice's face had changed fleetingly, becoming pale and pinched, with an expression that was almost savage. I wondered if she had been drinking, or was on some medication that had worn off. Either way, there was clearly something wrong with her.

'I was just trying to be neighbourly,' I added in what I hoped was a friendly tone. 'I certainly didn't mean to be intrusive.'

'No,' she snapped. 'I don't find your behaviour neighbourly at all. You're like your great aunt, always sticking your nose in where it's not wanted.'

'What are you talking about?' I blurted out, momentarily too taken aback by her words to move. 'What did Lorna do?'

She hesitated and seemed to grow calm again, although I had the impression she was struggling to control herself.

'What does any of this have to do with my great aunt?' I asked her again.

Alice sighed. 'I'm sorry. I'm afraid I'm not a sociable person, naturally. That's why I came to live here. I don't really want to have anything to do with other people. It's not a very attractive quality, I know. But you – and before you your great aunt – well, living next door – I'm afraid I must come across as very unpleasant. I'm sorry.'

She seemed genuinely contrite so I reassured her that I wasn't offended. Aware that her mood could change again, I was keen to leave. At the same time, I didn't want to appear rude.

'It can be difficult with neighbours, I know,' I said. 'Complete strangers, thrown together like this. I understand where you're coming from.'

Alice brightened up. 'Before you go, let me show you something I've been working on in my garden. Wait, let me get my torch.'

Having been curious about Alice's garden since my arrival in Ashton Mead, it was difficult to refuse the opportunity to see it for myself. She seemed eager to show it to me, and her eyes glowed with excitement as she took a large metal torch out of a drawer in the kitchen.

'Be careful where you walk,' she warned me as I followed her outside, clutching my winter coat around me. 'You don't want to trip over.'

36

AFTER MONTHS OF SPECULATION about what might be concealed in Alice's garden, at last I was on the other side of her metal fence. At first there was nothing to see but an overgrown tangle of bushes. The moon was out, and with the help of Alice's torch we picked our way among stout weeds and tall brambles, along a pathway flattened by being walked on many times. Carefully we walked towards the tall tree in the far corner. Barely able to control my curiosity, I followed her to the corner of the garden. Under the shelter of the magnificent tree, she bent down and pulled at several rusty bolts which appeared to have been cemented into the ground. Having slid the bolts across, she grabbed hold of a thick metal ring which was attached to what looked like a paving stone. Grunting, she raised the stone slab. Peering under her arm, I saw a large black hole.

'There was a historic building on this site once, centuries ago, but now only this old bomb shelter remains. Come on, you'll find it fascinating,' she went on as I hung back. 'It was originally a crypt of some kind. I discovered it by chance in an ancient document when I was researching the country, looking for a house to buy.' She grinned, her face a shadowy mask lit from below by her torch as she urged me to step forward. 'Go on, take a look inside. I'll hold up my torch so you can see. You'll be surprised how interesting it is.'

Intrigued, I stepped forward, and felt a hand shove me in the back.

'There you go!' she cried out exultantly as I toppled into the darkness below. 'I said you'd be surprised!'

I tried in vain to clutch at something, and succeeded only in scraping my palms on the abrasive surface of the wall. That was painful, but it probably slowed my descent slightly. In the terror of my fall, I barely registered the sound of the stone slab falling shut above me, leaving me in darkness. Landing on my front, with what felt like a sprained wrist and bruises on my knees and elbows, it flashed across my mind that my long padded coat had protected me from even worse injury. In that instant I knew, with horrible certainty, that Alice had been there when Lorna had plummeted down the stairs. But this was not the time to be thinking about my great aunt's death. I was alive, and needed to focus on saving myself.

The foul smell of something rotten made me gag. Doing my best to cover my nose with my sleeve, I dragged myself to my feet. My legs were shaking so violently I could barely stand. Reaching up and stretching to my full height, I discovered my fingers could touch the ceiling. By dint of feeling my way, I found a corner of the stone slab which Alice had dropped over the opening to the cellar. Taking a deep breath, I pushed against it with all my might. It didn't even budge. With a curse, I recalled the bolts which Alice had tugged across before raising the stone. Even without the bolts keeping it in place, it would have been a challenge to move the heavy stone with the tips of my fingers. As it was, the task was impossible. Even if I managed to find something to stand on, the slab was securely fixed.

Frustrated, I fell back, nursing my injured wrist and trying not to give way to despair. Remembering the box of matches in my pocket, I struck one with difficulty and looked around. The flame flickered in my trembling hand. Before the match went out, I saw a narrow chamber with stone walls and a low ceiling. A small air brick in the ceiling allowed some ventilation. The damp ground beneath it indicated that I might have limited access to water, but only when it rained. I struck a second match and stared helplessly at the air vent. It was too small to poke my hand through, even if I were able to prise it out. There was no way I would be able to escape without shifting the heavy stone slab that was fixed in place by a number of heavy metal bolts. My situation seemed hopeless.

The match flickered and went out. Left in darkness, I panicked and thumped on the wall for a while, but there was no response. All I succeeded in doing was make my grazed hands smart even more. Abandoning my futile efforts to attract attention, I felt my way cautiously along the wall in the darkness, reluctant to waste my limited store of matches. The wall seemed to go on forever, although the chamber was small. At last I completed a circuit of the four walls of my prison and sank to the floor to examine my injuries. Touching the palms of my hands, I winced and struggled not to break down in tears, feeling the skin raw and bleeding. I lit one more match and looked around the cramped cold cell, searching for a way out. Overhead, cobwebs hung in delicate strands.

There were no doors in the bare brick walls, and no windows. Only the small air brick let in a thread of moonlight along with a meagre breath of cold air from outside. Cemented in at the top of the wall, it was almost out of reach. However loudly I shouted, I doubted anyone would be able to hear me. My own house was empty, apart from my small dog, and Alice had no other near neighbours. If I hadn't already been desperate to escape, the thought of Poppy waiting frantically for my return made me determined to break out of my cell. Even though it was almost impossible that anyone would hear me, I stood on tiptoe facing the small air brick and yelled for help at the top of my voice. It was difficult to take deep breaths in the rank air of the cellar. At last I fell back, exhausted and hoarse.

The most likely outcome of my plight was that I would eventually starve to death but, apart from my emotional distress, my immediate physical problem was the cold. I had suffered cold before, but never to this extent, and never so hopelessly. The air seemed to freeze my lungs with every inward breath, and when I sat down it felt as though the cold was seeping upwards through my clothes and into my bones. Tugging the sleeves of my coat down to cover my hands, I tried to keep my fingers moving inside my gloves. Clambering to my feet, I stamped on the ground and wriggled my toes, and jumped up and down on the spot. It occurred to me that it might be more sensible to sit down and conserve my energy, but at the same time I knew it was important to try and keep warm. At last, worn out by my efforts, I lit another of my precious store of matches and examined my prison more carefully.

And that was when I noticed something moving and realised I was not alone.

37

WITH SHAKING FINGERS, I struck another match and raised it in front of me. Peering into shadows, I made out a face, the eyes blinking as though dazzled by the flickering flame.

'Who are you?' I asked, although I had already guessed the identity of the soiled and stinking creature sprawled on the floor in front of me. 'You're Sophie, aren't you?'

'Sophie,' she repeated in a hoarse whisper. 'Sophie. That's my name. Yes, I'm Sophie.'

She didn't seem particularly curious about me, nor did she ask me why I had joined her in this subterranean dungeon. Standing under the air brick, I lit another match and asked her how long she had been there.

She shook her head and her matted hair swung around her ashen face. 'I don't know.' Her voice sounded dry and cracked. 'I've been here for... I don't know how long... I tried to keep track of the days but I lost count.'

'Weeks? Months?' I asked.

She shrugged. My match went out.

'I've been here longer than I can remember,' she whispered, 'but I can't tell you how long. It doesn't matter now.'

'What's the last thing you remember, before you came down here?'

'I remember we'd been in lockdown,' her voice reached me in the darkness. 'Because of the pandemic, you know?'

'I know,' I said. 'I remember it well.'

'My mother and I, we'd been at home for two years. We had everything delivered by the local shop, because it wasn't safe to leave the house.'

'Someone must have been out, making the deliveries,' I pointed out, but she ignored my interruption.

'I was planning to go travelling as soon as the lockdowns ended. My mother didn't want me to go. We argued about it. But then the war broke out and my mother brought me here, where it's safe.'

'What war?' I asked.

'The world war.'

In the darkness she couldn't see my puzzled expression. It was difficult to take in her situation, but it sounded as though Alice had lied to her daughter to prevent her going away. It wasn't yet clear to me why she had done that. Then the pain in my wrist reminded me how Alice had thrown me down into the subterranean chamber – cellar or crypt, or whatever it had once been – and I had my answer. Sophie's mother was obviously insane.

'How do you survive down here?' I asked, turning to the practicalities of our situation.

I was down to my last few matches so I crouched on the floor and we talked in the darkness. It seemed to be an effort for Sophie to speak, and her responses were erratic. Most of my questions had to be put to her several times before she managed to answer and after a while she fell asleep, or at least stopped talking, while I still had many questions. Someone must have been bringing her food and water, or she would have starved to death, but the place stank of excrement. It was surprising she hadn't died of typhoid or cholera or some other foul disease that flourished in such squalid conditions.

'What have you been eating?' I asked her.

She didn't answer.

In a futile attempt to distract myself from my physical pains, I resumed walking cautiously around the shelter. It was dark, but I needed to keep moving. It was perhaps a waste of my strength, because I didn't know when I might expect to eat again, but I couldn't stay still. Something had been preserving Sophie's life and there was no reason to suppose the same would not be the case for me, but I couldn't rely on that. Alice might fall ill, or die, and no one would ever know where to find us. In her madness, Alice might simply abandon us to die under the ground.

Exploring the walls with my fingers, searching for any sign of an exit I might have missed, I discovered a tap. Turning it on, I was relieved to feel ice cold water trickling from it. There was no way of knowing whether the water was safe to drink, but thirst drove me to risk it. After washing my injured hands as thoroughly as possible, I slurped water from it. Presumably Sophie had been drinking from the tap for months and she was still alive, just about. But that didn't explain what she had been eating. I wondered how long I could survive without food. The thought made me realise how hungry I was.

Fear prompted me to return to the air brick and start shouting again. There wasn't much point, but I had to do something. I refused to simply lie down and wait to die. Sophie might have given up. I had no idea how I might behave if I had been down there for weeks or months. But I had to get out for Poppy's sake. The fact that it was Sophie's mother who had locked us in made the situation far more complicated for her than it was for me. I could loathe Alice as well as fearing her, but Sophie now had to hate the woman she had probably once loved more than anyone else in the world.

Sophie might be beaten, but so far I still had my health and strength and my spirit was not yet broken. It would increase my chances of escaping if I could remain fit and strong. That was going to be difficult if we weren't properly fed, but at least I could keep walking up and down. Perhaps I might even be able to appeal to Alice's maternal feelings when she returned to feed us, as she surely must. After a while, a faint light penetrated the cellar from the air brick. As my eyes grew accustomed to the semi-darkness, I was able to make out shapes. Sophie barely moved but she shifted her position on the floor and let out an occasional moan. I had given up trying to persuade her to speak to me, but I kept talking to her anyway, in the vain hope that the sound of my voice might help her cling to some thread of hope.

After what must have been hours, the light coming through the air brick faded. I was too cold and stiff to do anything but drag myself painfully along, really slowly, with one hand on the wall. Finally, when I could barely move, I heard the stone slab open, and a beam of light from Alice's torch illuminated the chamber. A few seconds later the door closed, shutting off the light, but not before a package had tumbled to the floor. Sophie scrambled over to it and tore it open. In the darkness, I heard her gnawing at the contents. When I lit a match and approached her, she shuffled away from me, clutching the contents of the package to her chest.

'Sophie,' I whispered, 'you have to let me eat.'

My voice sounded hoarse and inhuman. It echoed eerily around the cell. Sophie whimpered but she was too feeble to prevent me from grabbing the hunk of bread and cheese she was holding. It tasted better than the best meal I had ever eaten and I wept uncontrollably as I devoured it, while Sophie moaned softly like a creature in pain. If she died, I was afraid Alice might abandon me. My hands shook as I lit a match and held out half of the bread.

'Here, take it.'

With a faint cry, Sophie seized on the food and retreated to a far corner, as though worried it would be snatched away from her again. Simple though it was, the bread and cheese restored my spirits. Now that I knew there was the possibility of survival, it was time to plan our escape. If Sophie helped me, we might stand a chance of overpowering Alice.

'I'm going to get you out of here,' I told her. 'We can do it if we work together.'

'No,' she replied. 'We can't. It's not safe out there.'

'You're wrong. It's perfectly safe.'

'Don't lie to me,' she replied angrily. 'Of course it's dangerous out there. Why else do you think my mother's keeping me here?'

'Sophie, listen to me, there's nothing to worry about outside this hellhole.' *Apart from your crazy mother*, I wanted to add, but didn't. 'Sophie, you have to trust me.'

'Why should I trust a liar?'

In vain I reminded her that I had voluntarily shared the food with her. She had been listening to her mother's delusions for so long, she was past understanding reason.

38

LYING ON THE FLOOR of the crypt, I worried about Poppy. I had put out her food before leaving to visit Alice, and she had enough water for a few days. But her provisions would soon run out. Wretchedly I pictured her running frantically around the house, searching for me. Gradually she would grow weak from hunger and lie down beside my bed, whimpering for me, as her life slipped away. I could hardly bear to think about her dying like that, abandoned and alone. If she had been with me in the cellar, we would have been able to keep each other warm. We had a supply of water, and she might have been able to catch rats and insects, and keep herself alive. As it was, she had been locked up in Rosecroft to starve to death, alone.

'We have to escape before we die,' I shouted at Sophie. 'We can't stay here.'

In the faint light from the air brick I saw her staring at me, and her lips seemed to form the word 'How?'

'Sophie, can you understand me?' I asked her. 'Speak to me.'

'We can never leave here,' she croaked. 'You can't get out even if you want to. There's no way out.'

That was certainly true. Besides, I knew too much for Alice ever to release me.

'So your mother's planning to just leave us here to rot?' I asked, anger giving my voice strength. 'Sophie, you do understand we'll die if we stay down here much longer. You must know that. I've only been here for a short time and I'm almost too weak to stand up, and you're really sick. Without medical attention you'll soon be dead. We have to appeal to her. She can't want you to die. You're her daughter. She loves you. She read me your letters...'

I broke off, realising the extent of Alice's insanity. She must have written Sophie's letters herself, losing herself in some deluded fantasy that her daughter was writing to her from overseas. Quite possibly she didn't even appreciate that the creature she had trapped in an underground cell was actually her daughter. Somehow we had to make her understand. I tried to work out how often she opened the door to throw down our food. If we were ready, we might be able to talk to her. But I was afraid that was a false hope.

By now I was fairly sure Alice had been responsible for my great aunt's death, and I wondered what had happened to provoke that attack. The answer lay in the notebook where Lorna had recorded her concerns about 'S' when Sophie had vanished. Living next door, Lorna was best placed to realise that Sophie had not actually left the lane. Presumably she had challenged Alice, who had responded by pushing her down the stairs at Rosecroft. It was a risky way to kill someone, as the technologist in the mortuary had pointed out. Someone falling down stairs was more likely to break a few bones than die, but Alice was beyond rational thought. Possibly she hadn't even intended to kill my great aunt, but had just lashed out in panic.

We would probably never find out whether she had killed Sophie's father as well. What was clear was that she was slowly killing me along with her own daughter. Convinced it would be impossible to reason with her, or appeal to her natural feelings for her daughter, it was difficult to see how we could possibly hope to escape. I resolved to bide my time and wait for an opportunity to present itself. But time passed, and nothing changed. When a parcel of food was thrown down to us, we scratched around in the dirt for crumbs, like animals. By now Poppy would be starving to death. I had no more tears to cry for her, only a sickening dull ache of grief.

The next time the door opened, I shouted up that Sophie was sick. There was no response from above, just a food parcel thrown down and the door was slammed shut, cutting off the light from above. I was close to despair, convinced that Alice actually believed Sophie was away from home, travelling. Crawling around on the ground, I came across a small metal bar. Carefully I stored it in my pocket. By watching the light that reached us through the air brick, and counting the intervals of darkness, I calculated that we were fed every afternoon. So when the light outside reappeared, I dragged myself over to stand underneath the stone slab that was the only means of entering or leaving the crypt. The next time our food arrived, I would be waiting. Summoning what strength I had left, I planned to throw my precious metal bar up in the air. If I could hit Alice, taking her by surprise, she might stumble and fall into the crypt herself. With Sophie's assistance, I might be able to clamber on top of her, haul myself out though the open entrance, and fetch help.

My plan was doomed from the start. In my confusion I had overestimated my own strength. The metal bar flew up only a short distance before dropping down to hit me on my forehead. I wasn't badly hurt, but the shock of the impact caused me to lose my footing and crash to the ground. So it was me, not Alice, who was injured by my attack. Luckily my missile only grazed my forehead. It could have blinded me. The food parcel tumbled after me. Dazed by my failure, I was overwhelmed by a terrible despair. My head injury stung and I tasted blood on my lips, and my hands and knees were bruised from my fall.

Too exhausted even to cry, I watched Sophie crawl towards the food parcel which had landed near me with a faint thud. In the dim light of the cell, I saw her eyes, wild and fierce, as she reached out. For one crazy moment I was afraid she was going to start tearing at me with her teeth while I lay too bruised and shaken to resist. Instead, she pounced on the food and slithered away. I waited for her to hand me some of the food we had been given, but she refused to share it with me and I was too weak to protest. A moment later, the door shut and we were left in darkness once more. Alice probably hadn't even noticed my feeble act of resistance.

Painfully I hauled myself into a sitting position. This situation could not continue much longer. There was not enough food to keep two of us alive.

'Sophie, if we both attack her, we might be able to overpower her,' I said urgently.

In the dim light I saw Sophie shake her head.

'We can't,' she said dully.

'Why not?'

'We might hurt her.'

'It's no more than she deserves.'

'She's my mother,' she protested weakly. 'She brings us food. If it wasn't for her we would starve. And you want to hurt her.' She began to cry.

That was the longest speech I had heard Sophie utter for a while, and neither of us spoke afterwards. Down there in our prison the hours passed slowly, while I counted the days, according to the darkness and light that reached us through the air brick. Another two days passed, and I felt myself growing weaker.

'Sophie,' I murmured. 'Sophie, I know she's your mother, but we're going to die down here if we don't do something.'

Sophie didn't answer. In the darkness, I could dimly make out her eyes staring at me, and I knew she was awake.

'You're as mad as your mother,' I told her crossly. 'You're both completely insane. Well, you might want to die down here, but I certainly don't. I'm getting out of here, whatever it takes.'

But my words were empty posturing. The truth was I could barely walk, I was feeling so weak, and it was becoming difficult to breathe in the stench of the cellar.

'We're dying in our own filth,' I told Sophie. She didn't answer. 'You poor cow,' I added, almost under my breath. 'You've not had much of a life, have you? And I thought my mother was bad.'

The next time the door opened, we heard a food parcel fall down the stairs but this time the door did not close

261

at once. Looking up, I saw Alice's outline lit from behind, and blinked at the shaft of light. The light seemed to lend me energy, reminding me of the world beyond our prison cell.

'Help us!' I croaked and to my surprise Alice answered me.

'What do you want?' she replied irritably.

It was like listening to a disembodied voice.

'You know what we want,' I replied. 'We want you to let us go. Let us go. Please, let us go. You can't keep us here.'

Behind me, in the darkness, Sophie whimpered.

'And you'll go straight to your friends and start spreading nasty rumours about me,' Alice retorted. 'I know you. You think I'm a fool, but I see straight through your lies. That's why I can't let you walk out of here. Do you really think I'm stupid enough to trust you?'

'You're wrong,' I replied, nearly choked by my tears. 'I won't say anything to anyone. Please, let me go. You can trust me. It'll be our secret. Think about what you're doing. If Sophie and I stay here we'll die. You don't want to be responsible for your daughter's death, do you? You don't want to be guilty of murder. And what about Poppy? She's going to die too. If you kill us, you will never be innocent again.'

I wasn't even sure what I was saying.

'Innocent, pah,' she replied, spitting on the ground. 'What do you know about innocence? I can't let you get in my way.'

'Doesn't it trouble you that you'll be a murderer?' I asked.

Alice let out a curious snort. 'Sometimes people have to

die. You have no idea what I went through with my snake of a husband.'

In that moment I was certain that my great aunt had not been Alice's first victim.

'So you've already gone down that route,' I muttered, before shouting up to her, 'Did you kill my Great Aunt Lorna too?'

Alice shifted at the top of the stairs. 'You need to mind your own business,' she said before the door closed behind her.

Her words reminded me of the last time I had spoken to Susie, and it hit me that I would never see my sister again. My last words to her had been spoken in anger. Along with remorse was the realisation that she would not think there was anything amiss if she called me and I didn't answer. Even my own sister would not notice I was missing.

39

ALL AT ONCE MY feverish slumber was disturbed by distant sounds above us. Too weak to make much noise, I shouted for help. As soon as I started calling out, Sophie launched herself at me. She knocked me to the floor with surprising energy, and lay on top of me, covering my lips with her skinny fingers.

'No,' she croaked in my ear. 'No, we mustn't make a sound. They'll hear us.'

'What the hell are you doing?' I mumbled, my voice muffled beneath her hand.

I did my best to throw her off, but she found the strength to cling to me. Her fingers felt like chicken bones pressing against my mouth. Clearly she was as insane as her mother. But already we were too late. Everything had gone quiet overhead. I was about to despair, when we heard faint scrabbling and a distant frantic barking. Before I could call out again, Sophie slapped her hand over my mouth again.

'She's my mother,' she whispered, sobbing. 'We can't do this. I won't let you. It's not safe out there.'

But even Sophie's misguided belief in her mother could not prevent what was happening. The door flew open, and we heard shouting and banging, and a dog barking frenziedly.

'Poppy,' I whispered. 'That's Poppy! Poppy!'

Sophie pressed her fingers more tightly against my mouth.

'Jesus, it stinks in here!' a woman's voice cried out in disgust. 'What the hell is this place?'

'Must be a cesspit,' a man replied.

'Smells like dead bodies,' another man said. 'Shit, I think I'm going to throw up.'

There was a muffled response before the woman yelled angrily, 'I don't care what's down there, leave that damn door open! And cuff that lunatic before she does any more damage.'

'Is anyone else hurt?' another man called out. 'Why isn't the ambulance here yet?'

At last I managed to pull Sophie's bony fingers away from my mouth, and let out a thin scream. She flung herself on top of me again, but she was too late to conceal our presence in the cellar. Already a blinding beam of torchlight was shining on us and several faces were peering down at us, their mouths and noses buried in their sleeves.

'I don't believe it! There's someone down here!' a voice cried out.

'Looks like there's two of them,' another voice chimed in.

'That must be her!' a familiar voice cried out. 'Emily! Emily!'

Dazzled by the light and crying with confusion, I knew we had been rescued. Too overwhelmed to speak or even to move, I closed my eyes and felt myself trembling uncontrollably. There was a thump as a man jumped down beside me, his feet kicking up dust.

'You're safe now,' he said gently. 'The police are here and an ambulance is on its way.'

Recognising the voice, I opened my eyes to see a face leaning over me. 'Toby?' I croaked.

Somewhere a dog was barking furiously.

'Poppy?' I murmured before I drifted into unconsciousness. 'Poppy?'

When I came to, I was lying on the floor in Alice's front room with no memory of how I had arrived there. Someone must have carried me up out of the cellar. It was evening, but even so I squinted in the unaccustomed light. There was no sign of Sophie. Alice was sitting on the sofa, weeping noisily. With grim satisfaction, I saw that her wrists were handcuffed. I am neither a violent nor a vindictive person, but in that moment I would have happily put a noose around her neck myself.

'You don't understand,' she was wailing. 'I can't let her go. She's my daughter. She's all I have. I have to keep her safe. The world is a sinister place. You don't understand how dangerous it is for a young girl. I have to protect my daughter, because I know. I know.' She began rocking backwards and forwards.

'What is it you know?' someone asked.

'I know how men can assault you and no one comes to save you and no one believes you. Afterwards they tell you to hold your peace and not shame them in front of the community. And you don't have a choice. Now she wants to go off travelling on her own. I can't let that happen. I have to keep her safe. I'm her mother. I have to protect her.'

'By locking her in your bomb shelter?' a voice replied.

I hoisted myself up on one elbow so I could watch what

266

was happening around me. A policeman in uniform was sitting on one side of the coffee table, beside a woman in a dark jacket. Alice was seated on the sofa facing them.

'You know your daughter's been rushed to hospital suffering from a life-threatening infection, dehydration, malnutrition, not to mention severe psychological distress,' the woman said severely. 'The paramedics are hopeful she'll recover but it's going to take time. If she'd been down there much longer she would have died. And it would have been your fault. It's lucky Toby came looking for Emily or your daughter would have died down there. Do you understand what I'm saying?'

'Yes, yes,' Alice muttered. 'You're the one who doesn't understand.'

'How could you do that to your own daughter?'

'You don't understand,' Alice repeated, her face set with misery. 'You've got it all wrong. I was keeping her out of harm's way. What other choice did I have? I only ever wanted the best for her. I couldn't let her go off on her own into the world. She's my daughter. I have to protect her.'

'The only person she needed protecting from was you,' Toby said, entering the room, and the policeman frowned at him.

'Leave the questioning to us, please,' he told Toby who was staring at me intently, as though he wanted to memorise every inch of my face.

'He wanted to take her away from me,' Alice said, glaring at Toby.

But I already knew she had lied to me about Toby. He wouldn't have hurt Sophie. He wouldn't hurt anyone. It was Alice's insane jealousy over her daughter that had led her to hate Toby for rejecting Sophie.

'Tell us again how your daughter ended up locked in a bomb shelter at the bottom of your garden,' the policewoman said. 'I'm doing my best to make sense of all this.'

Alice shook her head and rocked backwards and forwards, the picture of misery. 'She wanted to go away. She said she would leave me and never come back. What else could I do? You don't understand. No one does. I can't let her go. She has to stay here with me, where she's safe. The world is too dangerous.'

There was a lot more along those lines, but I was too exhausted to listen to the crazy ramblings of a maniac. Shortly after that, I was hoisted onto a stretcher, although I insisted there was nothing wrong with me that a hot shower and a good night's sleep wouldn't cure.

'You're going to be thoroughly checked out and that's that,' Toby said. 'They need to x-ray your wrist, and they're going to put you on a drip as you're severely dehydrated.'

'Where's Poppy?'

'Don't worry about Poppy. Hannah's taking care of her. You just concentrate on getting better.'

'Take her to the vet,' I whispered. 'You have to make sure she's okay. And whatever you do, don't let anyone tell my mother what's happened. I'll talk to her in my own time, but I don't want her stressing over me just yet. Not until I'm strong enough to cope with her fussing.'

Toby reassured me he would do everything I wanted, and told me not to worry about anything.

'I'm so pleased to see you I could kiss you,' he whispered as I lay on the stretcher waiting to be carried off to the waiting ambulance.

'Well, why don't you?'

'Because you smell like a pig's arse, and you don't look much better than that either.'

I laughed but the pain made me gasp.

'I think I've broken my ribs,' I whispered.

'Just as well you're going to hospital then, isn't it?' he replied cheerily, but I could see he was worried.

40

THE NURSING STAFF AT the hospital were kind, but they were busy and had little time to stop and chat. The other patients in my ward were mainly elderly and mostly asleep in between meal times. I could have been in a coma for fifty years and woken up in an old people's home. Only the woman in the bed next to mine was lively enough to be sociable. She chattered for a while, telling me how she had fractured her shoulder and assuring me she would be leaving soon. Eventually she paused for long enough to hear why I was there.

'I fell down some stairs and landed on my wrist, but it's sprained not broken, and I've fractured a rib,' I told her.

That was easier than explaining how I had been imprisoned in a disused bomb shelter by a lunatic.

'You were lucky,' she said. 'It could have been worse.'

'Yes,' I agreed. 'It could have been worse.'

She was right, although she had no idea quite how lucky I was. All the same, despite my good fortune in so narrowly escaping death, I was miserable in hospital. The bed was hard and I couldn't get my pillows in the right position. My chest ached every time I drew breath, and the pain kept me awake. Worst of all, they wouldn't allow

Poppy to visit me. I missed her more than I would have thought possible. After a wretched spell in hospital, I was overjoyed to be sent home to recuperate.

My reunion with Poppy was emotional, at least for me. All the time I was in hospital I had worried she would have forgotten me, or would be cross with me for having abandoned her. But she was ecstatic when I returned home, and trotted after me wherever I went, reluctant to let me out of her sight even for a moment.

'It's all right,' I told her. 'I won't leave you again, I promise.'

If she understood what I was saying, she didn't believe me, and it was weeks before she stopped whimpering whenever I left the room. It was only seven weeks until Christmas and I was not sure whether I would be fit enough to host. I discussed my concerns with Hannah.

'Don't be ridiculous. Of course you can't do anything,' she said. 'But that doesn't mean you have to cancel your Christmas. Tell all your family to come to Rosecroft as planned, and me and my mother will look after everything.'

I protested, but she insisted.

'You know my mother loves cooking. She'll be over the moon when she hears about this, so don't worry. We'll do everything. You won't have to lift a finger. Just tell us how many we're catering for and leave everything to us.'

With my mother and father, my sister and her family, there were six of us, plus Hannah and Jane, and Toby and his mother. I didn't admit to anyone that I had once considered inviting Alice to join us. Hannah suggested we have our Christmas lunch in the tea shop where there was plenty of room, and a large oven. I was relieved at the offer, and so it was agreed.

'I don't really have any choice, do I?' I said, and she shook her head, smiling.

Somehow my mother had discovered that I was injured, with a swollen but thankfully not broken wrist, a fractured rib, and more bumps and bruises than I could count. She invited me to stay with her until I felt better but I assured her it was unnecessary; Hannah and Toby were on hand to take care of me.

'Toby?' my mother pounced on the name. 'Who's Toby?'

I laughed at her eagerness. 'Toby's a friend of mine in Ashton Mead. You met him last time you came to visit.'

'Oh yes,' she said vaguely. 'Yes, of course. I remember him.'

I wasn't sure she did, but I let that pass. It wasn't important.

'Hannah and Toby are looking after me and Poppy,' I assured her.

'Hannah and Toby?' My mother grunted. 'Well, if you change your mind you know you're always welcome to come home. Your father and I can take care of you. You know it would be our pleasure. It's no trouble at all. We'd love to have you.' She hesitated. 'You can even bring that dog of yours, if you want. You know I've only ever wanted you to be content with your life,' she added, sounding wistful. 'I've always known I can't make you happy, of course. I mean, a woman needs more in her life than a mother's love. But I've only ever wanted to see you settled and happy. You know that, don't you?'

For an instant, her words reminded me of Alice's obsession with Sophie, and I shivered.

'Yes, I know that, and thank you, mum. I appreciate

your concern, really I do, but Rosecroft is my home and my friends are here.'

She sniffed.

'Anyway you're all still coming to me for Christmas,' I said.

'If you're feeling up to it. Don't overdo things, Emily.'

I assured her everything was under control and I wouldn't have to do anything, and eventually she was satisfied.

Between them, Hannah and Toby came to see me at least twice a day to take Poppy for a walk. It cheered me up seeing them, especially Toby. Poppy adored him and I could no longer fool myself that I wasn't becoming fond of him. But one thing was still playing on my mind. Finally I plucked up my courage and challenged him about his relationship with Sophie. I was lying on my sofa with my feet up and he was kneeling on the floor, petting Poppy.

'What relationship with Sophie?' he replied.

'You never told me exactly what happened with her, from your point of view.'

Toby looked puzzled. 'You were there,' he faltered. 'You know what happened better than any of us.'

I shook my head and winced as the movement pulled on my sore rib. 'No, no, I mean what happened with her when you were younger, when she wanted to go to the prom with you. What happened?'

Toby looked faintly mystified. 'Nothing happened.'

I was not ready to let it drop. 'But you were keen to go out with her at one time, weren't you?'

'Good lord, no. That was never going to happen. For a start, her mother wasn't impressed with me, although I don't think anyone would have been good enough for her.

Still, her mother's opinion counted for a lot with Sophie.' He shrugged. 'I had no idea Alice was batshit crazy. Still, it didn't matter to me, because I was never keen on Sophie anyway. I mean she was nice enough, that is, I'm sure she still is very nice, but she was never anything special to me. She was just another girl living in the village. And besides, she's four years younger than me. That might not sound like much, but it's a lot when you're a teenager.'

I wondered if he was protesting too much. 'But you asked her out?' I said.

'Well, actually she did the asking, but it didn't mean anything. We were teenagers.' He laughed, and looked embarrassed. 'I never had much luck with girls. I've never been very good at talking to people at all, really. I get on better with the kids I teach. And dogs. Especially one little dog who's staring at me right now, wanting me to play with her.'

He turned back to Poppy and began teasing her with one of her toys.

'So you never argued with Sophie?'

'Argued with her? No. Never.'

'And you never hit her?'

'What?' Looking up at me in astonishment, he dropped the toy and Poppy seized it and ran off. 'Whatever gave you that idea? I've never hit anyone in my life. What would I be doing hitting a girl? Or anyone else, for that matter. What are you talking about?'

He was clearly astounded by my question. Meanwhile, Poppy ran back, dropped her toy at his feet, and gazed at him expectantly. When he didn't immediately pick it up, she barked. He grabbed the toy and waggled it just out of her reach, making her stand on her back legs.

'It was something Alice said,' I muttered, cross with myself for letting her fool me.

My gullibility had caused me no end of trouble, resulting in my being taken in first by Ben, and then Alice.

'I was no more than a fleeting teenage fancy for Sophie, and I never reciprocated her feelings. Like I said, she's a nice girl, but she's not really my type.'

'What is your type?'

Toby smiled at me. Before he could answer, we heard the front door open and Hannah came in. Toby leapt to his feet, and said he was going to be in trouble for not having taken Poppy out yet.

'Hannah's going to give me hell,' he muttered as he hurried off to find Poppy's lead.

I bitterly regretted having listened to Alice, and hoped it wasn't too late for me and Toby to become a couple.

41

FORTUNATELY MY INJURIES WERE not severe and there would be no long-term damage. As one of the nurses pointed out, it was lucky I hadn't hit my head when I fell. That could have caused brain damage and possibly been fatal. Thinking about my great aunt, I shuddered, and did my best to feel grateful for my relatively minor injuries, despite the pain I was suffering. My rib in particular mended quickly, although I had to be careful not to laugh, which was difficult when Toby visited me. He kept me posted about what was going on in the village, and his anecdotes were hilarious. When I scolded him for being so amusing, he told me it was impossible to go to the local shop without hearing some new rumour.

'Maud is such a gossip,' he said, as he related an anecdote about Tess who worked at The Plough, or the village butcher, or the local police officer who had kicked in my back door to rescue Poppy. He had been afraid to break a window in case the broken glass hurt her, but by the time she was found, she was too lethargic to move. Most of Maud's tales were too preposterous to take seriously, but somehow she kept up a steady stream of them.

'Where does she get all this from?' I demanded when he had finished a story about Tess dislodging an optic from its holder and smashing an entire bottle of vodka behind the bar.

'It was late at night. Maud told me she suspects Tess had been drinking heavily that night, because she was off duty.' He lowered his voice. 'Maud thinks Tess poured the vodka into another bottle and then smashed the optic when it was empty. It was after closing time and there was no one there to see.'

'Then how does Maud know about it?'

Toby shrugged. 'She has a fertile imagination, I guess.'

'That's ridiculous,' I said, remembering how he had said the same to me when I had suspected Alice had murdered her daughter. 'There would have been vodka all over the floor.'

'Cliff believes it evaporated overnight, but Maud seems to think it evaporated into Tess's bottle.'

The weeks passed pleasantly enough, and every day my pain lessened until I was scarcely troubled by it at all. Although I was strong enough to take Poppy for walks myself, Toby insisted on accompanying me when he could, in case Poppy tugged unexpectedly on her lead and hurt me. I assured him it would be fine, but there was no arguing with him. Mild-mannered though he was, it seemed that even meek Toby could be stubborn.

'Have you never had a girlfriend?' I asked him on one of our walks together.

'I did once.'

'What happened?'

'She dumped me.' He paused, and I waited for him to go on. 'I think she was freaked out by what happened to my mother,' he said at last. 'I was devastated at the time, but I don't blame her. Anyway, she met someone else soon after we split up, and I've heard she's engaged.' He paused. 'Actually, she might be married by now. We lost touch.'

'I'm sorry.'

'Yes, well, it was probably for the best. It's all water under the bridge. But I found it hard to trust anyone after that.' He sighed. 'I guess I'm just unlucky when it comes to relationships.'

'Join the club,' I said. 'But you mustn't give up, not if that's what you want. I'm sure there are plenty of women who would love to go out with you.' I paused, afraid of revealing that I was one of those women. 'If you keep looking, I'm sure you'll meet someone one day.'

Toby and I had grown close since Ben's departure. Only now, hearing how he had been dumped, did I understand why Toby was so sympathetic towards me. He wasn't in love with me, as I had allowed myself to hope. He just empathised with me after my break-up with Ben. I was glad I had never revealed how I felt. It would have been humiliating to confess that I was falling in love with Toby, only to discover that he didn't reciprocate my feelings.

'You've been a good friend to me and Poppy,' I said, in case he thought I was hoping for something more. 'But you're probably better off being single. I know I am.'

Toby looked away and didn't reply. Scampering ahead of us, Poppy barked as a small bird skimmed past overhead, its feathers fluffed out against the cold. We walked on in silence for a while, each of us absorbed in our own thoughts.

Christmas went off without a hitch. My sister and her family drove to Ashton Mead, picking my parents up on the way. It was a long drive for them, and I was worried they would all be tired and crotchety when they arrived, so I was really pleased when my sister fell in love with Rosecroft at first sight, just as I had done. My arrival there felt like a lifetime ago. I was sorry she did not see it for the first time in the summer, when the roses were in bloom along the path, and wisteria hung in delicate purple droplets around the front door. But the house itself was as beautiful as ever, the yellow stone soft in the crisp light of a winter's day. Toby had taken care of the little patch of grass in front of the house, and tidied up the flower beds where Poppy had scuffled around in them hunting for worms, or burying half-eaten carrots or chewing toys.

My nephew, Joel, had shot up since we had last seen each other. If he had not arrived with his parents, I would have struggled to recognise him. Taller than me, and slender, he was developing into a good-looking young man with mature ideas. He hit it off with Poppy at once, which was a relief, as he played with her and kept her happily entertained for hours. He also got on well with Toby, and from across the room I saw the two of them engrossed in an animated discussion and laughing together, while Poppy tugged at a toy Toby was dangling in front of her, just out of reach of her snapping teeth.

After a few drinks, Susie insisted on helping me clear up, even though there was nothing to do.

'Toby seems nice,' she whispered to me when we were alone in the kitchen, nudging me and giggling like she used to do when she was a teenager.

'I know, he's very nice.'

'What are you waiting for then?'

'What do you mean?'

'If I was single, I'd make a play for him myself!' She giggled. 'It's obvious he's crazy about you.'

'You're sloshed,' I scolded her. 'I knew we shouldn't have opened another bottle. Toby and I are good friends, but nothing else is ever going to happen between us.'

Turning away, I saw Toby standing in the doorway and hoped he had not overheard me. There was no time to worry about that, because we had to set off. Toby went to fetch Naomi in his car, and my family and I walked to the tea shop where Hannah and Jane were waiting for us. They had pushed several tables together, and Hannah had gone all out with the decorations. Tinsel and streamers were strung across the walls, and in one corner of the room a real Christmas tree was hung with colourful baubles and flashing fairy lights.

'It's beautiful,' I cried out, and Hannah beamed with pleasure.

'Just make sure Poppy can't reach any of the fairy lights,' my mother said. 'And be careful none of that tinsel falls down. It's toxic for dogs.'

'Suddenly you're a dog expert,' my father teased her.

Initially wary of Poppy, my mother now seemed to regard herself as my dog's chief protector, and constantly warned me about potential hazards. She had no experience with dogs, but my mother was never one to let ignorance hold her back from voicing her opinions. It was irritating, but I did my best to ignore her, assuring her that Poppy was fine.

When we were all seated at the table, Jane brought out an enormous turkey accompanied by the traditional trimmings: stuffing, pigs in blankets, bread sauce, and lashings of gravy, while Hannah served brussels sprouts and crispy roast potatoes. Everyone laughed and joked, and ate and drank far too much. After lunch, my sister whispered furiously to Joel who promptly claimed he was unable to move. He promised to take Poppy for a walk later. Hannah said she had to clear up and absolutely refused to allow me to help her after my sister and mother said they wanted to make themselves useful. So it was left to Toby and me to take Poppy and Holly for a walk down by the river. Even Poppy had eaten too much to bound around with her usual exuberance, while Jane's old dog plodded contentedly behind us. The village streets were deserted and a fine dusting of snow had begun to fall, too light to settle.

'You know if you hadn't found me, I would be dead by now,' I said.

It was the first time either of us had broached the subject of my incarceration in Alice's subterranean cell.

'It was Poppy who led us to you,' he replied. 'I heard her barking and barking and knew something was wrong because you weren't answering the door. When I tried to look in through your letterbox, I saw Poppy had crapped on the carpet. She was sitting by the door, whimpering. I called out to her trying to reassure her, and kept trying your phone, but I couldn't get hold of you. I knew you'd never go away and leave Poppy alone in the house for so long, so I had to do something. That's when I called the police and insisted they break down the door.'

'Maud had a spare key,' I told him. 'You didn't have to break down the door.'

'I was afraid we'd find you unconscious, or...' he said and broke off, unable to finish the sentence. 'Poppy was shut in your house, famished and distraught, but you weren't there. Even though she was clearly starving, Poppy refused to eat anything, and dragged me next door to Alice's house. I was sure she was trying to lead us to you, but there was no sign of you anywhere. Poppy kept barking and barking and scratching at Alice's back door and she refused to leave, so we decided to investigate. We went outside, thinking she just wanted to get out and explore, but she dragged me straight down to the bottom of the garden. Even then we had no idea what had happened.'

'How could you?' I agreed. 'No one could have imagined the truth.'

'We thought Poppy was barking at squirrels, when she kept barking at that tall tree in the corner of Alice's garden. She was determined not to leave. In the end we took a closer look around, and that's when we found the door in the ground. So if you want to thank anyone for saving your life, it should be Poppy.'

Poppy gazed at me quizzically, with her head tilted to one side.

'Thank you,' I whispered, reaching down to scratch the back of her neck. 'Thank you for giving me back my life.'

Epilogue

ONE SATURDAY MORNING, MY windows vibrated and looking out I saw a lorry pulling up. Slipping on my shoes, I went outside to investigate what it was doing there. It was a bright mild spring morning, and as I opened the front door, birdsong greeted me. The first buds were beginning to break through in my garden, and along the street trees were in leaf. A large removal van had parked next door, and two burly men in blue overalls jumped out of it. An elegant young woman was standing on the pavement, her hair neatly tied in a low ponytail at the nape of her neck. When she half turned towards me, I saw that her make-up was impeccable. She faced the removal men with an expression of rigid determination, while I hovered nearby. As the two men went to open up the back of their lorry, I stepped forward to greet her.

'Hello. I live next door. Are you moving in?'

'Moving out,' she replied shortly. 'What do you want?'

I hesitated and she eyed me warily. It should have been no surprise that I failed to recognise her since I had only seen her soiled and stinking, trapped in a dark underground cell. Since our rescue, my wild fellow prisoner had been transformed into an immaculately groomed young woman. She scrutinised me, a flicker of recognition in her vacant eyes, and I was uncomfortably conscious of my washed-out jeans and shabby T-shirt.

'Oh my goodness, you're Sophie,' I blurted out. 'I hardly recognised you. I'm Emily.'

'Yes,' she replied curtly, ignoring the hand I held out. 'I know who you are.'

Whatever feeling had been visible in her expression faded, until her eyes were blank. Sleek and emotionless, she reminded me of a shark. I shivered.

'So you're selling the house?' I asked her stupidly.

'My mother won't be coming back here, and neither will I.'

'After what happened, I didn't for one moment think you would,' I said. 'I'm sorry, I know she's your mother, but they need to lock her up and throw away the key.'

'She hasn't stood trial yet,' Sophie said coldly. 'They tell me she's insane, and everyone seems to think she's dangerous. That's because everyone knows your story.'

Her words sounded like an accusation, as though her mother had never imprisoned us both in her bomb shelter at all.

'Hardly a story,' I retorted. 'She did it to you too.'

As well as trapping us in a damp cellar, Alice had admitted to the police that she had pushed my great aunt down the stairs, and attempted to set fire to my house by posting a lighted firework through the letterbox. Her confession had been splashed all over the media, even making the national news headlines. A series of journalists had hounded me for a while, but eventually they realised I wasn't going to answer any of their questions and left me alone.

'That's why they'll never let her out,' Sophie said. 'She should have kept her mouth shut.'

It was a curious turn of phrase in the circumstances, but I let it go.

'Well, we're both safe now,' I said, smiling at her. 'Let's be thankful for that.'

'They're never going to let her out. Never.'

I wasn't sure whether Sophie's voice expressed satisfaction or resentment.

'So you'll finally be able to go off on your travels now?' I asked her.

She shook her head. 'No, I'm moving to Swindon to be near my mother.'

'You want to live near her?' I repeated in disbelief. 'Why would you ever want to see her again?'

'I can't abandon her now, can I? She's my mother. I'm all she's got.'

Listening to her words, I felt a profound sadness. We had been rescued from our physical prison, but Sophie had not been able to escape the emotional snare of her mother's madness.

'You ought to get right away from Alice,' I urged her. 'You can do anything you like with the rest of your life. I thought you wanted to travel and see something of the world?'

'I don't expect you to understand,' she said.

Without another word, she turned away and followed the removal men into the house where she had been held captive for so long. Almost her entire life, really.

'What's that removal van doing outside?' Toby asked when he called in to see me later that afternoon.

'Don't worry, I'm not going anywhere,' I smiled. 'It's for next door. Sophie's selling up.'

'That's hardly surprising. After everything that happened in that house, you'd think she'd want to get as far away from here as possible, and never look back.'

'She's going to live in Swindon,' I replied, and he shrugged.

Stooping down, I scratched Poppy gently under her chin, and she licked my hand.

'Do you think Poppy knows she saved my life?' I asked Toby.

He took my free hand in his. 'Of course she doesn't understand what happened,' he replied, smiling. 'She's a dog. But I know how close I came to losing you and I'd like to stick around to make sure you stay safe from now on.'

As I thanked Toby, I thought that nothing terrible was likely to happen to me again, as long as Poppy was in my life.

Acknowledgements

I would like to thank all the team at Crime and Mystery Club for having continued faith in my stories: Ion, Claire, Ellie, Hollie, Paru and Sarah. This book would never have happened without you. My thanks also go to Jayne and Steven for their skilled editorial work, to Nick for his eagle-eyed proofreading, and Steve for his brilliant cover design incorporating Phillipa's lovely original artwork. Producing a book is a real team effort, and I am fortunate to have such a dedicated team of experts supporting my writing.

I am grateful to the owners of a certain little rescue dog.

As for the real Poppy, who inspired this story, I wish you a long and healthy life filled with happiness, treats and walks in the grass.

If you enjoyed *Barking Up the Right Tree*, look out for *Barking Mad*, the next Poppy Mystery Tale!

Emily has settled in the picturesque village of Ashton Mead, where she lives with her puppy, Poppy. Life is finally going well for Emily. She has a cottage of her own, a job she likes and friends. Then she stumbles on the body of a woman who apparently drowned in the river.

The other villagers suspect foul play and are quick to blame Richard, Emily's next-door neighbour and a newcomer to the village. But Emily finds it hard to believe her friendly neighbour could be a cold-hearted murderer, and when she meets his attractive son, Adam, her feelings become more complicated.

Determined to find out the truth behind the death in the village, Emily travels to London to track down the man with whom Richard's wife was having an affair. Unfortunately for Emily, her visit does not go as planned. Instead of helping clear Richard's name, she finds her own life is in danger...

CRIMEANDMYSTERYCLUB.CO.UK/BARKING-MAD